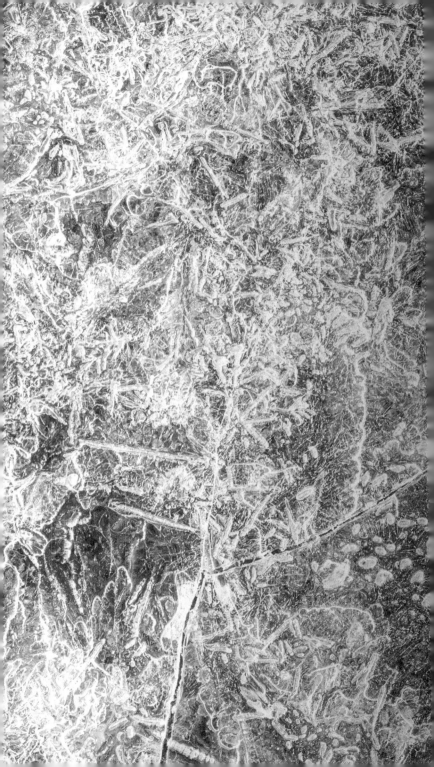

STICKS AND STONES

S. MASSERY

S.J. SYLVIS

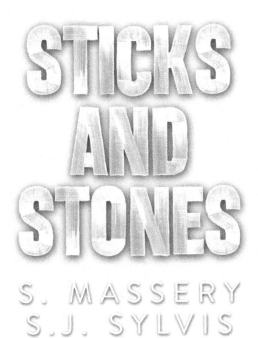

STICKS AND STONES

S. MASSERY
S.J. SYLVIS

Sticks and Stones

Copyright © 2023 S. Massery & S.J. Sylvis

Published: S. Massery & S.J. Sylvis Books LLC
Cover Design: Black Widow Designs
Editing: Jenn Lockwood Editing | Studio ENP
Proofing: Emma Cook | Booktastic Blonde

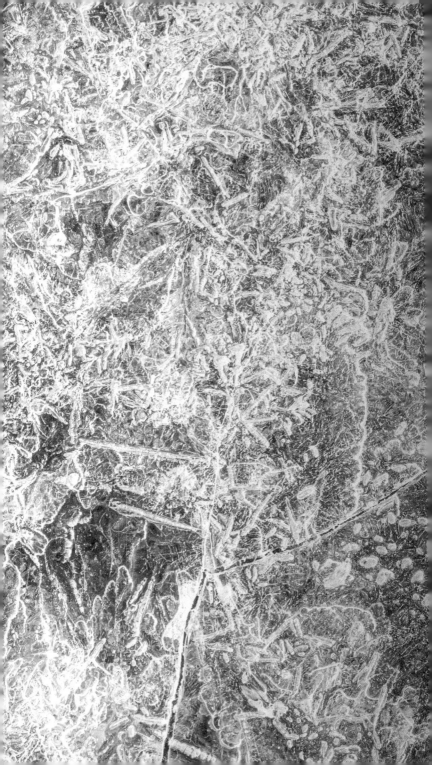

To our hockey romance era girlies
Thanks for taking a chance on our first co-write

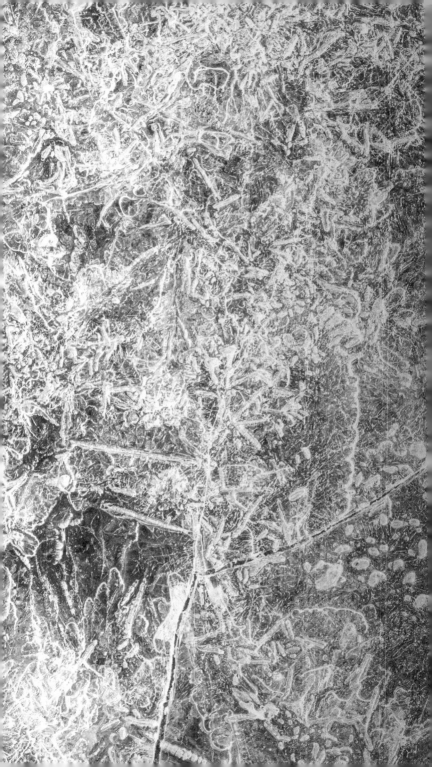

A NOTE FROM THE AUTHORS

Dear reader,

If you're familiar with S. Massery's work, you know to expect dark content. This story is a little lighter than her *Hockey Gods* series. S.J.'s *Bexley U* readers are in for a slightly darker ride. Please note that there is light bullying, talk of sexual assault, and kidnapping.

Sticks and Stones may break our bones…

xoxo,
   Sara & S.J.

CHAPTER 1
WREN

PAST

HIGH SCHOOL IS SUCH A BORE. I rest my head against my palm. Mr. Anderson is reviewing the periodic table for the seventieth time this semester. My eyelids grow heavier. There's a flick on the back of my head, and I quickly sit up and turn to glare at my foster brother, Evan. He gives me a jerk of his steely chin, and I roll my eyes.

I mouth the words, "I already know this stuff. Leave me alone."

He rolls his eyes right back at me, while Stone, Evan's best friend and the most popular jock in the senior class, whispers something in his ear. I squint but slowly turn, push my hair behind my ear, and try to pay attention.

It's not that I don't enjoy Chem. I actually *love* science, and Mr. Anderson knows that, which is likely why he doesn't get on me when I fall asleep during class. Not to mention, I think he and the rest of the faculty at West Ridge High know my life story and feel sorry for me. The shitty thing about living in a small town and having a druggie for a father? It's *always* on the front page of the paper.

Yay, me.

I'm thankful for Evan and his family, though. If it wasn't

for Rebecca and Stephen, I would still be in my former foster house on the corner of 1st and 2nd. How the Rowes became foster parents is still a mystery. They tried feeding me leftover cat food for dinner once.

"All right, there's a pop quiz during tomorrow's class. Make sure you study those elements tonight so you can all graduate and avoid summer school."

The bell rings, but Stone's deep, smooth voice floats throughout the room and cancels out all the shuffling of papers and scooting in of chairs. "Isn't the point of a pop quiz that it is supposed to be a surprise?"

I huff sarcastically and gather my things. "He has to give people like you fair warning so you don't flunk."

I send Stone a flirty but devilish smile because that's how our... *friendship?*... works. He picks on me, and I *attempt* to pick on him.

"Shut up, *Sticks.*"

That godforsaken nickname. Stone started calling me *Sticks* the first time I moved into Evan's house before being thrust back with my father for a short time. All the time I spent with my father was brief, but that one took the record because it lasted a total of seventy-two hours.

When I finally asked Stone why he called me Sticks, he admitted that it was because my legs were so skinny they resembled sticks. Naturally, that set a line of fire down my spine. The whole reason I was so skinny was because I was hardly eating due to my father's bad habits.

Anyway, the nickname stuck, and the only reason for that was because Stone knew it bothered me.

"Shut up. Both of you." Evan comes over and grabs my books out of my hand.

I follow him down the hall to break for lunch.

I brace myself for the lecture I know is coming.

"How is it going at your dad's?"

Stone is beside us, but he's buried in his phone with his

heavy brow line furrowed. A few of his hockey teammates bump knuckles with him, and then he goes right back to his phone.

"It's fine," I lie.

Evan's green eyes harden, and his mouth forms a straight line. "Wren."

I feel my face pale. Truth be told, it's far from fine, but Evan shouldn't be concerned. It's almost summer, which means I can bounce back and forth between his house and Jasmin's in between my shifts, and then come August, I'll be at Shadow Valley University, and all will be well.

Jasmin is my other saving grace. She understands me more than most people because she knows what it's like to be in the system: lonely.

"Stop lying," Stone says. "Your legs are lookin' quite thin these days."

I stop walking and stick my foot out to trip Stone, but he's just as good on the linoleum floor as he is on ice.

He stops a mere inch from my shoe and smirks at me. "Nice try."

"Will you two fucking stop for three seconds? I swear, you're like toddlers."

I reach for my books, but Evan holds them up above his head so I can't grab them.

I exhale, blowing my brown hair out of my face, and cross my arms. "He started it."

Evan laughs. "See? Toddlers."

Stone continues down the hallway, putting his arm around Cassandra, the junior who has likely slept with the entire senior class. Maybe even with Evan, too, which makes me want to throw up.

Evan is like a brother to me. It irks me to no end when girls try to be my friend just so they can get closer to him, and it irks me even more when they openly admit the things they want to do behind closed doors.

Evan slowly lowers my books and pushes them back into my hands. "You've got dark circles under your eyes, you're falling asleep in Chemistry, and your jeans are looser than normal."

Embarrassment floods me, and if it were anyone else, I'd fool them into thinking I was fine, but Evan knows me too well.

"Wren, what's going on?"

I look away and watch my peers pile into the lunchroom. "Same ol'," I admit before shrugging. "It's fine, Evander. It's not too much longer until August. I've been living in this hell-hole since I was born."

Evan lowers his voice when he bends his head down to the crook of my neck. "But you shouldn't *have* to live like that. Just come stay with us. Mom has been worried sick."

And have my dad show up like a fucking lunatic? No, thank you.

"I'll stop by later and say hi."

Evan grits his teeth and starts walking backward into the lunchroom. "Well, put some makeup on those bags, girl. Or else she might lock you in your room and not let you leave."

My room.

There's a dip in my chest that I ignore to save myself the trouble. There's no room for guilt or heartache in a life like mine.

Evan throws his keys from across the hall. I catch them and send him a thankful smile as I turn and walk out the doors.

He knows when I'm struggling. Naps in his car during lunch used to be a thing of the past, but now that I'm back with my dad, they're starting up again.

Except, the moment I step into the school parking lot, my entire body freezes at the sight of the police car off to the side with a meaty-looking German Shepherd sniffing his drug-smelling nose all around the parked cars like he's ready to tear someone to pieces.

Oh, fuck.

I whip my attention to Evan's car—the same car that holds my purse. The same purse that has a secret package inside from my father who pleaded with me to take and deliver. *"Just this once, Pumpkin."*

Without even looking inside the package, I knew it was drugs.

My father continues to pretend I'm still that seven-year-old girl he left at a bus stop to go get high one evening. I climbed on a big, black, smelly bus and rode on it until morning—where CPS was waiting for me to place me into foster care.

But I'm seventeen, nearly eighteen. I know what drugs are, and I know what the law does to people who are in possession of them.

I wait until Principal Howie and the three loitering police officers have their backs turned, then I duck down below the bushes and crawl my way over to the third line of cars. My heart flies, bumping harshly against my ribs just as the branches of the bush scrape against my back.

With each army crawl against the ground, my heart beats a little faster. Not only would I get in trouble if the drug dog sniffs out the package in my purse, but Evander would get called out of school, along with his parents.

They are the very last people on this planet that I want to disappoint, and although they know my life isn't easy, and know I don't do drugs, they will be hurt that I didn't turn to them the moment my father started his bullshit.

My fingers go underneath the passenger door of Evan's car as I continue to kneel against the parking lot pavement. A piece of gravel has definitely dug into my knee if the piercing pain has anything to say about it. I stay crouched down and feel for my purse until the thin strap touches my finger. I quickly pull it out of the passenger door and dig for the tiny package that fits in the center of my palm.

It's wrapped in a dark cloth, but I know if I lift the fabric, it'll reveal tiny rocks in a clear plastic bag.

I hate my life.

Stuck doesn't begin to describe how I feel, kneeling in the school parking lot with a package of drugs in my hand as the police and their dogs slowly approach all the cars.

What should I do?

I scan the grassy hill beyond the parking lot, wondering if I should just throw the package over there, but after turning back toward the snarling dog who is getting closer and closer, I know that isn't a viable option.

Just then, my eyes focus on a big, black, brand-new F150 three spots down from Evan's.

It's Stone's.

I know it's his, because it is often outside Evan's house, and not to mention, it is one of the nicest vehicles in the school parking lot. His rich daddy wanted the best for him.

I gasp.

His dad.

Stone's father is the hotshot of the town, and if there is anyone who can change the direction of a court sentence, it's him.

Stone will get a slap on the wrist.

I, on the other hand, with my last name having a reputation—no matter how smart I am and how good my grades are —will lose my academic scholarship, and I will be appointed some washed-up lawyer who won't care what happens to my future.

I am not going to bring Evan down with me either.

The gravel beneath my knees is now digging into my back. I slither underneath Evan's car and continue rolling. I'm staring up at the undercarriage of Stone's truck. I gulp back the guilt I'm sure to be submerged in later this evening and slip the little package in the tiniest nook, knowing the drug dogs will still find it.

My father and Stone are both going to put big, red targets on my back for this.

I won't be delivering the package to whatever druggie my father is dealing with, and Stone will no doubt know who was ballsy enough to put drugs in his truck with the police yards away.

But it really has nothing to do with being ballsy and everything to do with simply surviving.

CHAPTER 2
STONE

LUNCH HOUR at West Ridge High is always chaos. The administrators try to control it, as if they have any idea what control looks like. There's a buzz that accompanies the cafeteria that is almost soothing. The chatter of hundreds, if not thousands of students crammed into the huge space.

We're at the center of it. Me, Evan, and the rest of the upperclassmen on the hockey team. We reign supreme in this school, and everyone knows it. The other students watch us like we're royalty—all because we're good at hockey.

Evan and I met when we were thrown on the same hockey team as kids. My dad didn't know what else to do with me, and he was desperate to distract me from the rest of our lives. Luckily for my father, Evan and I traded insults and clicked immediately.

I smirk at that thought. Not that he notices.

Evan started as a teammate and quickly became something akin to a brother. I swear, nowadays I spend more time at his house than my own.

I eye my best friend. He shifts in his seat, his gaze bouncing from the door to his food. There and back, like a fucking yo-yo. He's ignoring the conversation of the guys around us, his brows slightly furrowed. Fidgeting.

Worried about his *sister*.

He got attached to Wren when she first arrived at his house as a malnourished kid, her dark hair greasy, her wide hazel eyes staring unblinkingly up at us. *Us*, because I was there, always hiding out at his house to escape my own—until she arrived, anyway. The weeks or months that she was there, I retreated.

It wasn't like I wasn't welcome. I still saw Evan all the time, hung out with him during the day, stayed over for dinner. But there was a definitive limit to how long his parents could handle three pre-teens, and I was usually the one to make things more chaotic.

Evan is worrying for nothing.

If that girl has to choose between sleep and food, nine times out of ten she picks the former. It's as if she doesn't sleep when she's at her dad's place, for reasons I can only imagine. She's skinnier lately too. But the system has checks and balances for these kinds of things. If something is happening... I mean, she could be on one of those diets, trying to emulate the popular girls. She has a social worker to check in on her. If something is really wrong—*again*—they would take her out of there.

I snap my fingers in his face. "Cut it out, dude. She's fine."

He runs his hand down his face, and his attention drops to his tray. "Yeah."

I give him a look that says I don't buy his bullshit, and he grimaces.

Evan's parents are softies. Like, some of the best people I've ever met. Wren wasn't their first foster kid, but she *was* the first one who seemed to fit into their family as easily as breathing. Something just clicked with them.

And I hated it. Hated that my best friend suddenly had a distraction, someone who pulled his focus away from playing with us. Someone who tagged along with him when we met at the basketball courts or teetered around on figure skates while we practiced our slap shots at the local rink.

The more I got to know her, though, and the longer she stayed with Evan's family...well, I guess I just had to work a little harder at my hate. It helped that I was able to turn my attention to hockey. That I had some distraction, an outlet for my anger. But she throws these freaking barbs at me all the time, and I push her buttons.

Sometimes it's fun.

The buzz in the cafeteria rises. It's like a tide coming at our table, a rush of sound that has the hair on the back of my neck standing up.

"Shit," Evan mutters. He scans a text, then shoves out of his chair. "They did a drug search—and found something, judging from the sound of it."

"Sit down," I order. "We're fine."

He drops back down and frowns. Evan wouldn't dream of touching the stuff, and neither would I. My coach would skin the whole team alive if he caught any of us doing drugs. Even something as innocuous as weed.

It's not worth the public humiliation that Coach would inflict on us.

As a result, I've been on the straight and narrow since I joined the team my freshman year. Once I realized I had a coach who could elevate my skill, I put everything I had into hockey. I saw it as a ticket out of the funnel my father was going to shove me into. The forced path into the corporate world.

I have more riding on the line than most of my teammates, though. I've got real interest from the NHL. Scouts keep coming to games. There have been whispers of drafting me in June. Signing on with a professional team will set me up for life.

It's all I need.

It's all I care about.

Everything else—my home life, family relationships, a "real job" in the words of my father—all gets pushed to the background. Nothing else matters when I'm on the ice.

Doing something to jeopardize that would be laughable.

"They're coming this way," Evan says under his breath. "I don't like the look of this, man. What if—"

"Stone Foster."

The room goes silent, minus the approaching footsteps.

Ice sweeps down my spine.

I pivot in my seat and eye the two officers who stride toward us, led by the rather skittish principal.

"Come with me, Stone," the principal says. "Now, please."

I narrow my eyes at her, but I rise anyway. I'm not in the habit of disobeying orders, especially with the whole school watching.

As soon as I stand, one of the officers is on me. He grabs my upper arm, squeezing my biceps like I'm going to bolt, and practically drags me with him out of the cafeteria. Like I'm no better than a scum-of-the-earth drug dealer? A miscreant?

They couldn't have found anything. Not in my truck, not my locker.

"Officer…" Principal Howie hesitates. "We need to call his father."

Funny, because I was about to use him as my only defense. The words, *'Don't you know who my father is?'* almost passed my lips. I lift my chin, although my skin is getting hotter by the second. There are a million fucking people in the hallways, all gaping at me.

At the scene the officers are creating.

But worse than this is any idea of my father finding out.

They move me into the principal's office and force me into a chair. I let out a huff, trying to suppress my irritation—and quell the sudden worry. Because this seems serious. The principal gives them an admonishing look. It's nothing compared to the one my father will shoot in my direction before he unleashes decades of legal crap at them.

Being a defense lawyer has its perks, I guess.

The secretary pokes her head in. "He's on his way."

I stare at the principal once the door has closed again, leaving just the four of us in her office. While I usually feel comfortable here—having never been in any amount of serious trouble—now, a bead of sweat rolls down my back.

"So, what's this about?" I glance at the two officers framing me in.

The principal sits and folds her hands in front of her on the desk. "We performed a drug search of the property, and we found an illegal substance on your car."

On, not in.

I press my lips together. Now is not the time to talk and get myself in even more trouble. I want to ask what they found and where. I want to ask who the *fuck* would think to plant drugs on my car.

But I don't because, if anything, my father trained me well.

To sit down, shut up, and wait for him.

I just never thought I'd need to take his advice.

Fifteen agonizing minutes later, the door opens, and my father storms through. He was clearly at work. His gray suit is perfectly in place, his tie knotted expertly. We used to share the same light-brown hair, although he started dying his a little darker to hide the gray at his temples.

His sharp gaze takes me in, then the rest of the room. "Principal Howie. Your secretary was not very forthcoming over the phone."

"We found methamphetamines on your son's truck," one of the officers says. "Enough to be considered a felony."

My father faces him. "Excuse me?"

The principal clears her throat. "Um, officers, have you met Daniel Foster?"

One of the officers pales, and it would be fucking amusing if my heart hadn't stopped at the mention of meth.

That's serious.

"I'm sorry, sir, but we have to take your son down to the station."

Fuck.

Dad's jaw tics. But it seems like he can't stop them—or maybe he won't—because he steps back and allows them to haul me up. I shake my head at him, trying to convey that it's not mine. That he's got to figure out a way to get me *out*. I mean, he's defended worse criminals than me—and more famous ones, to be sure. They emerged with their reputations intact.

No one speaks to me. One of the officers tries in the cruiser, but the other stops him.

Meth. On my truck, not in it.

The truck my stepmother bought me with my father's money as some sort of bribe, or penance—I never figured out which. I just started driving it.

Who the fuck would plant drugs on *my* truck?

It doesn't click until my father escorts me out of the police station six hours later. My body aches from sitting on a metal chair, and my throat is dry. Who would've known they were doing a search? Who would've left school just before lunchtime?

Only one person comes to mind.

One person who has connections to that world of drug dealers—who has been *living* with one.

Wren Davis.

"Reckless."

My spine snaps straight.

Dad sneers. "You're *reckless*. And stupid. Dealing drugs on school grounds? Do you *want* to flush your life down the toilet?"

"No, sir."

"They wanted to file felony charges. The only thing protecting you is our last name. My last name. And the leniency of the prosecutor who happened to owe me a favor." His voice is glacial. He glances at me, then back to the road. "This is going to reflect poorly on both of us, no matter what you do."

I exhale. "I know."

"This goes beyond, Stone. If you needed money, you could've come to me—"

I grit my teeth. "I don't."

"And if this is some sick sort of rebellion against your stepmother…" He grimaces. "You need to accept her."

I shake my head and glance out the window. He thinks I'm guilty. He got me out of it by the skin of my teeth, but he still thinks I did it. Maybe because he's used to defending guilty people, and his conscience just doesn't give a shit anymore. Or it's eroded any possibility of people being innocent.

He turns into the school parking lot. It's dark, and there are only a handful of cars left. The night janitors', probably, and my truck. It sits alone.

I grab my backpack and climb out of Dad's car.

"Come straight home."

I grunt my acknowledgement and slam the door. Once I'm safely in my car, I dial Wren's number.

She answers on the second ring. "Stone? I heard what happened—"

"Cut the shit, Sticks," I growl. I'm holding my phone tight, my other hand gripping the steering wheel like it might save me from driving to her dad's place and throttling her. "I know what you did."

Her breathing hitches. All the confirmation I need, really.

"You're dead to me," I declare. "If you see me coming in the hallway, you better go the other fucking direction. If I so much as hear your voice or catch you looking in my direction, I'm going to tell my father that the drugs were yours. And then we'll see who comes out of this unscathed."

"Stone…"

"Do me a favor, Sticks, and fuck off." I hit the end button and toss my phone into the passenger seat.

Only a few months until graduation. I just have to pray that the NHL doesn't catch wind of this or else my whole future will be derailed. And if it is, I'll have no one to blame but Wren Davis.

CHAPTER 3
WREN
PRESENT

TWO BOXES AND A WEATHERED BACKPACK.

That is all I have to my name as I stand outside my foster brother's house with a slightly mended heart because, let's be honest here, a broken heart from someone like Brad doesn't do more than dent the walls I've built over the years.

I take one step forward but three steps back when an elderly man on a bike whooshes past me, mumbling something about college students ruining his day. I roll my eyes and readjust my cardboard boxes. *Why bike this close to Shadow Valley University if you don't like college students?*

"Give me those boxes, right now." Evan pops out of his front door and hops down the front steps with as much ease as I have breathing.

I spin and hide my smile. "I've got it. Just show me the way."

Evan's hand finds the worn strap of my backpack, and he spins me back around. "Excuse me?" His eyebrows reach the top of his forehead, and he gives me a look I've seen multiple times over the years.

I grin and put my boxes on the sidewalk before letting his warm arms envelop me in his classic, brotherly hug.

He may not be blood related to me, but I can say with full transparency that I have never felt safer. Being hugged by any biological family member gave a slightly different feeling than it did when Evan hugged me.

"You good?"

I pull away and glance at his warm eyes, catching moving gray clouds behind his head. I lie and nod, but by the way his lips purse, he knows I'm lying.

"Well, come on. The rest of the guys want to meet you."

I try to steal the boxes back from Evan, but his parents taught him to be a gentleman, so he holds them up above my head until I surrender and follow him through the threshold of my new home.

A pang of guilt backs every step over the creaky floorboards of the hockey house.

I shouldn't be here.

Yet, here I am.

It was the best choice, given the circumstances. What's a girl to do when she stumbles upon her steady boyfriend of the last year banging a sorority girl on their kitchen counter?

Jasmin says I should burn his belongings, but I usually try to avoid breaking the law, because the last thing the Davis name needs is another crime attached to it.

The moment Evan and I turn to the left, I'm the center of the room. Heat swipes up my neck and wraps around my cheeks like a snake as I stand beside him, staring at several of his teammates.

I'll admit it.

I'm not a fan of hockey.

I have never been to a game, so I don't recognize a single one of them, and although this is my second year at Shadow Valley University, I hang with the academic crowd versus the jocks. Just like in high school.

The first guy stands and slowly walks over to me. I tip my

chin. He's a freaking mammoth. *What on earth does he eat for breakfast?*

"Hi, Wren. It's nice to meet you. I'm Taylor."

His hand is there for the taking, so I gingerly take it, although I'm the furthest thing from a docile college girl. Once I shake his hand, his toothy grin appears.

"I'd like to volunteer as tribute to be your roommate. You can sleep in my bed."

Everyone in the room snickers.

I look at him, unsure if he is kidding or not. When he winks, I realize I'm in way over my head in my new living arrangements.

"With me, of course," he adds. "But I won't touch you."

Evan places my boxes on the floor and slaps the six-foot-something hockey player over the head. "I told you guys to be fucking normal. She's my sister."

"Be normal?" Another hockey player replaces Taylor, slipping in front of me quickly. He smiles and shows off his missing tooth. "How can we be normal with someone this gorgeous standing in front of us?"

Most girls would have giggled and blushed.

But I'm not a normal girl.

"She was just cheated on. Cut the shit." Another guy pushes Toothless away and rolls his eyes. "I'm Sullivan."

His hands land on my shoulders, and I'm suddenly being pulled into his hard chest. His hug is nice, but I don't wrap my arms around his waist because, to be honest, I'm a little thrown off balance.

My world has shifted dramatically over the last week. I'm damn good at dodging the punches, but right now, I'm tired.

So fucking tired.

Evan leans in. "We call him Sully because, well, he looks like a monster, but he's actually the nicest of us all."

"Including you?" I peer through my thick eyelashes.

"Because not many people would let a Davis live in their house on a moment's notice."

Evan grimaces, but he doesn't comment on my personal dig. Instead, he introduces the last roommate, and by the time I follow him upstairs to my new room, I'm certain I've memorized their names and matched them with their faces. *Taylor, Grant, Sully, and Archer.*

"It's not huge, but it works."

I laugh. "This is a huge room and an even bigger house, Evander. You all are just...big."

Evan throws his head back and lets out a loud laugh before placing my boxes on the floor. "Don't let them hear you say that. Their egos are already too much."

"All hockey players' egos are too much," I counter.

Warmth fills the air around me while I stand in a small bedroom with Evan showing off his adorable, goofy grin that he only reserves for those he actually feels comfortable with. I do a spin, checking out every nook and cranny, and I'm happy to report that there are no holes in the walls or spiders in the corners of the ceilings, *and* there's an actual bed that's mine.

Not shared with a cheating boyfriend or filthy from previous foster kids.

"Déjà vu," Evan says, inching toward the door.

His eyes spark with what I can only describe as relief.

"Just like old times," I half-joke. My lips curve into a sad smile.

Evan grips the top of the doorjamb before pushing himself off. "Yeah, but this time, no one's gonna force you to leave."

He shuts the door, and I stand there alone, feeling half relieved but half scared. If there's anything I've learned from the moment I was born, it's that when things seem too good to be true, that usually means they are.

CHAPTER 4
STONE

"THIS IS AN OPPORTUNITY OF A LIFETIME." I cross my arms, then uncross them. I'm jittery, *anxious*, and I hate this fucking feeling. Like my life is balanced on this decision, and someone else is holding the reins. "I have to go."

My father's gaze is on whatever bullshit paperwork is in his hands. He's working. He's always working. But with some big trial coming up, it's been almost impossible to get his attention. Even when I need it.

Especially when I need it.

"Dad."

"One moment, Stone."

I clench my jaw and turn away.

He practically lives at his office downtown. He's on the third floor, in the corner office of the clock tower building his law firm took over last year. His windows overlook a busy street, another building across it—the library—and a fucking park. How idyllic. He's got rooftop access in this building and everything.

He once took my step-monster and me to a work party. We dressed up and drank cocktails. Well, they did. I snuck the free glasses of champagne when no one was watching, got so drunk I puked in the privacy hedges surrounding the roof, and was escorted home by Dad's assistant.

That was before my body-is-a-temple mentality. Before I got serious about hockey.

Before I realized Dad doesn't give a shit about anything that doesn't touch his image.

A billboard just went up with his face on it. He's smiling in the photo, with some slogan about saving innocent people from the justice system. *In Foster, We Trust.* I'd think nothing of it—except that he's getting too big for his britches—if I hadn't overheard a conversation where he talked about running for governor next term.

Then he'd truly be insufferable.

"Okay." Dad sets down the file and faces me. His hands are in his pockets, his face relaxed. "What's the opportunity of a lifetime?"

The whole spiel about attending this new school—I have to repeat it?

I bite the inside of my cheek hard enough to draw blood. The metallic taste is grounding in a way, and I relish it on my tongue. It sharpens my focus in the same way a hockey fight does.

"You've heard of Mike Aster?" I question.

He shakes his head and motions for me to get on with it.

"He's only the greatest college hockey coach of all time. He's already been put in the hall of fame." I take a deep breath. "And I was accepted to the school. I met him, and he said he had heard of *me*—"

"Of course he's heard of you." Dad rolls his eyes. "You've worked hard. The NHL doesn't draft every hockey player to come out of West Ridge, you know."

I know that.

I signed a contract with the New York Guardians last year when I turned eighteen. Their draft was nerve-racking, but I did it. I was a sixth-round pick after speaking with their coach a few days prior. They knew my intentions of doing two years at college. To improve. To play against higher-caliber players. To get stronger.

One year in, and I know I've made the right decision. This year, technically my sophomore year, will be my last in college. I take the minimum, easiest classes. Or the interesting ones. The school knows I'm only there for a short while, but I like to think of it as a symbiotic relationship. They let me play and take low-brow classes, and I win them championships.

Or so it's supposed to go.

"I want to transfer," I spell out. "This coach I have now, he's okay, but—"

"You want the best."

"Yes."

That seems to be something my father understands.

"You think your team will win the Frozen Four?"

I'm convinced he only knows what the Frozen Four—the final four games of the NCAA Tournament—is because I used to talk incessantly about it. Evan and I would pretend we were playing that final championship game, the score tied. Everything boiling down to *that one moment*. We loved the rush of it.

"I do," I answer, keeping my voice steady and my body relaxed. If he missed my fidgeting earlier, all the better. There's no sign of it now. "I need to play with the best to be the best, Dad."

"Send the information to my secretary. What we need to do to set you up at school financially." He frowns. "I trust you can sort out the rest?"

"I've got it all covered." I back toward the door. "I'll leave you to it. Bye, Dad."

He's already shifting back to work mode, picking up the folder and scanning it again. His head is bent, his tie loosened, and his suit jacket off.

Downstairs, I climb in my car. My bags are packed. I

wasn't going to take no as an answer. While I expected more of a fuss from him, I won't look a gift horse in the mouth either. I have his blessing. I'm getting away from the step-monster.

It's a two-hour drive to Shadow Valley. I crank the radio and sing along, lighter than I've felt in *years*. Since the arrest, Dad has kept me on a tight leash. He insisted on drug testing me every week for over a year, going so far as to stand in the bathroom with me to make sure I didn't cheat when the tests kept coming back clean.

Because I don't do drugs.

The cops in this town stare at me as I pass. As the son of a defense attorney, I'm sort of used to it. I had their attention before I was accused of doing anything wrong. But now, they're suspicious.

As soon as I'm out of the city limits, my singing gets louder. I've got a terrible voice, but it doesn't stop me from belting along to the classics. Nirvana and Blue Oyster Cult. You can't tell me 'Burnin' For You' isn't the best fucking song on earth.

The drive passes quickly that way, and before I know it, I'm pulling into Shadow Valley. I visited Evan here last year, after our seasons ended, and met his hockey teammates. I knew they were guys I wanted to play with, and with their coach? Of course I was going to make it happen.

Besides, if we win the Frozen Four, I have a better chance of the Guardians taking me onto their team immediately, instead of passing me off to their AHL affiliated team. I want the majors. I want the best.

Dream big or go home, right?

I park on the street and sling my bag over my shoulder. I'll come back for the rest when I figure out which room is mine.

"Anybody home?" I push the door open and step through. The huge house has a frat feel to it, although it's removed from frat row. The wide porch out front, the brick, the little balcony overhead. It's charming and probably not a place six guys should be living.

"Hey, man!" The big guy, Sully, comes around the corner. "Evan's upstairs. I hear you're joining us this year?"

I grin and slap his hand. "Yeah. You think you're ready for me?"

He chuckles. "I've seen your highlights. I'm just glad we're on the same team now."

"Oh, fuck off," Evan calls. My best friend strides into the room. He seems healthier, like he spent the summer in the sun. He stops in front of me. "Your room is upstairs."

"Okay."

"I'll, uh… I'll show you."

Sully chuckles behind me. I wave him off and follow Evan to the stairs. The downstairs is even bigger than it looks from the front, but we skip a tour in favor of seeing where I'm sleeping for the next ten months.

"There are six of us? Six bedrooms?"

Evan doesn't answer.

"Dude." I catch up to him and grab his arm, spinning him to face me. "What's up with you? If you don't want me here…"

"No, no. It's not that." He makes a face. "It's just that we had an emergency pop up the other day…"

"An emergency like what?"

"Well, you just have a roommate, is all. It couldn't be helped."

I grunt and motion for him to go on. Instead of talking, though, he steps up to the first door on the left and cracks it open.

"This is yours."

I eye him, then enter.

It's a miniature explosion of *stuff*. Not a lot of it, but what is there has been spread everywhere. Clothes, textbooks.

But more importantly, *girl* clothes. *Makeup.*

"What the fuck is this, E? You knew I was coming. We've planned for this since I got accepted."

Yeah, sure, it wasn't absolutely fucking decided until I got in my car today. My father played a large part in that. But honestly, I was going to come here whether or not I got his blessing. I would've paid for it myself.

Dread turns my gut over. There's only one person Evan would do this for.

"Please don't tell me you let *her* have my room."

"Half," he mutters. "Half the room."

"There's only one fucking bed! How is that half?" I pace in a circle, kicking her clothes in the process. I stop and point at him. "I want her out."

"Out? She's got nowhere to go."

"Bullshit." Damn, I'm *seething*. I haven't been this angry in…well, probably since the last time I spared a thought for Wren Davis. "Move her into your room."

He glares at me. "How weird would that be? She's my sister. I have a girlfriend—"

"You do not."

"I have a girl that I hook up with on a semi-regular basis," he corrects. "Suck it up, Foster."

A door slams downstairs. Without a doubt, I know exactly who it is. The one person with the worst fucking timing on the face of the planet.

I plant my hands on my hips. "Does she know about this little arrangement?"

His expression turns guilty. "Well…"

"Evan?" Her voice—her sweet, melodic, *evil-as-shit* voice —floats toward us. "What are you doing in my—"

She appears in the doorway and stops. Her face goes pale, and horror fills her eyes.

"What is he doing here?" she hisses at her pseudo-brother.

I take a seat on the bed, very deliberately ignoring the shit she has strewn across it. I can't stop staring at her. At how different she seems. There are circles under her eyes, sure, but that comes with every college experience. Lack of sleep and whatever. But she's no longer the skinny little kid with insomnia. She's…well… She's something else.

And as I wage an internal war about whether I like what I see, her nose wrinkles. Like *she* is disappointed in what she sees in *me*.

But you know what?

I'd rather use that to my advantage.

I lean back and smile at her. "I'm moving in, Sticks. Welcome to Hell."

CHAPTER 5
WREN

WELCOME TO HELL.

Looking at Stone Foster in my new bedroom is exactly what I would imagine if I were to be face to face with the devil himself. A handsome, smug, cocky, *evil* monster. The hate in his blue eyes is fleeting and quickly replaced with a vengeance that I feel down to my bones.

"No," I whisper, beginning to shake my head.

It is just like old times—being in a room with Evan and Stone, feeling like the odd one out. Evan always included me, being the best foster brother there was, but Stone always shut me out, irritating me, hating me, picking on me.

But we aren't teens any longer.

We are adults, and Stone is obviously out for revenge. I smelled it the moment I stepped in the house. Call it a sixth sense, or maybe I am just used to constantly having to watch my back. I've been on edge since the moment I planted the drugs on his truck. Only, the other people out for revenge are even worse than Stone. Maybe that's why I'm not shaking in my shoes, staring at him from across the room.

"I'm leaving," I say. I send a quick glance to Evan who is clearly panicking.

"No, you're n—"

"Thank fuck. See ya, Sticks." Stone leans farther back on the bed, and his arrogant, proud smile is all I see.

"Stone," Evan warns. He steps in between us.

I'm near the door, ready to dart, until I look past Evan's shoulder and latch onto Stone's glare. It's full of disdain, and I can't even blame him. And *God*, why does he look *so* good? Blue eyes the color of the sky surrounded by thick, dark eyelashes. A heavy brow line that makes him look dangerous —which is completely accurate—and even though he's smiling at me like the prick he is, his smile is absolutely perfect. The angles on his jawline should be illegal, and there's a messed-up part of me that wants to know how sharp they feel beneath my palm.

"What?" Stone pulls his steely gaze away from me and puts it on his best friend. "I had dibs on the room first, right? She should be the one to leave."

Irritation flies down my spine at his need to push me out. I've been pushed around all my life, and I've grown a little more of a backbone over the last two years.

"I was here first. Finders keepers, losers weepers."

Stone glares, and I can't believe that was the first thing I've said directly to him in two years.

"No one is leaving! You both need to grow up. This little hatred game you two have been playing is done."

"The fuck it is." Stone stands, and if we weren't separated by Evan, he'd be towering over me like a nightmare.

I remember the day like it was yesterday. Stone doesn't understand why I did what I did, but truly, it was a life-or-death situation for me. I *had* to get out of Maysville, and my full ride to Shadow Valley was the only way I was going to do that.

"She's just using you." Stone's cold accusation parts my lips, and a rushed gasp flies out.

"What?" I cross my arms and stand tall. "That isn't true."

Evan throws his hands up and walks toward the door, bypassing me and my tantrum. He's disappointed, and I instantly feel bad.

"You two need to hash this out. I'm sick and tired of having two important people in my life hate each other." He turns and looks us both in the eye. "Figure it out. Neither of you are leaving this fucking house until you do."

The door slams, and Stone is completely unbothered, and it's obvious that he feels zero remorse. *Typical.*

He sits back on the bed with strong arms holding him up from behind. His muscles flicker with each thundering beat of my heart. "There's a nice tree out front that you'd be perfect for. Those sticks of legs you still have will blend in perfectly."

I roll my eyes. "That's the best you've got? The stick joke?"

"Why are you even here? You had nowhere else to go? I find that hard to believe."

I stand with my back against the closed door and recross my arms. I'm wearing my Shadow's shirt, and if I don't leave soon, I'll miss my second shift, and the dinner crowd gives better tips. I'm beyond grateful to have a steady waitressing job that works around my school schedule, and I'm not going to screw it up by being late. "Do you think I'd stay in a room with you if I had any other choice?"

He chuckles, and it's frustrating how it sounds the exact same as it did two years ago. "Have you seen me, Sticks? Of course you'd want to stay in a room with me." He reaches back and grabs the other pillow, closest to the wall, and throws it on the floor, along with the thin blanket that was at the foot of the bed. "I get the bed."

"How gentlemanly of you," I snide.

Stone stands and shrugs. "I'm the hockey player here. I need the rest."

He walks toward me, and I want to run, but I don't because that's just not who I am. I've been face to face with much more dangerous people than Stone Foster, even if he does absolutely loathe me.

"What do you need to rest for?"

He's standing a mere inch away, and my heart is flying through my chest so fast I'm certain he can see my pulse pounding against the side of my neck. Stone is completely relaxed, though. His breathing is level, and the moment his lips part, I'm surrendering to his breath against my face like it's a wicked spell.

I gasp when his hands latch onto my forearms, but I don't dare pull away when he flings them onto the door behind me with a little too much force. His knee is between my legs, and I'm so frozen I can't even breathe. Heat paints my cheeks when he stares at my chest. His eye twitches, and his body puts off so much hate that it should scare me.

"The Shadow Bar and Grill?"

His laugh is full of sarcasm, and I hastily pull my arms out of his grip. He steps away, and I finally can breathe again.

"That's what you need rest for? A fucking waitressing job?"

He rolls those cold blue eyes of his, and I put my back to him, flinging the door open with so much force it hits the back of the wall. I'm halfway down the hall when he calls out from behind me.

"See you later, *roomie*."

————

MY SHIFT AT SHADOW'S ENDS TOO QUICKLY.

I'm back at *home* and staring up at the light coming from the window in what *was* my room until my past decided to come bite me on the ass.

Evan's texts are burning a hole in my back pocket, and part of me wants to tell him why Stone hates me so much, but

I don't want the pity, because knowing Evander, he'd understand why I did what did.

He would be disappointed, but he knows my living situation and family drama better than anyone.

Stone knows of my past too.

But he has a cold heart, so of course there is zero compassion or sympathy on his part. *Except*...Stone never did tell Evan the truth. The only thing Stone did after the whole ordeal was pretend I no longer existed.

Too bad he has to share a room with me now, and after reading Evan's texts, I know I have to suck it up and play nice because if there is one person in my life who I don't want to upset, it's him.

"Get in here, girl! We made dinner."

I peel my eyes from the second-floor window, and three happy grins stare back at me from the door. The smell of Thai food slips out past Evan's teammates and pulls me toward the door without much protest. I can't say no to stir-fry noodles and curry, even if I did eat a hamburger on my break.

"Wow, this smells..." I pause at the open containers from Touch of Thai splayed out on the coffee table in the living room surrounded by empty plates. I laugh. "I thought you said you made dinner."

"*Made* as in...put it on a plate." Evan snickers after landing a quick peck on my temple. "The rest of the food is in the kitchen."

Suddenly, I'm fifteen years old again and uncomfortable at the thought of someone taking care of me. *Should I give them money for dinner? Should I say I already ate? Should I pick up dinner tomorrow night?* The last thought sends a rush of panic down my spine because how the hell can I afford to feed hockey players on my measly waitressing salary?

Instead of asking any of the questions on the tip of my tongue, I smile and walk into the kitchen, leaving Evan, Sully, and Grant in the living room as they rewatch some hockey game on ESPN—probably of themselves, knowing how hockey players are.

The moment I step foot on the tiled floor, I pause and almost retreat.

There he is, all tall and broad-shouldered, leaning over the counter like he owns the room. I don't make a single noise, something I managed to master all those years ago, sneaking through foster homes while my temporary guardians were asleep so I could find loose coins in the couch cushions or some leftover food that was usually spoiled in the back of the fridge.

"Hungry, Sticks?"

I stay quiet because I don't trust him. He's probably poisoning the food.

"There's a nice spot out back." Stone peeks over his shoulder, and his lips tip in a devilish grin. "Perfect for sunlight. I'll water you every other day, and I picked up a bag of soil after practice." He spins around and leans against the sink, holding a white-and-red container that has Touch of Thai written on the front. "I thought if we just buried those sticks of yours, they would morph into a tree trunk, and you'd be set."

I hate him.

I hate that I'm letting him bully me.

I hate that I understand why he's bullying me.

"Clever," I say, moving farther into the kitchen. Nerves fuel my steps, but I refuse to show him any sort of guilt or any type of cowering. I will make this work between us, mainly because I truly have nowhere else to go—I can't afford it.

"I thought so," he replies.

I catch the quick grin on his lips, and alarm bells ring in the back of my head.

"Here you go."

He's holding out the container of Thai food, and I gingerly reach up and place my hand on it. Our fingers brush, and heat whooshes all the way up my arm and into my chest, burning me from the inside.

"Did you poison it first?"

Stone keeps his fingers resting against mine. "No, I prefer to watch you suffer slowly. Makes it more rewarding."

His hand is gone a moment later, and that's when I realize the nonexistent weight of the Thai container. I peer inside and see that it's completely empty.

"Enjoy dinner, Sticks."

His evil, menacing laugh is more of a threat, and I'm suddenly wondering what is more uncomfortable: sleeping in a room with someone who hates me or sleeping in the back-seat of my old, barely running Honda.

CHAPTER 6
STONE

I LEAVE the kitchen before I can see Wren's reaction. As soon as I heard the guys welcoming her home, I hurried to scrape every last remainder of food into a different container, which is now buried at the back of the fridge.

The slightest tinge of guilt presses down on me, but I shrug it off. If not for her, I'd have a better relationship with my father. I wouldn't have had to all but beg him to let me continue my journey with the NHL. I wouldn't have had to apologize to the head coach of the New York Guardians on the night before I signed with them, making up some acceptable excuse.

Most embarrassing moment of my *life*, and I thought I was going to watch it all go down the drain. Every late night practicing my slap shots, every sprint, every drill. For nothing.

I don't trust her not to stab me in the back again.

I close myself in my room, leaning against the door for a moment while I formulate a plan.

Wren Davis is fucking dangerous to be around. Those big hazel eyes seem to look right through me, and sometimes—well, most of the time—she doesn't like what she sees. It's obvious from the hate in her expression.

Just as well. I can't stand her guts.

And every moment in this house puts me and my team-mates in jeopardy.

What's stopping her from bringing more drugs into this house? Who knows what she's gotten into since I last saw her. Drug dealing would be the least surprising thing about her, especially knowing her family history.

The sooner she leaves, the better.

There's just one problem, and his name is Evan fucking Mitchell. My best friend loves her like a sister. A treacherous snake of a sister, but a sister nonetheless. Which means I can't just kick her out like I want to. For all intents and purposes, I need to play nice.

Nice-*ish*.

I push off from the door. Her stuff is everywhere. It's really, actually awful. In the closet, I spot a plastic bin. It has a line of tape and some other last name written on it, so it's clearly a relic of a past housemate.

Easy enough to reuse.

I swipe all her makeup and clothes into the bin. It's a little depressing how *everything* fits. The stuff hanging in the closet, in the drawers. My bags are still stacked along the wall, waiting for…

Who the fuck knows.

Me to man up, I guess.

I snap the bin's lid closed and kick it under my bed. Then I promptly strip her blankets and sheets to replace them with ones I brought from home, and something hot pink falls out. My eyes widen.

I snatch it up with two fingers, glaring at it.

It's a sex toy.

The idea of her getting herself off on that bed is oddly erotic. And *now* I'm picturing my arch-nemesis naked, her legs spread, the toy—

Fuck off, Foster.

I remake the bed and stuff the sex toy under my pillow for future humiliation. Then I unpack. I take up every single drawer and hanger.

Inhaling deeply, I look around and smirk to myself.

There's no trace of Wren, except under my bed and under the pillow.

I only hope she cleaned that thing after using it.

I flop on the bed with a book in one hand, earbuds firmly in my ears, and my other arm stretched over my head. And then I wait.

Finally, the door cracks open, and Wren slips in. It takes her a minute to close the door and turn back around, her shoulders rising like she's working up her defense. My gaze flicks from the book to her, then back again.

Her mouth drops. "What the hell, Stone?"

I ignore her.

I can hear her—my music isn't even playing—but she doesn't know that. Maybe I should actually switch on the music and drown her out. But part of me is curious. I've never had anyone to needle like this. No one who grinds my gears enough to try to destroy.

It's kind of gratifying.

"Where are my things?"

She comes over and whacks my leg.

I look up at her, taking in her furious expression. The poor foster kid doesn't like her stuff messed with, evidently.

"Are you intentionally being a bag of dicks, or does it come naturally?"

I barely suppress my snort. I yank out one of the earbuds and drop it on my chest. "Excuse me, what was that?"

Her face is turning red. In a moment, steam might pour out of her ears. *God, I hope so.* It would have a featured place in my mental gallery of her.

"My. Things."

I sit up and dog-ear my book, dropping it onto the bed

beside me. "Sorry, not sure what you're talking about. You have things?"

Her expression tightens. "I swear, I will go get Evan—"

"Okay, okay. Calm down, Sticks. I was just preparing your space. Making it nice and cozy for you." I lean down and drag the bin out, cracking it open. "Hey, there's even room for you in here."

She stops moving. Her gaze is glued on her things all shoved rather haphazardly in the bin. To be fair, it's a decent size. She wasn't lacking in *that* much stuff.

"We can switch off with the bed," she finally says, jerking the bin farther away from me. She drops to her knees and rummages through it.

"No, we can't."

Her hazel eyes are greener today. Or maybe it's just the room...or her t-shirt.

"You should shower," I add. "You smell like sweat and overcooked food."

"Fuck you," she seethes. She grabs handfuls of clothes and her toiletries and darts for the door.

I wiggle my fingers at her and put my earbud back in.

She returns an hour later, her long, dark hair caught up in a towel on top of her head. She's in a threadbare t-shirt that does nothing to hide her nipples and shorts that barely cover her ass.

"You walked around out there like that?"

Her sigh is her only reply.

I toss my book on the nightstand and point to the pile of blankets. "There's your shit. Surely you can make a nest like a good little rat."

Her eyes narrow, and she takes her time working the towel out of her hair. She throws the wet thing in my direction. It hits my chest, and the scent of her shampoo assaults my nose. I make a choking noise and drop down on the bed.

"Is that fucking lavender?" I cough out.

"What's your problem?"

"I'm allergic. My throat is going to swell—"

"Oh my God." She rushes me. Her fingers dig into my wrist, trying to pry my hand away from my throat. "Jesus, Stone, I had no idea—" The panic written across her features is what breaks me.

I burst out laughing.

She falls away from me.

"The expression on your face," I wheeze. "I actually thought you cared for a second. Damn, Sticks, you could've fooled me."

"That's not funny." She pats down her shirt and pivots away sharply.

Not funny. Was she trying to be funny when she put the drugs under my truck?

"Some pranks just don't hit right, do they?" My voice is cold. "We have an early morning."

I reach for the light and click it off before she can react, leaving her standing in the dark. I put my earbuds back in and crank my music. Because fuck her. I can't let my guard down again.

———

I WAKE BEFORE MY ALARM, AND I'M IMMEDIATELY CONSCIOUS OF the second body in the room. Her breathing is deep, and when I carefully roll over, I spot her form in the low, early morning light. She's created a makeshift bed with the blankets and sheets, and she's so deeply burrowed in it all I can make out is the upper half of her face and her fan of dark hair.

She didn't prank me in the middle of the night. I sort of expected to wake up with whipped cream on my palm and a feather on my nose, or my palms glued together, or my hand left in warm water.

Nothing.

Instead, I swing my legs over and immediately knock something over.

Cold water soaks my feet.

I swear under my breath, jerking at the sensation, and hit something else. More water.

"What the fuck?"

I switch on my phone's flashlight and shine it at the floor.

She's surrounded my bed in half-filled plastic cups, like a petty, prepubescent child with a stick up her ass. I smother my laugh at that. *Sticks with a stick up her ass*. I gather as many cups in my hands as I can, moving them to create a barrier between our sides of the room.

There's nothing I can do about the water that's already spilled, soaking into the rug. But I *can* repay her. Or at least make it difficult for her to get out of her pile of blankets. Once the army of cups has her surrounded, my side of the room is free and clear to walk around.

I sop up the water with the towel she used on her head last night, and her breathing doesn't even change.

After I'm showered and dressed, I pull her sex toy from where I kept it under my pillow. Was that what she was scrounging for last night?

Well, I'll return it to her. *Happily*.

I head downstairs. The other guys must not be early risers, and that's fine by me. My step-monster is the sort to sleep in too. Over the summer, mornings became the only time I could hang out in the house and still have a sort of refuge from her.

I write a note for Wren, taping it to the toy, and drop it on the kitchen table. It stares at me as I make my coffee and cereal. I wolf both down, now a hundred percent sure I need to get out of the house before this explodes in my face. Although, I would *love* to see her reaction…

No, fuck it.

I switch the toy on. It buzzes to life with surprising vigor, and my jaw goes slack for a moment. She puts *this thing* inside her? Fucking hell, no guy is ever going to please her if she's used to a cock that vibrates. It's got a little extra arm on it that I assume is for her clit.

Stop fucking thinking about her.

My shoes are on, and my bag is by the door. Everything is organized. Prim and proper.

The toy goes back on the table, and the buzzing is a thousand times louder against the wood. The thing jumps and jiggles. It's going to wake someone up, for sure. Or die trying.

I head out for my run and hope like hell someone will fill me in on the reactions later.

CHAPTER 7
WREN

WHAT AN AMATEUR.

Stone obviously has no idea what it's like to have to sleep with one eye open at all times. I hear him this morning from my surprisingly comfy pallet on the floor. I've slept in worse places than the floor of a secure house on a college street, that's for sure. And I'm sure, much to Stone's oblivious state, I know how to fake sleep and keep my eyes shut.

The door latches, and I spring up and laugh at all the cups that surround me. To be honest, I'm a little disappointed. After placing the cups around his bed last night, I assumed he'd dump them on my head like the asshole that he is, but instead, he placed them around me. Surely he knew that I was going to wake up skeptical.

I pull my hair up into a messy bun and push the covers off my legs, letting the cool air wash over my heated skin. I slowly stand and tiptoe over the cups and head to the bathroom to get ready for class.

I take more classes than most sophomores in college, but that just comes with my degree. I knew choosing a BS in Chemistry was going to be vigorous and demanding, especially because I had to keep up a 3.5 GPA for my academic scholarship, but proving to the world that a Davis can be more than a drug dealer is pretty much at the top of my bucket list.

Although, when some people found out that I was becoming a chemist, they made the joke that I was only doing it so I could help my father make drugs—as if my *real* goal in life is to be cooped up in a disgusting trailer full of cockroaches, playing around with methylamine and hydroiodic acid.

After rinsing my face and throwing on some makeup—which was all hurled into the stupid plastic tote that Stone threw my shit into—I open the bathroom door and hear a noise coming from downstairs.

What the hell is that?

Two doors open down the hall, and sleepy hockey players emerge with their lack of shirts and flickering abs from stretching the sleep from their bodies.

"What's that noise?" Archer's entire body takes up the hallway because of the width of his shoulders.

Taylor follows closely behind.

"I don't know," I answer.

They both stumble past me toward the noise. I decide to go, too, having a terrible feeling that it has to do with Stone, since he isn't in his bed.

The farther I go down the stairs, the more my heart beats. It's a familiar sound. It sounds like vibrating, and I'm suddenly panicking because Stone put his fucking hands on my stuff last night, and that's something I truly do not like.

"Oh, fuck." Archer is standing in the threshold of the kitchen.

All I can see is his stupid, large shoulders shaking with laughter.

Taylor doesn't smother his laughter with his teammate. He howls and throws his head back to the ceiling before looking over his shoulder with devilish eyes that show each and every dirty thought going through his head.

I'm going to fucking kill Stone.

"What is going on?"

I snap out of my plans of choking Stone in his sleep and turn at Evan's voice. He is the very last person I want to see my bright-pink vibrator that I use more often than not, even when I was still in a relationship with Brad.

Shit, shit, shit.

Evan's brows furrow. "Wren? What's wrong? Why are you pale?" He pauses. "And what the fuck is that godforsaken noise?"

I whoosh around and squeeze past Taylor, who is *still* laughing, and try diving toward the table before my foot catches on the cabinet, and I fly to my knees. The hard tile breaks my fall before Archer's hands are around my waist. He hauls me up, but I claw to get away so I can grab onto my vibrator—which is *still* gaining all the attention.

Oh my God.

The moment I turn it off, I let out a breath, but when I meet Evan's disgusted look, I wish I would stop breathing altogether.

"Is that…" His face scrunches after he looks from it to me. "Fuck!" His hands slap over his eyes, and now there is more laughter than before.

Everyone is awake.

Everyone is staring at me holding my pink vibrator in the middle of the kitchen.

The only person missing is Stone.

"Oh, shut up!" I place my hands on my hips, which looks ridiculous because I'm holding a pink, dick-shaped vibrator that just so happens to have an extra part on it for *more* stimulation. "You act like you've never seen a vibrator before!"

"I have!" Evan turns around and bends over at the waist. He's dry heaving. "I've just never seen *you* with one! Fuck."

"Bro." Grant shrugs. "She's not even your real sister. You can't honestly say that you've never thought about having sex with her." He glances at me.

Does he think I'm deaf and can't hear him?

"I mean, look at her."

"I'm right here!" I shout. I sigh agitatedly while planning Stone's death. "Ugh, move."

I'm ready to plow through my roommates, but Taylor clears his throat.

"Don't forget your note."

Fury backs my every move. "What?"

A yellow sticky note is dangling from the ends of his fingers, and I snatch it quickly, reading over the contents.

Missing something, Sticks? No surprise you'd need this — who wants to touch a girl with sticks for legs? It's no wonder your boyfriend cheated on you.

Ouch.

I don't let his insult wound me for too long. Instead, I crumple the piece of paper and throw it in the trash before smoothing out my shirt and walking through the kitchen, past the rest of my housemates who are now eyeing me with a little more twinkle in their eyes.

Except for Evan. He's trying to hold back vomit.

His hand grips my forearm to stop me from squeezing past him. "Let me guess? Stone?"

I shrug. "Just some roommate drama. Don't worry about it, big brother."

The one person who should be worrying is Stone. I know how to rise to a challenge and play games.

And he should know better than anyone that I can play dirty.

———

THERE ARE LIGHTS SHINING THROUGH THE BEDROOM WINDOW from a car driving down the street, and by the sound of the bass, I know it's Stone. He always blared his music in high school when coming to Evan's house, and I see that nothing much has changed. I recognize the song 'Burnin' For You' and tap along to the beat underneath the covers with my vibrator glued to my other hand.

I'll admit, my little plan for tonight sounded a lot better this morning when I was simmering with anger over what Stone had done, but I don't give up easily, and there is no way I am retreating when it comes to him. What he did was totally uncalled for.

Granted, placing drugs on his truck in high school teetered between unjust and impartial, but at least I had a good reason.

He's just being an asshole. He is still that same haughty, cocky, superior boy from two years ago who enjoyed inflicting misery on my life.

A door shuts downstairs, and heat races to my fingertips. There's a delicious twist in between my legs at the thought of doing this in front of Stone, but I'm blaming that on the excitement of irritating him. There is a chance my plan will backfire, but either way, I'll piss Stone off, and that is the most important thing at the moment.

My breath is trapped between my lips, and my chest is full of unshed oxygen. I hear him talking to one of the guys down the hall about their practice. They all got home before him, and knowing Stone, he stayed late to practice more because he just *has* to be the best.

"Yeah, I'll meet you downstairs at 6, man."

My eyes are open, and his tall, shadow-like form stands in the door. I can't see if he's scowling, but I have a pretty good imagination.

"Get up." It's not a request.

"I won't get up," I say. "But I sure will get off."

I smile deviously and press the button the very second he shuts the door and flicks the light on, showing off that stupid scowl of his.

Game on, Foster.

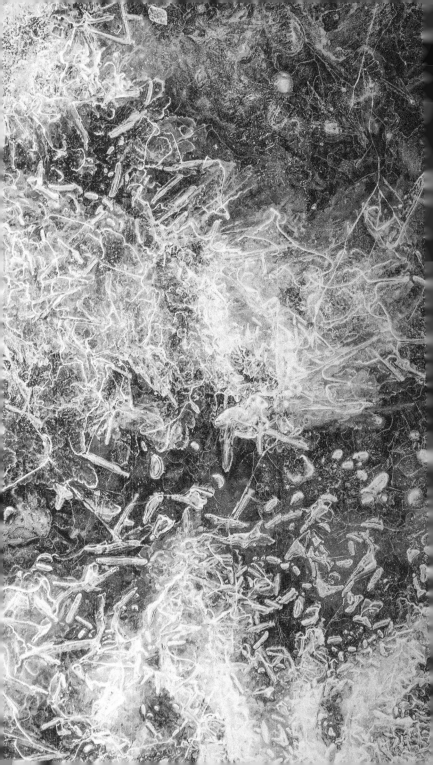

CHAPTER 8
STONE

BUZZING FILLS THE ROOM.

I glare at Wren, her lower half concealed under a blanket —*my fucking blanket*—as her eyes roll back in her head.

"Fuck," she groans. "This feels so much better than you could dream of doing."

My heart kickstarts, and before I can think better of it, I stride forward and try to rip the fucking blanket off the bed. She's got a hold of it, though, and it only goes down enough to reveal her bare knees. She keeps the other part firmly covering the apex of her legs...where her hand is undoubtedly wrapped around the base of the pink vibrator, her panties pulled to the side. If she's even wearing panties.

"Nice try." She laughs. It's raspy, her pleasure overriding her humor.

If there's one thing in the goddamn world I should *not* be doing, it's watching her masturbate.

"Get out," she says, an echo of my order. "So I can get off in peace."

I swallow and back away until I'm not close enough to touch her. In fact, I press my back against the door in an effort to resist drifting closer. But I can certainly *smell* her. It's like every part of my being is now hardwired to focus on her. To find *her*. The hate that comes with that is almost overwhelming.

Yet, it's not enough to stop my dick from reacting. From stiffening in my running shorts.

"What's wrong, Stone? Never seen a girl bring h-herself to…" She arches, her pretty mouth opening as the words fade.

She's got to be fucking joking.

I want to strangle her and take over the job in equal measure. Both things would probably be *ill advised*. I'd have to chop off my hands after.

"Keep going." My voice is fucking hoarse, but I suddenly want to call her on her bluff. "I think I'll stay right here and watch you come, Sticks."

Her gaze sharpens, and her movements slow. She closes her legs, trapping the blanket, her hand, and the vibrator between them. It muffles the buzzing. Yet, now I can see that she's definitely *not* wearing panties. The smooth expanse of her slim legs, all the way up to her hip, is bare.

"You're killing the mood, *Foster*."

Her gaze ticks down to my groin, and her cheeks go red. Redder, anyway, since she's already flushed. But this is different. She's embarrassed I'm turned on? I'm fucking embarrassed, too. Whoever thought I'd see the day where we're in *this* predicament? Or any predicament at all.

"I'll tell Evan you got an erection from looking at me in bed," she threatens. "*Then* who do you think will be the last woman standing?"

I jerk away from the door, just enough to get it open. The thought of her fucking herself is going to do my head in, but it's her jabs that kill me the most. I make it out the front door without any of the guys noticing, and I pat my pockets for my wallet and phone. They're the only things I really need for where I'm going.

In the cool autumn air, the heat crawling under my skin finally dissipates. And so does my hard-on. Fucking finally. Traitorous dick.

I spare one glance up toward the window. Not that I expect to see anything, but it doesn't exactly bring me any comfort not to either. I break into a run.

Running—or any sort of exercise—usually clears my head. It's what I would do when my step-monster was on my case too much, or when my dad was out for a fight.

I end up at Shadow Bar and Grill. Not exactly cream of the crop here in Shadow Valley, especially since they hired Wren, but it'll do. If I can get a hockey fan to wait on me, they won't ask for my ID. It's practically tradition.

The bar is strangely packed. There's an NHL game on the screens, and I nod to myself. If I hadn't distracted myself, I would be in the hockey house with the guys, probably watching the game in the living room.

I slip onto a stool and order a double shot of whiskey. The girl doesn't even blink, although she does give me a weird fucking smile. She brings it and leans on the bar across from me. I pick up the small glass, mirroring her expression and raising the shot in a toast. Then I down it.

"Rough night?"

"Rough doesn't even start to cover it." I slide the glass back toward her. "Another."

"Yes, sir."

I imagine those words coming out of Wren's mouth, and I swallow the liquid.

Two more, and I might not feel anything at all.

That's how it goes. The bartender disappears, leaving the bottle in front of me, and I pour myself a fifth. I brace my forearm on the bar and stare at the amber liquid for a long time.

My thoughts are all fucked up. What was Wren trying to prove? That she's as screwed up as me? I already know she likes to toe the line of impropriety. Or blow right past that line. *I* haven't done anything to sabotage her entire fucking life.

I trace my wrists. It's a weird thing, being handcuffed. The metal was cold, the vise grip on my skin tight. After, I had sores that took a few days to fade. My dad said he saw that when people tried to fight them.

That gives me an idea.

Better payback than our immature tricks.

Wren needs to know that I'm serious about her getting out. I can't think around her. I certainly learned that I can't sleep around her. The sooner she's gone, the sooner my life goes back to normal. Eat, sleep, hockey. She's fucking with the middle one, and I have a feeling the longer she stays in the house, the more she'll fuck with the latter.

"I get off in fifteen," the bartender says, suddenly back in front of me. One of her buttons is undone, giving me a view of her cleavage. "You know, in case…"

"I'll be here." I smirk. "You go to SVU?"

"I'm a junior." She smiles. "Brittany."

"Stone."

Her smile widens. "I know."

Ah, so that's how it is. This is what I came looking for, right?

"Well, *Brittany*, let me buy you a celebratory shot." I gesture to the glass.

She pours it and raises it to her lips. Total fucking flirt. And a puck bunny, *obviously*. We haven't even started our regular season, but she knows my name?

The fifteen minutes pass quickly. The whiskey kicks in.

And the next thing I know, I'm in the bathroom hallway with her pressed between me and the wall, and she's sucking on my lower lip. But my mind keeps glitching back to Wren. Like how she looked when she moved the vibrator or—

The girl in front of me drops to her knees and fumbles with my running shorts.

I grab her and guide her back up. "Sorry, baby, public BJs aren't my thing." I kiss her to soften the blow, although *fuck* if I hate every second of it. I pull back. "See you around."

The walk home is long and cold. Autumn is slipping toward winter with a vengeance this year. It does little to sober me up, but my mind is clearer by the time I get home. The house is dark, and I tiptoe—then crash into something.

Oops.

No one comes running, so I continue up the stairs to my bedroom, my jaw fucking set. Wren's not keeping the bed. Not when our season is about to start, and I need to concentrate. And *sleep*. I can't afford to have her drive me out of the house every other night. I can just imagine my dreams swirling down the drain.

I almost expect her to be waiting for me, to kick on that vibrator again just to torment me. But when I open the door, I find her passed out in the middle of the bed. Her lips are parted, she's snoring softly, and she's exchanged my blankets —now in a pile on the floor—for her own.

No.

Not happening.

Before I can really think about it, I scoop her up into my arms. Blankets and all. Her head lolls against my shoulder, and I'm surprised by how light she is. I mean, I knew she was skinny. Everyone can see that just by looking at her. But it's one thing to watch her, and another to touch her.

The fact that she didn't wake up is telling. That orgasm must've worn her out.

Don't think about that.

I carry her as carefully as I can out the door and into the bathroom. I almost fall over setting her in the tub. I go back and retrieve her pillow, tucking it between her head and the porcelain, then open my phone and take a picture.

Is the tub the most sanitary place in the hockey house? No.

Will she be mortified when she wakes up? *I sure fucking hope so.*

I carefully pull the curtain around the tub, obscuring her from view. No need to ruin the surprise to the guys. I use the toilet and brush my teeth, then stagger to bed. I drop my blankets back on it and crawl in.

And yeah, maybe I jerk myself off to the sounds she was making earlier. Because while my dick didn't respond to the bartender, it sure as hell does to the thought of Wren.

But soon after that, the used tissue tossed in the direction of her shit, I fall into the best sleep of my life.

CHAPTER 9
WREN

SURPRISINGLY, I feel well rested. After Stone stormed out of the room last night, I finished my business—quicker than I'd like to admit—and lay there for at least an hour, trying to wind down. Anytime Stone's voice crept into my head, I pushed it away because there was no way in hell I was going to sleep thinking about him.

Especially after getting off.

It was...sort of enjoyable turning myself on while he stared at me. It was erotic in a way and something I'd never done before. I wasn't one to put on a show, and last night was just that. *A show.* I made it to the finish line a little too quickly, and deep down, buried under denial, I knew it wasn't from irritating him. It was because of the look in his eye. It was full of ravished hunger, and it was *hot.* Even if that pains me to admit.

The outline in his shorts sent tingles to every inch of my body, but if it were anyone else standing there, like one of the other hockey players—except for Evan, of course—I'd be just as turned on.

If not more.

My eyes flutter open, and the ache between my legs is

growing more present the longer I replay last night. *Stop thinking about it, Wren.* There's a faint noise coming from somewhere nearby, and I quickly pull my eyes open altogether, because apparently, in my lust-driven state, I'd forgotten all about the fact that Stone and I still share a bedroom, and it's his turn to retaliate.

And he *will* pay me back. I am certain of it.

My brows pull in, and I reach up tenderly and rub the sore spot on my neck. I'm staring at a chrome shower head and am thoroughly confused. *What the hell?*

"Ahh."

A breathy noise comes from the left, and that's when I quickly pop up and pull open the shower curtain.

Grant flies backward with his dick in hand and piss streaming throughout the bathroom like a water hose with too much pressure.

"Oh my God!" I yell, dodging a stream of pee and using my blanket to block the fiery liquid. It smells like he hasn't drank water in days, but that is the least of my worries.

"What the hell, roomie? Make yourself known next time!"

Grant tucks his dick away, something I am unable to pull my attention from.

Wow.

"I..." I am too stunned and confused to even form a sentence. *Why the hell am I in the bathtub?*

My blankets are damp with warm pee, and I scowl.

"Let me guess? Stone?" Grant is leaning against the vanity countertop.

My hands find my hips, and Grant follows my movements with his slow, lazy grin before walking off, chuckling.

"You two are somethin'," he mutters.

I hurriedly hop out of the tub, rush over to the sink, and wash my hands, because I'm pretty sure I have Grant's pee on them, and then stalk my way down the hallway, ignoring the rest of my housemates because they are all standing near their doors, waiting for the next showdown.

"Stone!" I fling the door open and fly into the room.

The sheets I was previously sleeping on last night are thrown on the floor, and he is asleep on the bare mattress with only a thin blanket covering his body.

Though, the word *covering* is a total exaggeration.

There lies Stone with his dark head of hair laying perfectly on top of his head with a relaxed face—not the usual scowl I'm used to—and his bare chest on full display. I stand with my lips parted as my heart beats a little faster. I dip my eyes past his angular jaw and land on the very defined stomach muscles rising slowly with his sleepy breaths.

The V leading to the rest of the blanket is so pronounced I can't pull my eyes away, and it's very obvious that he is well-endowed. It's beyond frustrating that he is so perfect, because what lies beneath his faultless body is a cold heart that's full of hate for *me*.

Stone's eyes remain closed when he rasps out a bark. "What do you want?"

Anger lashes at me when I think about him putting his hands on my body while I was sleeping, but of course, not before the throb in between my legs makes itself known for a split second. "What else did you do to me while I was sleeping?"

His eyes fly open, and they're full of heat, resembling a blue flame. "I guess you'll never know, Sticks. Will you?"

I slam the door with my foot, blocking out our audience. I am almost positive I smell popcorn, and it wouldn't surprise me if they guys popped some kernels and put lawn chairs in the hallway to watch the show.

"That's pushing it too far."

The dip in my voice causes me to straighten my shoulders and wipe the mess from my face. Little does Stone know—or *care*—but I do, in fact, have some trauma in my past that I'm not quite over yet.

Stone slowly sits up and lets the blanket fall even farther down his body. "You think me putting you in the bathtub is pushing it too far, but fucking yourself with your vibrator isn't?"

Stone quickly gets out of bed, and I turn to avoid getting a visual of his penis before he puts shorts on. I refuse to show him all my cards right away.

God, he's fucking hot, and it's so annoying.

I don't look at him until his breath warms the top of my head.

His lip is curved up on one side, and his blue glare burns me from the inside out. "I mean, we both already knew you had a strange sense of humor, yeah?"

Stone's hands are on my hips, and my back is pressed against the door in a millisecond. He moves with agility, and it takes me by surprise.

"Who puts drugs on someone's truck as a joke but can't deal with some innocent roommate pranks?"

My breaths are shaky, and I know he notices. I try to backpedal and explain why I'm acting so stupid, but it comes out jumbled. "I... I... I don't like to be touched when I'm asleep."

His eyes squint, and his grip on my waist weakens, but only for a second. His face morphs right back to stone—no pun intended—and he whispers in my ear with angry precision. "Then don't get yourself off in my fucking bed."

And with that, he pushes me to the side, pulls the door open, and walks with ease down the hall, letting his housemates know that he'll be ready for practice in ten.

———

THE FEW CLASSES THAT I HAD IN BETWEEN MY FIGHT WITH STONE and my shift at Shadow's help my mood tremendously. Space is the best thing for Stone and me because, after this morning, I was starting to think I should find a new room to stay in.

Surely one of the other housemates would be fine with me staying in their room, although I have a feeling it would put an idea in their head that I am interested in them, and that is a bad idea to think about, let alone act on, because that's the entire reason I'm in this situation right now.

"You headin' out, girly?"

I exchange my waitressing apron for my bag and slip the strap over my shoulder. "Yep." I sigh and open my phone to check if I have any messages. "I'll see you for tomorrow's lunch shift." *If I make it that far after staying in a room with Stone for another night.*

Walking out of the door and saying goodbye to the rest of my co-workers and a few loyal customers—who are my favorite—I click on my messages. I have several from Jasmin. Nerves tingle my skin as I climb into my car, hoping that it'll come to life even though the *check engine* light has been on for nearly two weeks now.

JASMIN

As your best friend, I think it is my duty to warn you before you get back to Evan's.

Take a breath. It could be way worse.

Text me when you get this.

What?

I quickly type her a text and silently thank God that my car *does* rev to life. Her message comes a moment later after I slip my seatbelt on, and when I look at her message, I find myself pressing on the brake and flinging my car into drive.

My phone flies to the floorboard of the passenger side, but it doesn't matter. With each quick stop of my car on the way to the rink, I look down and see the photo of me curled up in the bathtub with a caption that's even more degrading than the viral photo of me posted from Stone's account.

> @stonefoster — homeless girl currently looking for a place to sleep and/or roommate. I found her trying to sleep in my bed without permission, so I carefully moved her to the tub until I can find her a new place. DM for more info. Rehoming fee is waived.

Rehoming fee is waived? Like I'm an animal instead of a human being?

It's foster care all over again, and Stone knows firsthand how humiliating that caption is, which is precisely why he posted it.

CHAPTER 10
STONE

I HAVE to shut my phone off before practice. My post caught fire, and it's been shared over two thousand times. Not to mention the likes and comments from people far beyond Shadow Valley.

At first, it was just other students. They were laughing at Wren the same way I was. But then the messages started coming in. Shit about her sleeping in *their* beds. Jokes about her being potty trained or if she knows any tricks.

Insinuating shit that they have no right to insinuate.

I put my earbuds in and warm up off the ice, ignoring my teammates. They're ignoring me, too, sensing my bad mood from a mile away. "Sweet Emotion" by Aerosmith takes me into the zone, and I crank up the volume on my outdated iPod until I can't hear anything else.

Hands yank the back of my shirt and spin me around. I barely have time to brace myself before Evan slams me into the wall. He's furious, judging by the way his chest is heaving. He's not an enforcer on the team. He plays clean. If someone needs checking into the boards or given an attitude adjustment, it sure isn't him.

But now he looks ready to murder me.

I rip out an earbud and stare at him. "What the fuck?"

"You have *no right*," he seethes. "That's crossing a fucking line, asshole."

I tsk and shove him away from me. It takes a second to click that he's talking about the photo. Of course he is.

"You're not even her brother," I snap. "And you gave her *my room*. She's pulling some crazy shit, and you don't even see it because you're so obsessed with having a sister. Some childhood wet-dream shit."

"You've got it so twisted!" Evan yells. "Take it down. *Now*."

I roll my eyes. "When Wren grows a pair and asks me herself, then I will. Until then…" I turn away from him and grab my skates. I finish getting ready, the Aerosmith switching to an angry Nirvana song. I block out the rest of the shit going on and get on the ice.

Coach doesn't like us listening to music while we skate, but he says nothing about warm-ups. Working with this coach has made all the idiocy of living in the hockey house worth it. I'm learning more, playing better. He's got a good team here, and I have nothing but respect for him.

It's why I begged my father to let me come to Shadow Valley.

It's why Wren has to be the one to leave.

She can work at any restaurant in any town. She'll probably be a waitress for the rest of her life, honestly. Once you're at the bottom of the barrel, it's damn hard to claw your way out.

I put my music away and inspect the practice schedule taped to the glass. Conditioning, then individualized drills. Conditioning usually means torture in Coach's language, but I can't deny that I'm going to enjoy the burn.

Coach comes out. We line up for sprints, and I avoid Evan. The whistle blows. I push everything out of my mind, focusing on being quick. The fastest that I can be. My muscles are screaming by the time he blows his whistle twice and calls for a break.

"Five minutes, then we're switching to drills." He steps off the ice.

The rest of us go for our water bottles on the bench. I uncap mine and yank off my helmet, dousing my head with half of it and guzzling most of the remainder. The cold water feels like heaven on my heated skin, and I pull off my glove to run my fingers through my hair.

Evan is still avoiding me, which is fine. I don't really want to get fucking yelled at again.

"Stone!"

The female voice cuts straight through me. It's worse than nails on a chalkboard. I turn toward the sound, my eyebrows already rising. It's impossible to mistake it.

And sure enough, Wren is marching out onto the ice like she fucking owns it.

"Stone," she calls again.

Why does she have to be so goddamn pretty? Her dark hair is braided, there's not a speck of makeup on her face, and her hazel eyes are lasered in on me. She's got on an oversized t-shirt and black shorts.

Definitely not fall-weather attire.

And the more I stare at her, I realize it's *my* goddamn shirt.

What the fuck?

It's unsettling. Which means she did it on purpose because she loves to fucking mess with me in unusual ways. Like the vibrator. Like wearing my clothes.

She makes it all the way to me on the far side, waving off Evan when he tries to steer her away. Her jaw is set.

She's damn lucky Coach went back to his office, or else we'd all be screwed. She's drawing her fair share of eyes, but so am I.

"You trying out for the hockey team, Sticks?" I put my

hands on top of *my* stick. "You can play with the one shoved up your ass."

She huffs. "You're unbelievable, you know that?"

I shrug. "That's why the ladies like me."

"*I* don't like you."

"You're no lady." I glare at her. "Is there a point to this? Or are you just trying to make a bigger fool of yourself?"

"You had no right to post a picture of me," she says, stepping closer to me.

She's in street shoes. Worn-out-looking Converse that are barely holding on to life. In my skates, our height difference is startling. I want to crowd her, intimidate her. I live for the hitch in her breath and the wobble in her voice that says I'm *affecting* her. That I can actually get through to her.

But maybe not with an audience.

Or…

"Well?" She actually stomps her foot. "Don't you have anything to say?"

I pull at her t-shirt. *My* t-shirt. "And what about this, Sticks? Do you have any right to wear my clothes?"

It's my Blue Öyster Cult t-shirt. I was—and still am—obsessed with them. Which makes total sense because "(Don't Fear) The Reaper" is a great song. And "Burnin' For You." Obviously. But it just makes her choice that much worse. Like she's invaded yet another aspect of my life.

She bats my hand away. "It was in my room. Finders keepers."

"Losers weepers." I skate closer, fisting the collar. "Take it off."

Her eyes go wide—and then she smiles. I get this weird feeling in my stomach as her smile grows. And suddenly, I find myself regretting my decision. Even more so when she grabs the hem in front and pulls it off in one sweep, tossing it at me.

Pink bra.

Pale, perfect skin.

My brain stops working.

Until I register the wolf whistles coming from behind me. From my teammates, who are getting an eyeful of her tits too.

I snatch her hand. She squeaks when I force the t-shirt, now fucking inside out, over her head. She fights me, but I get the shirt back on her in record time. But now her hair looks like she was just fucked, and the way she's glaring at me...

"What's wrong, Stone? Afraid of a little skin in the game?"

I manage a laugh to hide my sudden, strange attraction. "Just trying to save you, Sticks. Wouldn't want anyone to think they could use you as kindling."

Her expression drops.

"No one would think twice about your barely there tits," I add. "Now, get to the point, or get off the ice."

Her voice is icy when she says, "You took a picture of me without my permission."

"Yeah, and?"

"And that's illegal."

I scoff. "You're out of your mind, Sticks. I mean, I guess you could sue me...but do you think you'd win against the Fosters? My dad has a whole team at his disposal, and you'd have whatever two-bit attorney you could wrangle up with the change under your couch." I tap my chin. "Oh, wait, you don't even have a couch. And it's not like you can sell *yourself*. Who'd want to buy some skinny, broke chick? So, good luck with that."

She lifts her chin. "Take the photo down."

"Take the photo down, *please*."

Her lips press together. For a second, I think she won't say it. Out of the corner of my eye, I spot Coach talking to Archer and Sully. They pivot him around subtly, putting his back to us, buying me a few more precious seconds before he sees Wren and blames me for having a girl on the ice.

"Take the photo down, Stone, *please*."

"I don't see why you're so out of sorts about a silly little photo, so I'll get around to it… eventually." I laugh. "That's fine, right? I mean, it's not like I can take it back. It has a life of its own. It went viral. But we can discuss that later. Right now, you've got to go."

I point her in the direction that she came.

She takes two steps and slips.

I manage to snag her arm before she hits the ice on her ass. She jerks out of my hold, muttering about being able to do it herself, and hurries forward.

Well, she tries.

Apparently, her sure-footedness is only connected to her anger, and that's run its course.

"For fuck's sake," I groan. "Up you go." I grab her by her hips and lift her off the ice.

Her back connects with my chest, and she immediately squirms in my grasp. I skate her to the door fast, skidding to a halt and sending a shower of ice spraying at the ledge.

When I dump her on the mat, she stumbles.

I shake my head at the sight of her, strangely at a loss. I just can't pinpoint why.

"Foster!" Coach yells. "Work with Maverick on passing drills. The rest of you need to tighten up your shooting."

I nod to him and head in the direction of Josh Maverick. He's a damn good player, although there's nothing he loves more than a fight. It's why he rarely starts—and nowadays, he ends up kicked off the ice more often than not.

We go to the far side, away from the other players. Through the glass, I find Wren. She's still fucking here, having taken a seat a few rows up and adjacent to where Maverick and I now practice.

Her gaze is locked on me. And she slowly peels the shirt off, turns it back the correct way, and slides it back on. The display grates on me. *Anyone* could've just seen that. But she's so fucking smug I can't stand it.

Always trying to one-up me. Always trying to put me in the worst spot imaginable.

"Focus," Maverick orders.

The puck sails past me and slams into the boards.

Wren smiles.

Fuck.

New rule: Wren Davis is not allowed anywhere near the hockey rink.

I glance back at her, and she's staring down at her phone. Her mouth is open, and I pause what I'm doing just to watch her. Because I don't think I've ever seen her look *that* shocked.

She answers it, rising from the seat and hurrying away.

The puck hits me in the gut, bringing me sharply back into focus. I flip Josh off and let the puck fall to the ice.

"Game on," I mutter.

CHAPTER 11
WREN

THE AMOUNT of anger I feel is more of a wrath than anything. The air is crackling with rage, and although I'm in hardly any clothing, I'm sweating. My hands shake as I watch Stone skate toward center ice with my nerves in the palm of his hand.

I sigh, flicking my eyes to Evan for a quick second before my phone vibrates. I assume it's Jasmin to make sure I haven't flung myself off the side of the building, but when I see the number flashing on the screen, my entire world shifts.

NHCF — State Prison for Men.

Oh, fuck.

I'm suddenly sucked back into a world I want nothing to do with, but old habits die hard because before I know what I'm doing, my phone is pressed up against my ear, and I'm accepting a call.

"He—hello?" I clear my throat and rush down the row of seats and up the aisle to block out the cutting of ice from the skates. I know, from past experiences, that the only way I'm going to get through a phone call like this is if I tune out all distractions and stay sharp.

My father may be a felon, but he's smart and the most conniving man I've ever known—even compared to Stone.

"Pumpkin." His voice is like a hand around my throat.

Too many emotions pour through me, and I'm embarrassed to admit that one of them is longing.

"It's been too long since I've heard that sweet voice."

Approximately two years and forty-two days.

I keep count.

"Yeah, it has been."

I rest my back against the cool, tiled wall in the hallway and stare at the locker room door. My legs are so wobbly that I eventually sink to the floor.

"You're not going to ask how I've been?"

My eyes shut, and I remind myself that he is locked away in one of the most secure prisons in the New England area. He can't hurt me, and he can't use me, though I know he'll still try. Otherwise, why the call?

"You're in prison. I'm sure you're just surviving at this point."

"It's not so bad here." He chuckles, and it hasn't changed over the years. It's still the same raspy noise full of hidden cynicism. There is always a hint of pessimism in every blank space of his sentences unless he is getting his way.

"That's good," I whisper, unsure of what to say. Part of me wants to hang up, but that same jaded little girl who still lives and breathes inside me is scared to death of the repercussions that always follow after being in contact with Jessie Davis.

"I'm a little upset that I haven't heard from you since I got locked up." His tone goes from cheery to displeased in three seconds flat.

This time in prison is like all the rest. Every single time he goes away, I have the tiniest sliver of hope that he'll recognize all the mistakes he's made over the years and change. It's the same kind of yearning that I had when I was five years old, hoping for my mother to come home to save me, even though

I knew, deep down, it was a far-fetched delusion. She was dead.

Jessie Davis may be my blood, but that's as far as our loyalty goes.

"Wren, are you there?"

I rub my hand against my clammy face. "I'm here."

"You know why I'm in prison, don't ya, Pumpkin? That's why you've been hiding from me."

I'm hiding because you're an unpredictable junkie.

"It's your fault."

It's a slap against the face, but I'm able to muster up the strength that I've been molding since my first foster home and slap him back. "It was either you or me, Dad. I chose me."

And I threw Stone Foster under the bus in the process.

It was funny how things circled back around. I pinned the drugs I was supposed to deliver for my dad on Stone's truck, potentially ruining Stone's future whilst doing the same to my father, which landed him in prison. Stone pays me back by posting that picture, giving my father and his little peddlers the perfect window to where I am. *I hate my life.*

"Well, now you owe me, Wren."

I flinch at the sound of my name coming from his end of the phone. He rarely calls me by my first name, and the only time he's done it in the past was when he was about to ask me something that I know I'll say no to now.

"I need money."

"Money?" I question. "For what? Your books?"

This isn't my first rodeo. It's a whole new world behind bars. Prisoners could buy things—snacks, attire, *drugs*. I eventually stopped putting money on my father's books when I moved in with Evan because that was when I learned what *normal* was.

My father chuckles. "No. Not my books. You put me in a bad spot. You didn't deliver when I needed you to, and that came with a price, and that price has been gaining interest since I've been here. If I don't find a way to pay...well, let's just say, I'm not safe."

"And what about all the times I wasn't safe while you were away?" My nerves tangle even further.

"You think you'll be safe if I don't pay up?"

I pull my knees up to my chin and rest it against them. The longer I talk to Jessie Davis, the more numb I become. I stare across the hallway, wondering when practice is over. The last thing I need is for Evan to find me like this because he'll know exactly why I'm in this catatonic state, and not to mention, it'll give Stone more ammunition.

"What does that mean?" I continue to stare. My nerves have disappeared, and I feel myself slipping. The fight-or-flight reaction is nonexistent, and now I'm in my dissociative phase, which almost always ends badly.

"Do you want my death on your hands, Wren?"

I swallow. The words leave my mouth without a second thought to what I'm actually saying. "You're already dead to me."

I know I'm still mentally here somewhere, because after I hear what I say to him, there's a sense of hurt somewhere in the back of my head. A tear slips down my cheek, but I'm too frozen to swipe it away.

There is a long pause on the other side of the phone, and more tears slide down my cheeks, but they're not backed with hurt. Instead, they're jammed full of unyielding fear. *What did I just do?*

"Remember this moment when the time comes, Pumpkin. Because I gave you an out, and you're going to wish you took it."

The phone call ends, but I keep my phone up to my ear for so long my fingers grow numb. There is ringing in my ears, so I don't hear the footsteps in front of me. There's movement, and the door is opening and closing, but I can't move. I focus on my breathing and the rising and lowering of my chest.

Archer's mouth moves, and that's when I see that he's crouching low, head dripping with sweat and his gray shirt speckled with wetness. His bag is beside him, and his blue eyes are darkened with worry. "Are you crying?"

All I can hear is my heart pounding in my ears.

There's a hand in front of my face and a snapping of fingers. I flick my eyes back to Archer and see that we're the only ones in the hallway. I take another breath, and after Archer bellows my name again, everything comes rushing back in.

A sob scrapes up my throat, and my shoulders shake. *No, no, no.* I don't cry, and it isn't easy to break me. There aren't many people who could even attempt to do so, but leave it to Jessie Davis to continue his main act and take me down with him every single time.

"Hey, hey. *Shh.*"

Archer's hands are around my shoulders, and then I'm pulled to my feet and crushed into his body.

I shake my head against his warm chest. I refuse to say a word. *It's fine. Get it together right fucking now, Wren.*

"Is it Stone? What did he do to make you storm out onto the ice like that? I can piss in his Cheerios tomorrow morning if you want me to."

I try to laugh, but it comes out as another sob. Archer's hand dips into my hair, tangling with the ends as he keeps my face pressed against his chest. His heart is steady, and I try to match the rapid beating with mine.

But it doesn't work.

My father's words are an echo in my head, taunting me with fear just like he's been doing since I was young enough to know what fear was.

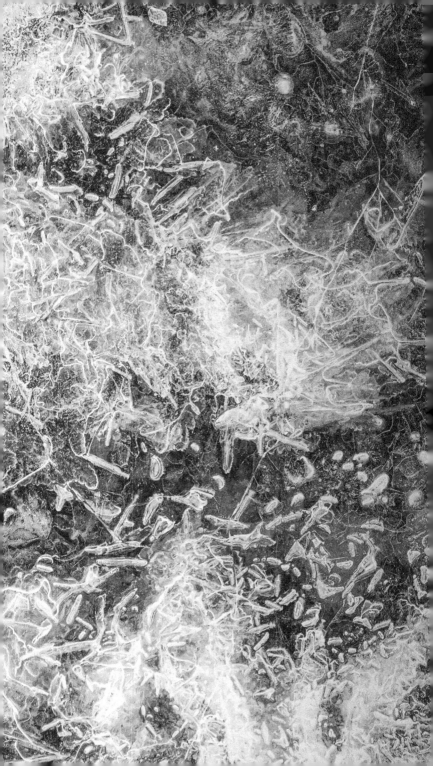

CHAPTER 12
STONE

I'M *STARVING*. More than usual after a practice. All I want is to go home and eat a giant plate of pasta, chicken, and salad. Which is weird, I know. But it's what we used to have when I'd get home from practice as a kid, and it's what I crave now.

That, and a little freaking stability.

But those days are in the distant future. Once Wren is out of the picture and I can just focus on hockey and nothing else, *then* I'll be able to concentrate.

With my bag slung over my shoulder, I wave goodbye to the teammates left in the locker room. Under normal circumstances, I'd wait for Evan and Sully, but they're both dawdling, Sully still getting dressed, and my growling stomach dictates my movements.

I round the corner and stop dead.

Wren.

Archer.

The first thing I notice is their embrace. The way he's cupping the back of her head and holding her to his chest.

The second thing is her panic. Her mouth is open, her chest heaving. There are freaking *tears* in her eyes.

And the thing about Wren is that I've never seen that girl shed a tear. Not when the social worker dropped her back off at Evan's house for the thousandth time. Not when people picked on her at school. Not when *I* picked on her at school.

But she's crying now, and Archer seems caught between confused and mortified. Our goalie is a big dude. And usually, the last person you want to pick a fight with is the fucking goaltender. But he looks *guilty*, stroking her hair like he has any fucking right to touch her.

Why is he touching her?

Why is she crying?

For some reason, that just spikes my anger. I drop my bag and rush them, ripping Wren away from him. She stumbles to the side, but I'm too focused on Archer. He belatedly realizes what has happened, which means he isn't prepared for my fist in his face.

Something pops in my hand, but the blood that comes pouring out of his nose is worth the sting of pain. He yells and pushes me away, but it isn't hard.

Fuck, I want a fight. I lunge for him again. He grips my shoulders and basically throws me into the wall, but I come back and get in a quick punch to his ribs. My hand is fucking killing me, but I hit him again in the stomach. He bends over, wheezing droplets of blood everywhere.

Archer runs his fingers under his nose. "What the fuck?"

"Don't you fucking touch her," I seethe. "You made her cry?"

"You're batshit insane."

I shove him, and he laughs as he goes backward. Only a goalie would be laughing and bleeding at the same time.

"Stay away from her." I point at him. My heart is going a million miles a second, the adrenaline bleeding into post-practice exhaustion.

"Stone!" Evan puts himself between us. His hand on my

chest is the only thing stopping me from taking Archer's head off. "What's going on?"

"He made her cry."

"No, I fucking didn't," Archer snaps. "I was *comforting* her."

I glare at him. "You can comfort her from a distance, asshole. You don't need to molest her to do it."

"You're a real piece of work, Foster—"

"Enough," Even snaps. "Archer, go. Please."

I raise my eyebrows at him, and the big dude finally stomps away. *Good riddance.* But when I turn back toward Wren, she's not crying anymore.

She's just as pissed as I was.

Am.

Fucking hell, she's got me all mixed up.

"Go to hell, Stone," she says in an even voice.

My eyebrows rise. "What?"

She grabs Evan's hand and drags him past me. "You should get familiar with Hell. You welcomed me there when we started sharing the room—but you're the one who's gonna be living there for the next few months."

They leave, and I stand there dumbfounded until Sully comes out of the locker room.

"What's up? I heard yelling."

I snatch my bag from where I dropped it and follow him out. We head in the direction of the hockey house. On a day like today, I need the fresh air.

"I thought I saw Archer being inappropriate with Wren."

Sully snorts. "You know you're like the definition of inappropriate with Wren?"

My jaw falls open. "What? No, I'm not."

"Yeah, you are."

I mean...*maybe.* "It's just because we've known each other forever. She's my best friend's pseudo-sister, which basically means she's my sister."

Biggest lie I ever told, especially since I can't stop thinking about her face when that vibrator made contact under the blanket. It's haunting me. *She's* haunting me.

By the time we get back to the house, all the lights are on.

Wren sits at the table with a bowl of mac n' cheese, Evan beside her. Along with Taylor and Grant, the two remaining housemates. Archer sits next to Evan, and the distance makes me feel somewhat better. All the guys have wet hair and contemplative expressions, which means she was talking shit.

Of course she was.

She came to this house with the goal of sabotaging us. Sabotaging *me*. Evan might be blind to her little act, but I'm not.

"House meeting," Wren announces without looking at me.

Sully chuckles. "You stepped in some shit, my friend."

He claps me on the back. I elbow him and take the seat at the end of the table, with Sully beside me. Wren's gaze still seems to go everywhere but at me.

"I'm in search of a new roommate," she says.

My jaw fucking drops. I mean, *yeah*, technically this is what I wanted all along. But now? I'm supposed to just let her go with one of them?

"You can share my bed, Wren," Archer says.

He meets my gaze and smiles.

Oh, the fuck she will.

"Over my dead body," I grit out.

"You're small," Taylor says, ignoring me. "You wouldn't take up much space in mine."

She smiles brilliantly at him. It's so fake it burns. Which means she's doing this to torture me, then.

"No." I ball my fists under the table.

Evan glances between us. "So, Stone, you want Wren to stay in your room?"

I make a face.

"It doesn't matter what Stone wants," Wren says loudly.

"It matters what *I* want. I'm not sharing a room with someone I can't trust. And he's at the top of that list."

Ouch. "Because of the stupid photo?"

"You still haven't taken it down," Evan points out. "Which you definitely should. Right now."

All eyes swing to me.

Seriously?

How did I become the bad guy?

I shake my head and pull out my phone, deleting the whole post and its million views. Well, shit. That actually accumulated a lot.

I toss my phone at Wren. "There. Check and see for yourself. But I'm not responsible for people who copied and reposted it."

She scowls, picking my phone up with her fingertips like it might be contaminated. She types something, then slides it back to me.

A new status update from Stone Foster: *I post pictures of sleeping girls because I'm compensating for being a shitty hockey player.*

I go to delete it, but Wren wags her fucking finger at me.

"You touch that status, and I guarantee I'll stay in everyone's room except yours."

"Well, you're definitely not doing *that*."

She gets up. "Come on, Archer. I want to check out your room."

He scrambles after her. Evan's laugh chases me as I follow them upstairs, stopping in the doorway. She flops on his bed while he stands in the middle.

"Hmm… Your bed is really comfy." Her gaze comes to me.

I fucking hate her.

"No," I snap. I brush past Archer and grab Wren, picking her up and carrying her out into the hall. I put her back on her feet, stepping away before she can hit me again. "Stop being fucking foolish."

"I don't know what your problem is," she snaps back. "Why do you even care?"

I roll my eyes. "Because you're a nuisance, and I can't concentrate with you around."

"Which is exactly why I should not be around."

"You think the idea of you pulling stupid pranks in other guys' rooms, taunting me about fucking them, is going to help?"

Her mouth falls open. "You think I'm going to sleep with them?"

I throw my hands up. "Yeah, maybe. I don't know what your kind would do to keep a roof over your head."

"Your kind," she repeats. She steps closer, her eyes flashing. "Do you mean *poor*, Stone?"

I lift my chin. "I mean the daughter of an imprisoned drug dealer. Are you following in your daddy's footsteps?"

Hurt flickers across her face, but it's gone before I can latch onto it. In its place is steely determination. "So you don't want me in your room, and you don't want me in any of theirs."

"Pretty much," I goad.

"Fine," she hisses. "Have it your way."

She storms off. I follow her downstairs, to a door off the kitchen that I've never opened. I thought it was a pantry. But she yanks it open and reveals a *tiny* room. It's got a single window with broken blinds covering it, and it's full of boxes.

"Evan," she calls. "Can you help me get these boxes out of here?"

He appears beside me, elbowing me hard in the stomach.

I grunt.

"Why?" he asks her.

She turns on the spot, her fists planted on her hips. "Because I just found my new room."

I gape at her, and all she does is smile.

"Now, I think this satisfies your requirements, Stone?"

CHAPTER 13
WREN

I HAVE LIVED in worse places. I have slept in smaller spaces too. The room is hardly bigger than a Harry Potter closet, but it works. I made a makeshift bed on the floor with the promise of Evan getting me a twin mattress, which I refused. I have my textbooks stacked beside my pillow and a small lamp placed on top, giving my new room a romantic ambiance. My clothes are folded nicely at the bottom of my "bed," and although there isn't much space to do homework, I can always use the kitchen table or go to the library like I have done in the past.

Truthfully, anything is better than sleeping in Stone's room.

This tiny room could have spiders hanging in the corners, and I'd consider them a friend over considering Stone one.

I lie and stare out the window at the moon and feel the uptick in my blood pressure. The way Stone ripped me away from Archer was completely uncalled for. I was shocked at first and then completely overtaken by a disarray of emotions.

It felt nice, for half a second, to have someone defend me.

Then came the blinding anger and betrayal. The entire

reason I was shaken up was because of Stone posting that stupid picture of me.

Now, I have to watch my back even more than before.

I squeeze my eyes shut tightly and breathe out through my nose. I hate that I let my guard down.

Not with Stone. I'm not sure I would ever trust him, even if he did attempt to come to my rescue with Archer's arms around me. I meant with myself and my father.

One month ago, I thought I was free. *Content.* Relaxed.

Now I'm stuck in a house with hockey players, careful of my every move, struggling to keep up with my demanding school schedule and cursing my sore feet from my extra shifts at Shadow's.

I turn to my side after switching my phone to silent and curl up on the wood floor blanketed by a warm quilt. I ignore the stiffness of my hip and attempt to block out my father's cold voice.

Do you want my death on your hands, Wren?
Do you want my death on your hands, Wren?
Do you want my death on your hands, Wren?
Do you want my death on your hands, Wren?

I sit up quickly and bring my knees to my chin, wrapping my arms tightly around my shins. My forehead is tacky, and my pulse is thundering behind my skin. I fling the blankets off my legs, hopeful that no one is awake in the house.

As tempting as it is to piss Stone off, the last thing my anxiety needs right now is another sparring with him—or better yet, another potential fight at his surprising need to be protective over me.

Like he has any right to do so. *Dick.*

The door creaks loud enough to wake each guy upstairs, but I pad on my tiptoes to the darkened kitchen and pray they all mind their own business. Especially Stone. The glow of the fridge illuminates the room, and I think back to when I used to live at Evan's house and his mom would already be in the kitchen with milk and cookies the night after I was thrust back into their care.

She never poked or made me talk.

She was just there.

The front door opens, and I quickly slam the fridge shut and peek down the hall. My erratic heartbeat is even faster than before, and I swallow my fear before I realize that it's just Evan prowling down the hall in his school jacket and sweats.

"Looking for these?"

My hand flies to my heart. "You scared me, Evander. Jeez —" I pause as I look at his hands. "Are those…"

My words trail just as quickly as my fear.

He walks over to the table after turning the kitchen light on and places the Ziploc bag of chocolate chip cookies on top. Then he swishes past me and opens the fridge, pulling out the milk before grabbing two cups. He nudges my shoulder. "Sit."

I shuffle over to the table, knowing very well that Evan isn't going to allow me to hide behind silence. His mom knew when not to ask questions. Evan doesn't care for my independence.

"Did you go all the way home to get these…for me?"

It feels like a chocolate chip cookie is stuck in my throat, but I refuse to cry again. I sit in silence as Evan pours us both some milk and unzips the bag. "Mom met me halfway."

A soft laugh escapes me, and I shake my head, pulling my knees up to my chin again as I rest my back against the kitchen chair. "You did not have to do that." I pull my gaze away from the cookies. "What did you tell her?"

"I told her your ex was being a dick, and you needed her famous pick-me-up."

He shoves an entire cookie in his mouth as I nibble on the one in my hand.

Once he swallows, he taps the table with his knuckle and shoots me a look. "Why were you crying, Wren?"

My eyes dart to my bedroom door, also known as the hall closet, and a lie climbs from my mouth. "I was just frustrated that Stone—"

"I went four towns over to get these cookies for you, and you're going to sit here and lie? Not a chance."

Shit.

It isn't that I don't trust Evan. I trust him more than anyone. But I'm not going to pile my trauma on his shoulders. *Again.*

"Wren."

"My dad called, okay?" My feet stomp to the floor in frustration, and I shove the cookie away.

When I peek back at Evan, his eyebrows are raised in worry. "Must be bad if you're turning down Mom's cookies. What did he want?"

I sigh. "The usual. Money."

"But you were crying."

Please don't remind me.

"You never cry, Wren."

I cried because the way my father spoke to me felt more final than before. There have been many threats over the years, but this time is different. He's desperate, and if the past is a window to the future, I know he'll do anything to save himself.

"I'm fine, Evan," I lie and force myself to smile. "And I do cry. Just not in front of you."

"Liar." Evan flicks a crumb at me.

I roll my eyes.

"When was the last time you talked to him?"

"Right before he went to prison."

Evan looks surprised, and I know he wants to ask more questions.

"Was it the photo? Did it push him to contact you?"

I nod and debate telling him everything, but the air around us grows tense. The skin of my exposed arms shows my chills. Evan's gaze moves behind me, and I know without looking that Stone is lingering in the shadows.

"Go back upstairs," Evan barks.

My chair screeches against the floor. Evan sighs loudly, knowing I'm finished with the conversation. I refuse to look at Stone as I walk the three feet over to *my room*. Stone doesn't move. He stands just outside the kitchen, blocking me from opening the closet door. I stare past his shoulder, knowing his eyes are pinned on me.

"Move," I demand, leveling my shoulders and bracing myself for impact.

His mouth opens. He licks his lips, and I know he's going to say something that's going to drive me up a wall, but to my surprise, Stone moves just far enough away that I can slip by him. My chest brushes his, and the way his warm breath skims my skin pisses me off. I want to fling the door open so far that it hits him in the face, but instead, I keep my cool and open it just far enough that I can slide in.

The door clicks a moment later, and if Evan wasn't watching us from the kitchen, I am certain that Stone would pull a chair over and push it up against the doorknob, locking me inside. Just to be an asshole.

"Lay off her."

I grimace at Evan's seethe. His voice lowers, but I have exceptional hearing. You don't grow up in foster homes and not learn how to eavesdrop.

"I did," Stone says in his normal tone. "Otherwise, I probably would have tripped her when she walked past."

"*Stone.*" Evan is angry.

"Relax. I'm kidding."

"Well, I'm sick of the jokes. I don't even want you to look at her. Not now."

"Not now?"

It's hard to hear, so I press my ear up to the crack.

"What's that supposed to mean? Is this because she cried? How was I supposed to know that a simple photo of her on the internet was going to make her have a mental fucking breakdown? Talk about sensitive."

"For fuck's sake, Stone. You have no idea what you're talking about."

There is a growl loud enough to make me pull back from the door.

"Haven't you noticed that Wren isn't on social media? That there are no pictures of her online? Like, anywhere?" There is a short pause before Evan continues. "Of course you didn't notice. You're too selfish to worry about anyone other than yourself."

"There is nothing wrong with being focused on myself. I'll worry about someone else when I get settled in my career."

"No, but there is something wrong with taking down innocent people just because you're blind to real problems that others have."

"You want to talk about taking down innocent people?"

My eyes widen, and I glance over to my things at the bottom of my makeshift bed. *I might as well pack my shit now.* Stone has every right to throw me under the bus.

"What?" Evan asks. He sounds completely fed up with his best friend.

"You first. What real problems does Wren have now that she's legally an adult and no longer the poor girl with sticks for legs who bounces around foster homes? Huh? Because from the looks of it, she's doing just fine."

"Just fine? She's sleeping in a fucking closet because of you."

"She isn't innocent in all this, Evan. You just can't see that because you're blind to anything she does."

"You're the blind one, Stone."

My legs shake, and I place my hand on the doorknob.

Their argument is quiet, but I have heard every word, and even though I hate Stone, I don't want to get in between them. Evan means too much to me to ruin their friendship.

"Fine, then open my eyes. Why was the photo such a big deal?"

My fingers tighten on the worn bronze of the knob.

"Her fucking dad called her. You posted that picture, and he tracked her down!"

It takes everything in me not to burst out into the kitchen to tell Evan to be quiet, but instead, I'm the one who stays quiet. I rest my head against the door, hating that my life has to be so complicated.

"Isn't he in prison?"

I suck in a breath, trying my hardest to push away the stress that is lingering in the back of my head.

"You think just because he's in prison that he can't torment her? That he can't threaten her?"

Footsteps move in front of the door, and I know they are taking their conversation upstairs.

Evan's voice lowers to a whisper. "You have no clue what it was like for her back in high school, Stone. Did you ever wonder why I didn't let you spend the night?"

"Yeah, I figured you just had a hard-on for her."

I make a disgusted face.

"It was because of her nightmares. She would scream bloody murder almost every night when she first moved in. So back the fuck off, because neither of us truly knows what she has been through."

I rest my head against the door and stay that way until their footsteps disappear. When I lie down, I stare at the moon again and think of anything but that phone call from my dad.

"*She's pretty good at this.*" *Gus nudges my dad with his bony elbow as they eye me from across the trailer.*

Sweat is trailing my skin and curls past my collarbone, down to the dip of my tank top. It's eighty-nine degrees outside and feels like it's one hundred and eight-nine degrees inside this trailer. The fire beneath the broiler has singed all my arm hair off, and although I am exceptional at math and know the difference between acids and bases, performing "science experiments" while my drug-addict father and his right-hand man watch isn't my idea of a fun summer.

"I know. I've been teaching her for years, and she's even better than I had imagined."

I glance at my dad and wish I could adjust the mask on my face. At least he had the audacity to give me the proper lab gear while I make one of the world's deadliest drugs.

So much for those "science experiments" my dad and I bonded over years ago.

He's been grooming me for ages.

"Ooh, she's good, alright." Gus's voice tapers off. His pinky is covered in white dust, and when he pulls his mask down, he sniffs the latest batch up his nose.

My father does the same beside him.

They have to test the product.

Or that's just their excuse to get high.

My dad's phone rings, and I grit my teeth.

"Can you take that outside?" I ask. I watch my tone, but on the inside, I'm fuming. "It's distracting."

"Anything for my favorite little scientist, Pumpkin."

I hold back a snort. Scientist. More like a meth cooker, but that's just semantics at this point.

The moment the door shuts, I go back to measuring while ignoring Gus and his slow eye movements. He has always followed my every move. He calls himself my uncle, but I know for a fact that uncles don't stare at their nieces the way he stares at me.

"Come over here, little one."

I stay quiet. My hand shakes with the spoon in front of me. I *glance at the door and wonder when my dad is going to come back. He doesn't do much when the men make comments, and there have been numerous times that he has brushed off their inappropriate touching, but I can't help but hope that he'll come to my rescue for once.*

"I said come here."

"I can't stop what I'm doing, or this batch will be ruined."

It's a lie, but he won't know the difference.

"Fine, I'll come to you."

My chest hurts, and my mouth goes dry. The beaker in front of me is beginning to boil, and if I don't focus, I'll fuck it all up, and I'm not sure what's worse—a punishment from my father if I waste product, or a touch from Gus.

"Don't touch me," I warn. I try to recall what I've already mixed, but I can't focus.

"Why not?"

"Because you'll distract me, and I'm trying to get this right."

"I'll distract you?" His breath is gross and warm and mixes right in with the sweat on my neck. "Like this?"

His sloppy lips touch my skin, and my eyes grow blurry.

"Please don't touch me."

I choke on fear from the slippery feel of his tongue, and the room grows black. Shit, shit, shit. Focus, Wren.

"Stop, please."

I'm crying, and suddenly, I'm not in my father's trailer. Instead, I'm in a jail cell, and my father is on the other side, smiling at me.

"Do it, Gus. She deserves to be punished."

A GASP OF AIR SURGES UP MY THROAT, AND ALTHOUGH I DON'T see Gus or my father in front of me, I'm still brimming with fear and clawing to get away.

CHAPTER 14
STONE

THERE'S something in me that just can't leave it alone.

I pace my room, which feels like all the air has been sucked out of it. I can't tell if it's because of what Evan revealed or simply because it's empty.

My gaze drops to the corner where Wren had made her little nest the first night. The blankets and pillows are gone, her nest relocated to under the fucking stairs. I *hate* that she's down there. I hate that she's still in this fucking house, but I hate more that she left this room and abandoned me to my own thoughts.

Because I'm battling guilt, too. Over posting that photo, of alerting her apparently psychotic drug-dealing father to her whereabouts, to potentially bringing back nightmares.

Evan didn't say that, per se. He came pretty damn close, though. He *did* insinuate that I was the current bane of his existence for hurting Wren. Which is…fair. I'd be more worried about that if I didn't know he'll get over it in a day or two. Life will go on.

Besides, it's not like Wren's dad is going to hurt her from behind bars. He's a dangerous guy—surely there's due process for shit like that. The prison is supposed to monitor contact. So while he can call her, there's a simple solution: block the number and move on.

My mind keeps drifting back to Wren, though. Stupid fucking Wren with her soft, dark hair and big hazel eyes. Her tiny body wrapped up in my arms, not anyone else's.

Wait.

No, she's never been in my arms. It doesn't even count when I ripped her away from Archer or when she crashed into my chest after I snuck up on her. And the way she brushed against me in the doorway, as she ran for her new little safe haven, has put permanent goosebumps on my arms.

Fuck Wren Davis.

My anger, an uncontainable restlessness, drives me back out my bedroom door and down the stairs.

Evan is long gone. The rest of the guys are asleep.

The house is so silent, my footsteps sound loud to my ears. I go to the kitchen and open the fridge door, scanning the shelves. While I'd love to guzzle a beer and pray for it to put me to sleep, I opt for a bottle of water.

It's the safer choice, seeing as how we're moving to a two-a-day practice schedule.

Our first preseason game is this week, and Coach seems... well, maybe *worried* is the wrong word. But concerned?

I'm not the only new guy on the team. It seems like there's been a massive transition in the past year or two, an outflux of the talented players Coach relied on, and an *influx* of...us. The new guys.

While I'm determined to prove I'm worthy of starting, while I relentlessly chased *this* school for *this* coach and *this* team, not everyone feels the same way. Hockey is my blood. But to some, it's a hobby.

There's no time for anyone to half-ass this season.

I close the fridge and sit on one of the stools. The water is halfway to my mouth when a loud noise doesn't just break the silence—it fucking decimates it. I start, dropping the bottle.

Water flows out of it onto the counter, running off the edges and hitting the floor in little streams.

"Shit," I mutter. I right the bottle and sop up the mess with the hem of my shirt. There are no fucking kitchen towels, and one measly square of paper towel proves...*ineffective*. I tear off my shirt and use it to soak up the rest of the water on the floor before I register the noise.

It was a scream.

I tilt my head, waiting for...

Well, I don't know.

Some sort of reaction from the rest of the house?

"No! *GET OFF ME!*"

Fuck.

I rush toward Wren's little closet, pausing only for the briefest of moments before I yank open the door. It's a swath of darkness and shadow. I flick on the hall light, and it illuminates enough of the tiny space to see her.

She's writhing on the makeshift bed, which is nothing more than a few blankets on the floor—which alone gives me another twinge of guilt. Her eyes are screwed up tight, her whole body tense. She jerks like she's trying and failing to escape someone.

I glance over my shoulder, waiting for the telltale sign of Evan running to Wren's rescue. Hoping for it, more like.

No such luck.

Her mouth opens. A yawning, wide stretch of teeth and tongue and gums, all pink and white and exceptionally ordinary...

Except, it's not.

And for some reason, I duck *into* the closet-room instead of backing away and waiting for someone else to deal with this. With her.

Someone much more qualified. Someone who gives a shit about what happens to her.

The door closes behind me, putting us in total darkness. Yet, when I drop to my knees and reach for her, it isn't hard at all to find her shoulders. To haul her upright and shake her slightly, even as the scream bubbles out of her.

It's loud. Bloodcurdling.

I slap my hand over her mouth, muffling the sound, and reach for the lamp with my other hand. That, I fumble with. It takes a moment for the light to click on, and I squint against the burning illumination. Then, I focus back on Wren.

"Wake up," I urge, peeling my fingers from her face and cupping the back of her neck. "Wren, *wake up*."

She does.

Violently.

She hits me in the chest, knocking me back into the door. It must've latched, because it doesn't move under my weight. And her eyes are wild, her hands patting down her body. She touches her face, runs her hands over her cheeks and lips and nose.

Her breathing is coming in short bursts, and her eyes remain unfocused.

I crawl closer until I can grab her hand.

"Wren, stop."

"Can't. Breathe."

"I know. It's okay, just slow it down."

She shakes her head, her hair swinging around her shoulders. She looks like she's still caught up in the nightmare.

I realize two things at once.

If she continues like this, she's going to pass out.

And...Evan is going to murder me either way.

So I grab her face and yank her forward, slamming my lips to hers.

I've kissed girls before. But tell me why *my* breathing stops as soon as our mouths are on each other?

Tell me why my heart fucking skips?

And most of all, tell me *why* Wren Davis kisses me back?

I lean into her, our mouths opening and tongues tangling. She tastes sweet, a faint remnant of sugar on her lips. Her hands creep up to my biceps, gripping me so tightly her nails cut into my skin. And her moan goes straight to my dick.

I nip her lower lip.

The little bit of pain breaks the spell, and she jerks away from me.

We're both breathing hard. She tucks her hair behind her cheeks, wide-eyed and confused. Gone is the cocky girl who drives me nuts. In her place is a version of her that isn't so...*guarded*. For just a moment, I can see who she'd be if she hadn't gone through the childhood she had.

But she's Wren, and I'm me, and as soon as she registers that, the walls slam back down.

"What the fuck are you doing?" she hisses.

I swallow. "You were screaming."

"Because of *you*."

"I don't believe you." My voice is low.

Her eyes inexplicably well with tears, and she twists sharply on her pallet of blankets away from me. She faces the wall, her shoulders so high they're almost touching her ears.

"Go away," she orders.

"Wren—"

"Go. *Away*."

I don't believe a single thing Wren Davis has ever said. And I don't believe this either. I reach out and grip her shoulder, pulling her back around. But the expression on her face— pure, devastating fury—has me releasing her just as fast.

"Fine," I spit out. My pride is more hurt than anything. "Stay in your little closet until the sun comes up. Hide from everyone—"

"I'm not hiding," she whispers raggedly. "I just don't want anything to do with you."

"Feeling's mutual," I snap.

I jump to my feet and slip out of the room, slamming the door shut behind me. I make it all the way to my room before I lose my shit. I have a silent freak-out for ten seconds, then I wrangle myself back under control.

Kissing the enemy is *not* allowed under any circumstances.

Even if the enemy is having a nightmare. Or hyperventilating. Or looking at me with those big, panicked eyes…

I flop on my bed and cover my face with my hands.

Why was my first impulse…? Why did I have to kiss her? I could've slapped her, that might've done the same fucking thing. *But with way less heat.* I can still feel the ghost of her on my lips, the little breathy noise she made, the way she started backward when it seemed to register who she was making out with.

We used tongue.

That's going to keep me fucked up for a long time.

I roll on my side and turn off my lamp.

The *only* solution to this is to go radio silent. Or, as I overheard my step-monster whispering one night, *stone-cold*. She hated when I froze her out—which I did often. I hated her. I wanted her gone. She wasn't a replacement for my mother, not even *close*. But she sure did try. So she got the cold shoulder, the icy, cutting remarks, and then…well, then I left for hockey camp. And that turned into hockey during the school year, which turned into the draft.

One more year of playing college hockey, and then I join the New York Guardians.

After tonight, I'm so fucking ready to get out of here.

CHAPTER 15
WREN

THE LACK of sleep is catching up to me. I can't decide what's worse—exhaustion from refusing to close my eyes or exhaustion from waking up with a hoarse throat from the nightmares and running into Stone lurking in the hallway, which is a nightmare in itself.

The only thing that has been passed between us other than a fleeting glare is the water I placed on his table the other night when the guys came into the Shadow's for dinner. I passed my table off to Nicki, refusing to wait on Stone even if the rest of my housemates weren't on my shit list.

Stone is on board with acting like the kiss never happened. I have been pushing the thought of his lips on mine clear out of my head, and if it slips in, I remind myself of my scream-induced nightmare. I'm practically training my brain to recoil at the thought of his mouth.

His little wake-up call worked, though. Stone's hot tongue against mine momentarily paused the bloodcurdling memories of the past, but the second I realized that I had fallen in another trap, I was even more ashamed. Stone kissing me felt like a punishment. A repentance for the past when I allowed my father to treat me like I was a piece of trash instead of his blood.

And if that wasn't punishment enough, I'm sitting in the back row of a make-up class for an elective that I never wanted to take in the first place—*Personal Finance.* Thanks to overworking at Shadow's and having non-stop nightmares, I accidentally slept in the other day and missed the test. Thankfully, Professor Walsh has some decency and has allowed me to take the test this morning instead of giving me an F.

If I were to lose my scholarship, I would truly be fucked.

At least with a chem degree, I have some hope in breaking the never-ending curse of being a *true* Davis.

"Pencils down."

Pencils clank against wood all throughout the lecture room. I finished my test twenty minutes ago but triple-checked my answers because I always triple-check them, even in a fruitless class like *Personal Finance.*

"How'd you do?"

I turn and meet the face of a brown-eyed guy with a smirk that has trouble written all over it.

I shrug. "Pretty good, I think."

The test was a breeze, especially when I am used to calculating complex reactions of substances and slaving over papers regarding what those substances may or may not produce when mixed.

"Good, good."

I turn away and pack my things. One more class and a shift until I can head into my little Harry Potter closet and avoid probing questions from Evander and glares from Stone.

"I haven't seen you in this class before. Have you been hiding back here this whole time? I usually sit up front, but I was late today, so I stayed back here."

"Oh, no—"

Another voice interrupts my response. "She's in the morning class."

I squint at the guy to my left. A quick tremor of fear fuels my movements, and I fumble with my backpack. "How do you know my schedule?"

The guy to my left smirks, and it's just as deadly as the guy on my right. "Always best to know the schedule of a girl as pretty as you."

I puke in my mouth.

He pays no attention to the way my face scrunches, because he leans back in his seat, looking more arrogant than anyone I've met before—even Stone.

"I hear you live with the hockey players."

"I heard that too."

I peek behind me, and there's a *third* guy. I am beginning to wonder if they planned to place me in the middle of their little trio. *Did they sit before or after me?* I'll admit, I'm on edge. My father's phone call and the reappearing nightmares have me rethinking every glance or interaction I have with someone.

"Yeah, so?" I say.

"So, do you maybe want to try sleeping at the lacrosse house instead?"

The snapping of a pencil catches my attention as it echoes down the aisle of seats. I scan for the culprit, and my heart stops for a second when I land on his russet-colored head of hair. *Are you fucking kidding me?* Stone *would* be in this class. I grind my teeth and hate that I didn't notice him the second I sat down. Granted, the test was given minutes after I arrived, but *still*. I need to be better about my surroundings.

"You are welcome to stay with us." The guy to my left is staring intently at me with his pencil lazily trapped between his long fingers.

He's wiggling it back and forth while biting his lip, and I want to laugh in his face at his attempt to sway me into their house.

Professor Walsh finally dismisses us, and I fling my backpack onto my shoulder. I have on my Shadow's shirt, and I hate that these guys now know I work there.

They all stand and walk with me. They're oblivious. I roll my eyes and want to say something flirty, just to irritate Stone, because although he's avoiding me just as much as I'm avoiding him, I know he's listening.

I don't have the energy to antagonize him today. It'll start another fight, and I'm tired.

"What do you say? Do you want to stay with us tonight?"

I stop in my tracks and grip my backpack tightly. There's a heap of students corralling around us, walking in all different directions to leave the lecture room, but naturally, the group of guys stops and waits with bated breath for my answer.

"Do I want to stay with you tonight?" I repeat, making sure I *actually* heard them right.

They all nod and elbow one another in excitement, and I'm left to stand there, dumbfounded at their confidence.

After releasing a soft sigh, I ask, "Is this your way of asking me to have a foursome? Is that what you guys think I do while staying in the hockey house? You think I just let those guys use me or something?"

"Isn't that how you pay rent?" one of them asks, and by the look of confusion on their faces, they truly believe it.

"She isn't a fucking whore, Gibbons." Stone's voice is feral, and although he's talking to them, it's the first time he's even referred to me since last weekend.

"Wasn't it you who said that? Was it a rumor?"

I spin around and send Stone a death glare, but he refuses to meet my eye. *Still avoiding me, I see.*

"Come on, Stone."

One of them laughs, and their hot breath ghosts the back of my neck.

"Share her."

Stone's face turns red, and the flickering muscles on the sides of his temples move with unleashed anger. I want to agree to move into the lacrosse house *just* to piss Stone off, but I refuse to be treated like a toy, being passed around by overconfident, arrogant jocks. I put my back to Stone, but before I can say anything, he grips my shoulder and pulls me back so hard I nearly trip.

He's in front of me, and his fists are by his sides. "If you ever insinuate her sleeping with you guys again, I will break each of your necks."

This asshole. He thinks he can start a degrading rumor about me but then get angry when someone actually tries to act on it? Or worse, come to my rescue?

"I don't need you to fight my battles for me." I step in front of him.

The lacrosse players chuckle and shake their heads at Stone's threat, but before I can say anything to them, Stone's hands are on my waist, and I'm lifted off the floor. He spins around and drops me down, all while refusing to meet my eye. He turns his back to me *again*, and I want to scream.

"Get the fuck away from her."

I want to bang my fists on Stone's back, but I don't. The lacrosse players walk past Stone, and one of them winks, but I keep my expression steady and poised. I wait until Stone takes a step in the opposite direction, but I'm not going to continue to ignore him like he wants.

"How dare you start a rumor like that about me?" I say, picking up my pace to match his stride. His jaw is as sharp as the knife in my back from the rumor he started. "What was your plan with that one? Are you trying to get me raped?"

Stone stops moving so abruptly I have to take a step back to stay beside him. He remains even-faced. I don't even think he's blinked. His chest is heaving, so I poke a little more.

"Are the nightmares that I'm having not enough for you? Wanted to add some more?"

His eye twitches, and I tighten my high pony with confidence. I said I was too exhausted to fight with him, but it's addicting at this point, which is terrifying.

"What was it you said again?" I ask over my shoulder when I reach the door.

If I don't hurry, I'll be late for my shift, and that's not an option. The more money I save, the sooner I can be in my own place without having to share a house with someone like him.

"You aren't sure what poor girls like me would do to keep a roof over their head?" I snicker. "Maybe I will move in with them. Would be better than sharing a house with a self-centered asshole who can't even apologize."

I smile deviously, but it falls when his voice skims my back.

"Takes one to know one."

My pony whips against my cheek when I turn. "Excuse me?" *Self-centered?* I am the very opposite of that. Years and years of saving my father from jail time, giving him all my money, and cooking drugs for him is far from self-centered. I gave up my morals for him. I gave up my sanity for him.

Stone keeps his dark and broody glare pinned above my head, and I almost lift my knee and ram him in the balls.

"You're so self-centered you planted drugs in my truck to save your own ass, Sticks. So shut the fuck up about being self-centered."

His eyes drop to mine unexpectedly, and my world stops for a second.

"And would someone *so* self-centered sleep three feet from you every night in case you start screaming and wake the whole neighborhood?"

My throat closes.

I'm defeated.

Stone beat me, and I let him.

"No one is asking you to sleep outside my door," I snap with hidden embarrassment.

I didn't know he was sleeping out there. The few times I've left my room for water after a nightmare coated me with sweat, he was always near but never asleep.

I probably woke him.

My cheeks burn, and he notices.

"Tell me if those guys bother you again," he demands, face etched with rage. He brushes past me, and the door flies open, allowing cool air to cover my heated skin.

I glance at the clock and curse because I'm going to be late for my shift.

And it's all Stone's fault.

CHAPTER 16
STONE

I SHOULD'VE KNOWN that damn rumor was going to bite me in the ass. One little mention of Sticks moving into the hockey house, one tiny insinuation that she's paying for the space in more creative ways... It didn't seem to get a foothold, but suddenly it seems like every guy and their fucking father are looking at Wren like she's walking around naked.

She hurries off to where-fucking-ever, and I head to the arena for hockey practice. The cold air is a welcome distraction as soon as I walk into the building. The locker room smells like old sweat and cleaning solution, but it brings a smile to my face, nonetheless.

There's nowhere I'd rather be than on the ice.

...Except for today.

Today, my thoughts are pulled toward Wren and that fucking kiss. And the lacrosse jackasses trying to get her to move into *their* house.

"Foster!"

Someone crashes into me.

I grunt under the impact, losing my footing and going

down hard. We're not in full pads today, and an elbow to my gut drives the wind from my lungs.

It takes me a moment to realize it's Grant. Our enforcer and D-man. He's thick as shit, and his weight keeping me pinned to the ice does nothing but enrage me. I slam my fist into his side, and he lets out an *oof*.

"Get off," I growl.

He jumps up and tosses his stick down, glaring at me. "What's your fucking problem?"

"I don't have a problem." I leap to my feet and drop my stick, too. It's either get rid of it or bash him over the head—and then I'd be in deep shit.

"Yes, you do. You look awful. You're playing like shit."

"I'm fine," I insist. "You're just a moron who doesn't know how to skate."

"You skated into *me*!" he yells. "Jesus, man, we're on the same team."

I roll my eyes.

"What's the problem here?" Coach barks, skating to a halt between us. His gaze bounces from Grant to me. "Foster? Marvin?"

Sometimes I forget that Grant has a terrible last name.

"Sorry, Coach," we both utter.

He shakes his head. "Not good enough. You're both done for the day. Get off my ice."

I open my mouth to protest, but Grant grabs my arm and drags me with him. Evan pushes my stick into my chest, and I catch it on reflex.

The whole team is staring.

Grant sighs as soon as we're in the locker room, and he makes quick work getting out of his gear. While I just...sit there.

"Speak," he demands. "The circles under your eyes are dark enough to convince me you've been punched in the nose. Why are you falling apart?"

I grit my teeth.

It's not in my nature to talk. Especially not about feelings. Dad used to say that emotions are dangerous. Let them leak out all over the place, and I'll have nothing left for hockey.

Okay, he didn't say the last part. My coach when I was fourteen said it, probably in an effort to stop me from picking fights with guys twice my size. He wanted my anger on the ice, and that was exactly what he got.

He used to call me Stone-Cold Killer. I'd smile at the time, but somehow it morphed into my whole fucking personality. Cold in every aspect—except when I'm around Wren. Then, it seems like I'm burning up on the inside.

"I haven't actually been sleeping." The words are out before I can stop them.

Grant goes still.

"I've been sitting outside Wren's room every night."

He glances at me, but I get the sense that he doesn't want to scare me off. "Why?"

"Because she has nightmares, and I'm pretty sure it's my fault." No, it's definitely my fault. "I just don't want her to think she's alone."

"She is alone," he points out. "She was in your room, but you freaked out, and now she's sleeping in a little closet."

I scrub my face. "Yeah."

"And you're sleeping on the floor outside her room because…?"

"Maybe it's what I deserve," I say quietly.

"Nah."

So easy. I stare at his back and try to come up with a reply. *Nah.* It's not what I deserve? According to Wren, I should be rotting in Hell. So that's what I'm busy doing. I'm fucking punishing myself.

No one asked you to sleep outside my door. Her words haunt me. Her face haunts me. That fucking kiss haunts me.

If you asked me two weeks ago if Wren Davis moving out

was a good thing, I would've said *hell yeah*. I would've packed her shit into garbage bags and tossed them out on the front lawn to be picked up by whatever new arrangement she organized.

But now…

No.

I force myself into motion, unlacing my skates and changing into my street clothes. Once I'm done, I nod to Grant and follow him outside.

"Want to get a drink?" he offers.

Which is how we end up at Shadow's.

Wren is busy with other tables, her dark hair coming loose from her braid in chunks that frame her face. She looks as tired as I suddenly feel, but she keeps moving.

Another waitress brings us beers. Grant and I sit in silence while I watch Wren. She disappears into the kitchen and comes out a few moments later with a tray of plates. Once they're down at a table, she tucks her hair behind her ear and goes right on to the next thing.

"Dude."

I scowl and turn back to Grant.

His expression is stoic. Not happy, not mad, just carefully blank. But the corner of his lips pulls up when he says, "You're so screwed."

"You're telling me," I mumble.

"We've got our first preseason game on Friday. What will it take for you to be ready?"

I sigh. "I'll be ready."

He scoffs.

Wren's panicked voice draws my attention back to her. It only takes me a split second to find her in the crowded bar— it's like I never actually stopped keeping tabs on her while talking to Grant. Some guy's holding her wrist, even as she tugs back.

I see red.

I'm out of my chair before Grant can get a word in, striding across the room. It isn't until I get closer that I realize it's another group of guys from college. Football assholes, maybe. I don't know. I don't really give a shit about what sport they play—just that they're touching Wren.

"You should really let go of her." I stop beside her and glower at the guy.

"Oooh, your tough fuck buddy has come to rescue you?" The guy sneers.

His friends laugh.

I tilt my head, then lunge for him. I grab the back of his head and yank forward, slamming his face into the table. There's a satisfying *crunch*, and Wren slips free. I release him and back away. He pushes upright. Blood pours from his nose.

"That was a warning." I point at him. "You go ahead and spread the goddamn word that Wren Davis is off limits."

"Stone—"

I whirl on her. "Save it, Sticks."

Her face is flushed, her hair wild. I have the indescribable urge to go caveman on her. Toss her over my shoulder, carry her outside. Fucking ravage her just to lay claim on her.

That's not how this works.

"You need to leave." She grips my arm.

It's only then that I realize the place has gone silent.

Grant comes up and guides me out. Wren follows.

"You're a monster," she calls. "All your talk about *me* being the selfish one. You just want me gone by any means necessary—"

"No." I whirl around and point at her. "All I want is to play hockey! And I can't seem to do that with you fucking with my head."

She stares at me. She has the audacity to look hurt by that. "You're kidding me."

"You jeopardize *everything* I want!" I jerk out of Grant's

hold and stride past her. Fuck this. I break into a run. I don't even care where I go—I just can't stay here.

I hate her.

I hate her.

I hate her.

Say it enough times and it might become true.

———

I'm just dozing off when Wren's door cracks open. The past week, she's cried in her sleep every night. But she's only emerged a few times. And in those times, we haven't spoken a word.

Evan and I are currently not speaking either. He's still pissed about the photo, and me being an insensitive ass, and also for not clearing the air with Wren. Any time he sees us in a room together, he scowls like I've broken his favorite pet and leaves as fast as he entered.

The light from Wren's phone sweeps over my outstretched legs, up my chest, and finally lands on my face. I squint up into it, more than a little confused about why we're breaking the pattern.

"Why are you still here?"

I shrug and raise my hand, blocking the light.

"Is it because you feel guilty?"

"I don't fucking know." My head *thunks* against the wall. Then, "Yeah, maybe I do feel guilty."

She hesitates. But only for a second. "Good."

I accept that.

She moves down the hall. The fridge light illuminates the kitchen for a brief moment, then recedes into darkness. I wait for her to come back and retreat into her room, but instead... she stops beside me.

Then she slides down the wall and sits next to me. She holds out a bottle of water.

"This is not a truce," she warns.

I smile and take it from her. "I wouldn't dream of that."

But one thing is sure: Wren isn't safe on her own. Clearly. I've already planned exactly what I need to do. I've already contacted my advisor and asked to switch into her Personal Finance class. *Easy.* Same professor, same work, different time of day. Because if there are assholes harassing her in my class, there will definitely be some in hers.

Just thinking of that angers me.

I got her full schedule, too. She's taking crazy-as-fuck science and math classes that made my head spin just reading the names. I *was* going to see about transferring in, but fuck that. But I can be in the same hallway when her class gets out...and happen to be walking in the same direction of her next class.

If she were to ask—which she won't. Because I'm stealth incarnate.

"You look like you're plotting something."

Okay, maybe not.

I eye her. "Aren't you tired?"

"Exhausted."

Her *smile.* Her sad, tired smile nearly does something to me.

My dick has a not-so-subtle reaction. I cover my groin with the water bottle before she can notice its rise.

Guess I'm not drinking that.

"So..." I shift. "You're tired, but you won't go to bed."

She nods slowly. "And you're tired, but you sleep out here."

I scoff. "I get plenty of rest. I can sleep anywhere."

"Stone."

"Sticks."

Her elbow drives into my side, fast and hard. "Don't call me that."

"Well, I like it, *Sticks*."

She jumps to her feet. "Why can't you just—"

"Why do you take it so personally? It's not a bad nickname. Sit back down, Wren."

I tug her hand, insistent that she actually *sit*. Because I don't want this to be over. Our weird, middle-of-the-night temporary truce. But when I do, she comes almost too easily.

And she lands on my lap.

We stare at each other for a beat, both surprised at the position we find ourselves in. I mean, in what world would Wren Davis ever actually touch me?

But she doesn't move, isn't trying to scramble off of me, and it's messing with my head. Especially with the way she's glaring at me like she wants to claw my eyes out.

I should not be attracted to her. I should not be attracted to her. I should not—

"You really fucked me up by kissing me." Her eyes narrow. "So this is just me repaying the favor."

I'm shocked into stillness when Wren kisses me. I can't even reciprocate. I'm just... She just...

My brain clicks together almost as soon as Wren gives up. She pulls away.

I don't let her get that far. I slide my hand around the back of her neck and draw her forward, crushing her lips to mine. It spirals into a mad frenzy. She's grabbing at my clothes, my hair. I bite her lip and taste blood in my mouth, and she whimpers. Not in a way reminiscent of her nightmares, but of pleasure.

It goes straight to my cock.

I'm sure she feels it pressing between us. Her fingers tug my shirt up and skate along the skin above my shorts' waistband, sending goosebumps coasting up my back and down my arms. I grip her hair harder, tilting her head to the side and leaning up into her.

When she palms my dick through my shorts, though, I see stars. I dip my hand into her shorts, dipping under her panties. Her slight intake of breath is the only tell that my fingers are affecting her.

She's soaked, though. I linger on her clit, then inch down and dip my fingers into her pussy. I want to taste her in the worst way. But I'm too focused on the noises she's making as I finger-fuck her.

Wren rolls her hips forward, grinding her clit on the heel of my palm.

"That's it," I whisper against her lips. We've stopped kissing and are just pressed together, open-mouthed and chasing pleasure.

"Fuck," she groans.

I bite her lower lip, tugging until she kisses me again. Harder. I've never been this turned on just by touching someone. Her hand is still on me, rubbing through my shorts. But that takes a backseat when she suddenly arches her back.

Her muscles tighten around my fingers.

Her orgasm face is something I won't be forgetting anytime soon.

When she comes down, I carefully pull my hand away. My fingers are wet, and her eyes are dark. Pupils dilated.

I lick my fingers clean and imagine it's her pussy.

One day I'll have her spread open for me to devour.

But the moment seems to fade, even with my raging hard-on drawing ninety percent of my attention. The shift in the air is clear enough.

She stands shakily, using the wall over my head for balance, and steps away.

Retreating.

"You know what they say," I call to her before the door closes between us.

She pauses, and I grin.

"An orgasm a day keeps the nightmares away."

Wren rolls her eyes and shuts the door. I reach for my water bottle and uncap it, chugging half. I lower it and resign myself to another night on the floor.

Because *fuck*. That was unexpected.

AN ORGASM A DAY *keeps the nightmares away.*

I can't believe that's what he said to me just as much as I can't believe it actually rang true. I didn't have another nightmare after shutting the door in Stone's face two nights ago, and I have refused to make eye contact with him since.

What was I thinking?

My plan was to irritate him because I could see him sulking outside my door, and I was already pissed about him coming to my rescue at Shadow's. He was messing with my head—so hot and cold, just like his nickname from high school, *Stone-Cold Killer.* I heard one of the guys talking with him in the kitchen, poking and prodding and asking why he was playing like shit, but he only grunted and stalked off.

It's probably because he's tired due to my stupid anxiety creeping up on me when I'm at my most vulnerable, whimpering and crying at all hours of the night. Not that I asked him to stay outside my room—that's all on him. Which again, messes with my head.

I slam my notebook closed and rub at my sore neck. I stand at the sound of Professor Walsh's dismissal. Personal Finance is the class I'd choose to skip out on for a nap if I had to pick, it is the least demanding of my course load, but I won't slack off when it comes to my academics.

"You look tired."

I freeze at the sound of a voice I'm not expecting. Stone is standing in the back of the lecture hall, resting along the doorframe casually. His book is trapped in his large hand as he ignores all the puck bunnies trying to gather his attention.

"What are you doing here?" I ask.

Everyone is staring at us.

He shrugs and walks beside me. "I switched classes to be in yours."

"What?" I slam on the brakes. "No."

He doesn't pay any attention to me. Instead, he pulls out his phone, and when I glance at the screen, he has an email open from an academic advisor with the heading: *Here is your new schedule.*

I rip the phone out of his hand, ignoring the quick brush of our fingers, and zoom in.

When I meet his eyes—*those annoying blue eyes*—I can tell he's pleased with himself.

"Did you seriously switch your entire schedule to match mine?"

Stone is so nonchalant with his casual shrug. "Yeah, except those godawful chemistry classes you're taking."

I wait for a beat, preparing for his jab over how ironic it is that I'm a chem major and used to cook drugs for my father, but surprisingly, he doesn't say anything, which leaves me confused.

"What? No remarks about my past *chemistry* skills?"

Stone walks beside me, eyeing everyone we pass with skepticism. I'm on edge. Not because of the staring from our peers but the death glares *he's* sending. The moment we're outside, I see that he has parked his car right beside mine. I pick up the pace, which is completely pointless because he's a hockey player, for fuck's sake—his endurance is much better, and one of his strides is three of mine.

"Why are you rushin' off, Sticks? You gotta work?"

I glare at him. He has on a backward baseball hat, and it's annoyingly hot. His jaw flickers with impatience, but his eyes scan all over my face like he's searching for something.

"What's it to you?"

I throw my bag and books in the passenger seat of my car. "Are you planning to show up and punch every guy who looks at me?"

He chuckles, and I feel it everywhere. I drop my eyes to his mouth and sweat at the sight. *Shit.* The other night was supposed to be a punishment to him. It was supposed to fuck with his head, but instead, it fucked with mine.

"If they need to be punched, yes."

"Well, don't," I snap. "They give me good tips."

I shut my passenger door and stalk over to the driver's side. The door creaks as I open it, and I half expect it to fall off its hinges. Stone watches me with amusement, and I'm growing more irritated.

"And why the hell did you switch your schedule to match mine? Are you trying to pay me back for the other night? Because this isn't messing with my head. It's just pissing me off." I'm lying right through my teeth. "Or is that your plan? To piss me off so much that I just leave the house altogether?"

Stone's hand falls to my bicep, and I pause at the touch. *Why does it feel different all of a sudden?* And why the hell am I not pulling away?

"I switched because I'm trying to prevent you from getting gang-banged."

My jaw slacks with a gasp. Stone's free hand pushes my chin up to close my mouth.

"I started a rumor, and it's biting me in the ass. This is me trying to fix it. I'm…" He lowers his voice so much that I hardly hear him. "I'm trying to protect you."

My heart thumps, and I know it's because there is a severely broken part of me that craves to have someone protect me. But just as quickly as I fall for his words, I climb back up and shut him out.

"Well, I don't want anyone's protection." I climb in my car with haste. "Especially not *yours.*"

I slam my door and rev my shitty car to life and speed away, hoping I can beat him home. But knowing Stone, he'll beat me because he refuses to lose.

And that's exactly what happens.

His footsteps are behind me, and I curse the fact that my car can't go over thirty miles per hour without vibrating the entire frame. I try to race up the steps to the house first, but Stone's a step behind me, cackling like a fucking monster in my ear.

"Those sticks of legs you have are quick," he whispers so close to me that his breath brushes against my neck. "But not quick enough."

I scan the house to see if anyone is home, but there isn't another beefy hockey player to be found anywhere. Not even in the kitchen.

"I'm fast when I need to be. If I truly wanted to lose your trail, I could." I open the closet door.

I stare at Stone standing in the hallway with his irking smirk. He finds this amusing, and I do not.

"I'm sly, Stone. You should know that better than anyone."

I watch as the thought flickers across his features, hardening the lines around his mouth and turning his smirk into a grimace.

Wren—1. Stone—0.

The smile tastes just as victorious as I feel, but when I turn and look at my room, I still. *What the fuck?*

I whip around quickly and level Stone with a glare. "Not only are you stalking me, but you're fucking with my shit too?"

Stone rolls his eyes. "I'm not stalking you, Sticks. Way to be dramatic."

My heart is beating with anger, and suddenly, I'm ten years old again, in a room with Winnie the Pooh wallpaper, looking at my stuff strewn all over the place because one of the foster kids thought I stole their lighter. They destroyed my things, and I still haven't gotten over it.

"At least clean up after yourself next time! Why were you going through my stuff?" I walk farther into my room, noticing that each of my notebooks is open, and my books are shuffled throughout. I peer back and snarl. "What were you looking for? Didn't do your homework and wanted to copy me?" I roll my eyes. "Just like high school. Constantly cheating...on homework *and* girlfriends."

"I wasn't in your fucking room."

He's standing behind me, and I know Stone isn't an honest guy, but I can tell by his voice that he isn't lying. I scan my small area again, and the panic sets in before the realization.

"Jesus, this is a mess," he says.

"Get out," I say, hating that my voice is less than confident.

Stone notices. I know he does.

"Wren. I didn't go through your shit."

He called me Wren. He knows something's wrong.

"Get *out*."

I push on his chest, and it must surprise him, because he stumbles backward. Before he can realize what I've done, I slam the door and flip the lock. I jump when his fists bang against the wood.

"Wren! Open the fucking door."

I ignore him and take a small step forward. I bend down and scoop up one of my notebooks. It's an older one, from high school. I kept it because I knew I'd have to refer to the easier equations to further my current labs in Organic Chemistry and probably even more classes throughout my junior and senior year. I run my finger over the soft pencil markings to ease my anxiety, but as soon as I flip to the last page, my eyes swell with moisture. It's torn, and I know *exactly* what was hidden in between what seemed like normal equations.

Not to mention, the scribble of messy handwriting left behind is the answer that I didn't actually need:

Your father says thank you for all of your help, Pumpkin.

I muffle a sob and shove the notebook away. Stone has given up on knocking, and I'm pretty certain he has left for practice. I refuse to open my door, though. Instead, I clean up the mess my father's *friends* have made and put everything back to where it was before. I should be thankful that they took the measurements for the best batch of meth we've ever made instead of taking me, but now they know where I live, and that's a problem in itself.

———

"ON YOUR KNEES."

Shit. Shit. Shit. I stare at the door to the trailer and hold back a sob. There's a gun pressed to the back of my skull, and I force myself to swallow the frog in my throat. I'm shaking with fear, and my hands have residue on them that is honestly so dangerous. My gloves are thrown off to the side of the table, and I watch as a cockroach scurries underneath the couch to hide from the loud voices.

"Where is he?"

The barrel digs into my head, and I whimper. "I don't know."

I don't. I really don't. My father is no knight in shining armor, but right now, his appearance would save me.

"Where's the money, then?"

He doesn't tell me where the money is. Why would he?

My shaky voice breaks through the pounding in my ears. "I don't know. I can... I can give you a fresh batch if that'll help until he gets back?"

Please work. Please work. Please work.

"A fresh batch? How old are you? You can't honestly think I'll believe a teenage girl is the one cooking."

The man has a large scar running down his face that stops just above his upper lip. There are scars all over his face, but the long one is what sends a chill down my spine.

"A fresh batch? We want something else."

"What do you want?" I shift my attention to the guy standing near the door. I'm eager. I'd do anything to get the gun off the back of my head. Fear makes you do wild things. I've learned that the hard way.

"You."

The gun becomes a little less forceful, and my body is numb. My stomach twists, and instead of swallowing my tears, I'm now swallowing regret. Shit.

"How old are you?"

The very tip of the gun comes around my neck, and my hair is pulled backward.

"Sixteen," I answer.

"Good enough for me."

A pair of boots are in front of me, and I'm pushed to my back. I'm on the floor with the cockroaches as my audience. I tell myself to stay strong and to just put my mind somewhere else, but the fighter inside of me can't fathom it, so I scream.

I scream so loud that my throat hurts worse than the force between my legs.

"GODDAMN IT, WREN!"

My throat burns when I gasp for air. I scramble backward and smack my back off the wall. My head is caught by someone's hand before it hits, and I hear my sob loud and clear.

"Look at me."

I can't breathe.

I can't do anything but shake.

I gasp and gasp until two hands cup my cheeks, stroking the skin underneath my eyes.

"Look at my eyes, baby."

I blink past the tears and find myself clinging to the blue for dear life. I grip his wrists so hard I'm positive I've made him bleed. He takes it, though. Stone says nothing. He continues to stare into my eyes, breathing slowly out of his mouth, trying to get me to do the same.

"You're safe," he whispers.

I'm too weak to argue, and I'm too weak to pretend like I don't need someone at this moment, because I do. Instead of pushing Stone away, I pull him in closer and bury my head into the crook of his neck, soaking his shirt with my tacky skin and wet face.

I feel the movement without opening my eyes. I'm in his arms, and he's moving me out of my room. My door has a hole in it. The wood is splintered. I locked the door before going to sleep, and I'm pretty certain Stone used his fist to break it down to get to me.

"*Jesus Christ*," someone says.

I shut my eyes immediately when I see the rest of my housemates standing in the hallway with concern etched onto their sleepy faces.

"Wrenny."

Stone pauses at the sound of Evan's voice, but I shake my head along his chest. I don't want to talk, and there is no amount of milk and cookies that can get me to. Instead, I listen to the thundering beat of Stone's heart against my ear and hold on tighter as he takes me upstairs.

CHAPTER 18
STONE

STEP-MONSTER

> Please call me! Getting things ready for your
> father's bday!!

I LET my head fall back against the wall and try to formulate a response. If I ignore her texts, in two days I'll get a call from Dad. Down to the minute, actually. I could time it if I wanted to run another experiment...

Dad's birthday isn't for two months. He'd want me to come home, of course. The perfect family picture—you know, father, son, and holy Stepford wife—for everyone to witness.

The step-monster will throw some huge bash, like she does every year. She treats his birthday like the most holiest of holidays.

Gag.

I'm actually surprised that she waited until now to reach out.

So it's with satisfaction that I shut off my phone and drop it to the kitchen table. Some of the guys have filtered through, but no one questioned why I decided to tackle my Personal Finance homework out here.

There are a thousand reasons loaded and ready to go for if they do ask. Reasons that have nothing to do with Wren Davis.

Archer plops into the chair across from me.

I glance up at him, then turn back to my laptop.

"Foster."

I sigh. "Yes?"

"You look like shit."

"Thank you so much, Arch." I roll my eyes. "Is that all?"

"You've got circles under your eyes. When's the last time you slept?" He leans forward, his brows furrowing. "When's the last time you ate an actual meal?"

"I sleep." It's not quite the convincing argument I hoped it would be.

He chuckles. "Okay, man. It's late. Normal people would be sleeping...*now*."

"Well, I've got homework. Stuff to do. Grades to keep up, you know?" I shrug and try not to glance past him to Wren's closet door.

"Hockey to play," Archer adds.

I wave him off. "I'll be ready for our game tomorrow."

We're playing the Bexley University Wolves at home to kick off our season. I'm not nervous. I feel like I've studied their tapes for hours. I know Theo, their team captain, is a force on the ice. And their goalie, Emery, has anger issues.

I look forward to pissing him off.

"It's just—"

"I'm *fine*." I glare at him. "It's fine. Everything is under control."

He nods slowly and pushes off from the table. I go back to the paper I've been trying to write. What kind of accounting class requires *essays*? The only saving grace is that it'll eventually be useful. I've got most of my initial signing pay from the New York Guardians sitting in a high-interest account until I'm ready to use it. That was Dad's accountant's idea.

I guess I could just rely on accountants, but I'd rather know myself.

The upstairs hallway light goes off. Its glow was visible down the stairs, in perfect view from where I sit. After a few more minutes, I close the laptop. My head was starting to droop.

I flick off the light and pile my stuff up, heading to wash up in the upstairs bathroom. Even if I'm sleeping on the floor outside Wren's door for the rest of the year, I can't let my hygiene slip.

It's when I'm on my way back that a sound makes my blood run cold.

Screaming.

I break into a run and slam into her door. It rattles, but it doesn't budge. The knob turns, but she must've flipped the deadbolt.

"Fuck," I growl.

Her screams are going to haunt my fucking nightmares.

I punch the door. Nothing. I mean, nothing apart from the terrified noises she's making. I throw myself against the door again. And again.

Until something cracks.

One more time, my shoulder throbbing, and the door snaps under my weight. I stumble in and find her in the darkness. My chest tightens. There's just enough light behind me to see her.

She's curled in a fetal position, tear tracks down her cheeks, eyes squeezed shut as she fights off an invisible attacker.

"Wren." I drop to my knees beside her, squeezing her arm. "Wake up."

She flails. Her hand catches my jaw, whipping my head to the side. If I wasn't so freaked out, I'd be impressed by her backhand. But she needs help being yanked out of this dream, seemingly locked in it.

I grab both her upper arms and shake her violently. "God-damn it, Wren!"

She wakes and scrambles backward. I go with her, catching her head before she can knock it into the wall. I don't need her to be traumatized *and* concussed. Her gaze is all over the place, her breathing wild. She's hyperventilating.

"Look at me," I order.

She's trembling. Her mouth opens and closes, but it's just sheer panic behind her eyes. I cup her face with both hands, catching her tears on the pads of my thumbs.

"Focus on my eyes, baby." *Baby*. I ignore that and hope she does, too.

I focus on my breathing. Her hands come up and squeeze my wrists. I exaggerate my inhales and exhales until she copies me.

"You're safe."

She finally seems to come back to herself. And when she registers *me*, she doesn't push me away. No, she fucking drags me closer. She winds her arms around my neck and buries her face in my shirt, hiding herself.

My heart cracks.

She was in here fighting for her life in her dreams. *Alone*.

I can't leave her. I scoop her up into my arms, ignoring how light she is. How reminiscent it is of the time I carried her to the tub—but then, it was out of spite. And maybe a little bit of lust. This is all concern.

The hallway light is on, and I squint at the brightness.

Archer and Sully stand in the doorway, eyeing the splin-tered pieces of wood. The deadbolt that ripped clean through the frame.

"Jesus Christ," Archer mumbles.

I eye him, and Sully elbows him. They both move out of my way. Grant and Taylor made it out of their beds too. They seem more confused than anything.

"You good?" Grant mouths.

I nod.

Evan is at the back of the pack. "Wrenny."

He steps forward like he's going to take her from me. I bare my teeth at him, stopping him in his tracks, just as Wren shakes her head against me.

She doesn't want him either.

He sees the look in my eye, and he's as confused as me. Well, he can get fucked. They all can.

I don't know how I went from hating her guts to...*this*.

She thought I went through her shit. It wasn't me, and I highly doubt it was any of the other guys. They respect her space, although there's certainly been an air of confusion around the house in the last week or so. Only Evan has caught me downstairs past midnight, but I assured him it was a one-time thing.

A total lie.

It's her face I pictured while being held in the police station. Her name I cursed when my father scolded me. When he made sure I knew I had to do better, to *be* better.

I never told Evan what she did. I made something up to explain why I was hauled out of the lunchroom and later arrested—something my ego did not anticipate needing to brace against. The questions, the jokes.

Now there's this.

Hurt flashes across his expression, but I ignore it and keep moving. Up the stairs, into the bedroom. I turn to close the door and find the rest of the guys in the hallway.

We don't need a fucking audience—but they probably deserve an explanation.

I do, too.

My body aches. I've never thrown myself at something so hard—no check in hockey could compare to the jarring nature of trying to break down a door. A door Wren locked to keep me—and the world—out.

But she can't keep me away. Not after tonight.

With her head tucked in the crook of my neck, her fingers curled in my shirt, the need to protect her grows stronger and stronger.

I kick the door shut and sit on the bed, resting her on my lap. I stroke her hair. "It's just us."

She shudders, her fingers tightening on my shirt before slowly relaxing. Her palm flattens. It's amazing how much heat is transferred from her to me.

"I'm sorry, Stone."

"For what?"

She lifts my hand and runs her thumb over my knuckles.

"Punching it didn't work. I just rammed it until the lock broke." I force a laugh to hide my sudden nerves. I'm not fifteen years old anymore, practicing how to talk to hot girls. "I'm fine..."

"But?"

There's always a but. And in this case, it's the elephant in the room. The reason for her screams.

"But I think I deserve the truth. You said someone was in your room. You freaked out about the picture I posted. Who is chasing you?"

I can't even tell her how much I need her to be honest.

She slides off my lap and scooches backward, until she's leaning against the wall. She takes my pillow and hugs it to her chest.

"I do owe you the truth." She looks away. "But I don't want you to hate me for it."

I eye her. "I doubt I'd hate you for it."

"You already hate me for..." Her jaw works. "For what I did in high school."

"Just tell me the truth," I reply. "Please, Wren."

She rubs her eyes and nods. "Well, you know my dad is into some stuff."

"Drugs." I withhold the obvious *duh*.

"When I was a teenager, he discovered I had an affinity

for…recipes." She tosses the pillow aside and jumps to her feet. "Recipes of an illegal nature."

Holy shit. "You were cooking his drugs?"

"Yeah. Well, you know. It's hard to find someone smart enough to not get blown up in that line of work." She tucks her hair behind her cheek and offers me a small smile. "But with that line of…work…comes other things. Mainly, bad men."

"But your dad—"

"He couldn't protect me twenty-four seven." Her expression falls. "And sometimes I think he didn't *want* to protect me from it all."

This is ridiculous.

"You were cooking meth, and he didn't even have the decency to keep you safe?"

She laughs. "Do you hear yourself, Stone?"

I stand, too. I run my hands through my hair. "This is only backstory, isn't it?"

"Yeah. So… I would go a few months with Dad, then something would happen. He'd get in trouble, or a neighbor would call the police, and I'd end up with the Mitchells."

Evan's family.

Wren clears her throat. "*Anyway*, I cut ties for good when I left for college. Dad's in prison, and it seemed as good a time as any for a fresh start."

I narrow my eyes. She got away from her drug-dealing father… "Until I posted the photo?"

She goes to the window and pulls back the curtain, peeking out.

"Wren."

"Yes, Stone, until you posted the photo. Then the phone calls started."

A chill skates down my spine. She's weirdly calm relaying all this information. Like she's not really comprehending it, just reciting the facts.

"Your dad?"

"He found me," she says on an exhale. "He wants me back in his operation."

I already know it was his drugs that she planted on my truck in high school. I already know she came from a bad family. That she didn't sleep when she was living there—or eat. She'd lose weight, she'd get dark circles under her eyes.

Evan would give her the car keys so she could nap.

I didn't suspect...

"Did they hurt you?"

She glances over her shoulder at me. Her dark hair is loose. I want to run my fingers through it. To tug it.

Get your head out of the gutter.

"No more than expected," she whispers.

I close my eyes. Everything in me goes white-hot, a burning rage like nothing I've felt before. I suspect I'm the one shaking now. I ball my fists and try to breathe, but it's not really working.

"Stone."

Wren needs protecting.

It isn't a matter of question. I fucked up, and someone is clearly out to manipulate her back into her father's operation —no, wait. Manipulate is too nice of a word. I have no doubt they'd drag her back.

"*Stone.*"

Her fingers run up my arms, looping around the back of my neck. She pulls me down until her breath ghosts across my lips.

Someone was in her room. They found her room and went through it enough to show her that they were here.

We need fucking security cameras. Or a bodyguard to follow her around, or—

"I don't want to go back to sleep," she whispers. "Can you help me with that?"

I open my eyes.

She's right there, her sometimes-green, sometimes-brown eyes so damn alluring, I have no doubt I could fall right into them if given the chance.

If you haven't already.

"Are you propositioning me, baby?"

She bites her lip to hide her smile and slowly nods.

Oh, fuck. I'm a goner—and judging by the glimmer in her gaze, we both know it.

CHAPTER 19
WREN

SLEEP USED to be a way to shut everything down, to hide, but I can't seem to use it as a pause in reality any longer. I'm afraid to sleep. I'm afraid that someone is going to come take me, after knowing they were in my room—so much that they're coming for me in my dreams. But at least when I'm awake, I can pretend that Stone Foster will protect me from all the bad in my life, even if I considered him one of those bad things hours ago.

Stone stares at the ceiling, showing off his chiseled jawline that is moving back and forth with temptation. "I can't say no to you."

He cups my butt and picks me up. I'm pressed against him and can feel how hard he is through the thin cotton of his pants, and it does something scary to me. I crave his touch, his mouth, his eyes. I want it all, and I want him to take away the fear I felt moments ago, trapped inside my little bedroom.

"Kiss me," I whisper, staring into his eyes. The last two times we've kissed, it wasn't like this. I'm desperate for an escape. I'm desperate for him to silence everything, and there isn't an ounce of hate or manipulation between either of us at the moment.

Stone swallows, his Adam's apple bobbing just above the collar of his t-shirt, and he stares into my eyes. He's like the Grim Reaper, sucking up my soul, and I'm willing to give it to him.

My back presses on the back of his bedroom door—the door that was supposed to be mine—and his fingers dig into the skin below my short sleep shorts. He kisses me, but it's so much more than a simple kiss. His tongue plunges into my mouth, and a groan rumbles out of his chest and vibrates. I kiss him back, burning all over. I'm wet, and needy, and I forget all about the nasty nightmare that sent me screaming minutes prior.

"Fuck." He leans back.

There are little red splotches creeping up his neck. He places my feet on the floor and pushes me forcefully to the back of his door again, shoving my shorts down to my ankles. I kick them off to the side, and it only distracts him for a moment because he takes his hand and dips it into the front of my panties, all while staring into my eyes. My heart beats a mile a minute when he teases me, gently brushing his finger over my swollen clit.

"Does it turn you on knowing the power you have over me, Sticks? I can't fucking resist you."

He removes his hand when I don't answer. I whimper, but it only lasts a second, because at the same time, he pops his finger into my mouth. I taste myself and can't see straight. I'm in a frenzy and claw at his shirt, pushing it up his chest and revealing his tight stomach and rippling muscles.

"On the bed." He's talking between clenched teeth, like it's taking everything in him not to fuck me against the door.

I'd be fine with it. Anything to stop the ache and feed me more distractions.

"*Now.*"

I'm on my back, and Stone wastes no time. He shoves at my shirt and reveals my bare chest.

"God," he whispers.

My back arches, and my legs butterfly, needing to feel him everywhere.

"*Perfect*."

I sigh when he gently bites my nipple. He releases the bud and places a soft kiss on it before moving to the next.

"Stone," I plead. His sheets bundle in my hands. "Please."

"That's a change," he notes before blowing cool air against my flesh. "You saying *please* to me."

His mouth against my skin is like the devil worshiping me, and I'm in a daze. My hand moves past his head as he continues to bite and suck. I place a finger on my clit and gasp with pleasure.

"Absolutely not," he bites out, sitting up quickly and snapping my arms above my head.

His blue eyes are hooded with pleasure, and I have never seen a hotter look. He's turned on, and there's a fire brewing in my lower stomach at the anticipation of him inside me.

"This cunt is mine."

My lip is trapped beneath my upper teeth, and I'm in nothing but a damp pair of panties. *Too much clothing*. The thought must cross his mind, because he dips down, and I hear the rip of fabric before the cool air of the room brushes against the slickness surrounding my clit.

"Open," Stone says just above a whisper. He taps on the inside of my bare thigh. "Let me see how perfect you are."

He hisses between his teeth when I willingly open my legs. I relax my flexing wrists as his hand loosens around my pinned arms, and when I feel his tongue slip inside me, I instantly tighten. He licks me so intently that the room caves in. His hum against my clit forces a cry from my chest, and I arch my back as his finger plunges inside me.

"I want to watch you come for me before I fuck you so hard you come faster than you ever have before, baby."

The dirty talk pulls me over the edge. I throw my head

back and chase the high. Stone drags his finger out of me and slams his palm over my mouth.

His whisper brushes against my ear. "Shh, baby. Evan will kill me if he knows what I'm doing to you in here."

I nod quickly and eagerly. Stone smirks at the way I follow his every movement with parted lips and a heavy chest. I'm in a trance. He slowly shoves his pants and boxers down, and I can't look away. *Shit.* My eyes widen when I look back at his face. All I see is his hot smirk. Stone is one of the cockiest guys I know, and right now I am all for it. I lick my lips and sit up.

He shakes his head at me, lowering his gaze. "I'm all for finding out how talented that bratty mouth is, but I'm not waiting another second before claiming you." The wrapper of the condom is trapped between his white teeth when he rips it open.

My legs fall to the side on their own, and before I know it, Stone is above me, gripping the top of his headboard and thrusting into me fast and hard. He catches my gasp in his mouth, swallowing my surprise and running his tongue over mine in the most sensual way I have ever felt. We match each other's rhythm, kissing each other so intensely I feel it everywhere. I can't hide from Stone Foster any longer. The desire is too palpable between us. My heart thumps each time he presses into me. His movements are fueled with power and redemption. He is owning me, and I'm letting him.

"Jesus fucking Christ, Wren." He pulls back and pauses our moving bodies. "This is…"

"Don't stop." I move closer to him.

His hand splays on my back, and he flips us around so I'm on top.

He skims down my body and pauses on the way we connect. His fingers leave marks in my skin, and his jaw flickers. "Give me all you got," he coaxes, rubbing his thumb over my clit.

The sight of his tongue licking his lips while he stares at me pushes me to move over him and take what he's giving me.

"I'll want every single fucking part of you."

I move fast, working my body at the same time I work his. The rough parts of his palms skim my skin. He touches every spot visible, like I'm going to disappear when this is all said and done.

And I just might.

My nails dig into his shoulders when I lean down and kiss him to silence my cry.

He kisses me back just as roughly, flexing his hips to meet me, and then we both stop abruptly. His teeth sink into my bottom lip, and the metallic taste mixes with the lust while he fills the condom that's still inside me.

My lip pops with a loud sound when he lets go. I take my thumb and wipe off my blood from his mouth before collapsing onto his bed. I'm out of breath, exhausted, and completely sated.

Shit, did that really just happen?

The dip of the mattress is the only indication that he's gotten up. I gently close my eyes, feeling sleep come for me. The silence of the room is comforting in a way, and although I'm still afraid to close my eyes and give in to the slumber, I can't stop it from happening.

"Sleep," Stone whispers from somewhere close by.

I inhale the scent of his pillow and submit to the warmth of his blankets when he drapes them over my bare skin.

"I'm here, and I'm not leaving, Sticks."

CHAPTER 20
STONE

THIRD PERIOD against Bexley University Wolves, and I cannot seem to get my shit together. When I'm checked into the boards for the fifth fucking time in as many minutes, I lose it.

I race after their captain, Brooks. He's got the puck and is charging down the center in an all-out sprint. He's slowed by my teammates. Grant skates to intercept, Archer prepares himself in the crease.

He passes the puck a moment before I catch him, slamming into him from behind and taking him down in a tumble of limbs and sticks. He curses me out and shoves me aside. Sully picks me up by the back of my jersey, spinning me away so I can't do something truly stupid.

We're *losing*. Badly. And while it's mostly my fault, the rest of my team has been coming apart at the seams. Our passes aren't connecting. No one's fucking shooting. The BU Wolves are skating circles around us.

And now their captain is glaring at me from across the circle.

I automatically scowl back.

The ref drops the puck, and Grant, ever the faithful center, gets the puck and flicks it my way. I take it and sprint toward the Wolves' goalie. But I fail to see the stick carefully edged into my path on time. It hooks around my skate, and I'm suddenly falling forward.

The whistle blows.

I leap to my feet and spin, finding Theo Brooks grinning at me.

"*FOSTER!*" Coach screams from the bench.

I really shouldn't punch him in his smug face, so I ignore him and skate for the bench.

Brooks is thrown in the penalty box for two minutes, and I'm benched for the remainder of the game. I pull my helmet and gloves off, then spit out my mouth guard. I run my hands through my hair and watch the time tick down.

Two minutes, then one.

We're 1-5. No fucking chance.

Thirty seconds.

Ten.

The horn blows, and the crowd is rightly lackluster. They just watched their home team lose by a mile.

Those of us on the bench get back on the ice, lining up to shake hands with the victors. I block most of it out.

I was awake for a long damn time after the mind-bending sex with Wren last night. One minute I was scared she was going to be permanently traumatized by her past, and the next she was writhing in pleasure on my cock. And she felt better than I could've ever imagined.

There's a permanent tingling sensation left over from Wren's body pressed to mine. Her head on my shoulder. She shifted there after she fell asleep, her hand sliding across my stomach. A lump forms in my throat just thinking about it.

I left her in that little room for too long. Let her whimper and cry, as long as it didn't get *too bad*. But she was having nightmares this whole time.

"You okay?"

I jerk out of my thoughts. Evan stands over me, his brow furrowed. We made it back to the locker room before he decided to confront me, at least. He's been weird all day, but I've ignored it—well, mostly just ignored *him*. How the hell am I supposed to explain the hold Wren has on me?

My attention moves around the room. The only ones left are my housemates, which presents the perfect opportunity. They're all in various shades of distress, annoyance, or concern—and it's all pointed at me.

"We need to have an emergency house meeting," I tell them.

An hour later, they're all seated around the kitchen table.

Except Wren.

I experience a weird déjà vu moment of walking in on her holding court in a similar fashion. Although, right now, she's working the last hour of her shift at Shadow's. It's bound to be busy after the game, which should keep her occupied until we've come to an agreement.

"What's all this, Foster?"

I glance at Grant, then down at the supplies I laid out on the table.

Wren told me the truth, and I feel oddly protective of it. I've been collecting her secrets like pennies since high school. I never told Evan about Wren's involvement with my arrest, definitely didn't tell him about me threatening her after.

But now's the time to share at least some of them.

"Wren's in trouble."

Silence.

Evan glares at me. "Stone—"

"Shut up, E." I take my time meeting the rest of the guys' gazes. "Listen. I wouldn't be coming to you guys if it wasn't serious. You all heard Wren screaming last night. You saw how she was."

Nods all around.

I sigh. "It's my fault. She's been having nightmares for weeks."

"And you've been sleeping outside her door out of guilt?" Sully asks. "Is that why you've been playing like shit?"

"He looks like shit, too," Taylor mutters.

I hold up my hands. "It's not an excuse. It's just an explanation."

"A shit explanation," Grant pipes up. "What are you saying?"

Evan's still glaring at me like I'm about to piss in his cereal. But if he had just told *me* the truth, even if it wasn't his secret to share, I would never have shared that picture online.

Could I have predicted it going viral? No. But that's unimportant.

"Wren comes from a bad family," I say. "And the photo I posted has brought down on her some attention she was avoiding."

"Hiding from," Evan spits.

I nod my acceptance. "Right. Hiding from."

"Who?"

"Well, her father in prison, for one." I wince. "I won't get into the details, but he's used her for years. And when the social workers caught on, that's when she went to Evan's house. But she always went back to him. Until he went away."

Archer leans forward, resting his forearms on the table. He's directly to my right, and he searches my face. "How can he hurt her from prison?"

"He's got people on the outside," Evan snaps.

"Furthermore," I hurry on before my best friend can take control of this meeting, "someone was in her room. Rifling through her stuff. It's what triggered the most recent—"

The room breaks out into chaos.

Maybe I should've led with that bit of information?

I lean back in my chair and wait for their outrage to

simmer down, and I tap the supplies in front of me. "That's what the cameras are for. They can sync to all of our phones. Just in the public spaces and outside, I'm not that big of a dick."

"And Wren?" Evan's voice is cold. "You didn't give her a chance to explain this to us—"

"She wasn't going to." I laugh. "You're such a fucking idiot, plying her with milk and cookies like that's going to solve anything."

"And cameras are?"

"So we can catch the bastard trying to get to her—"

"Shut up." Archer stands, knocking his chair back. "You two need to figure your shit out on your own time."

I look away from Evan and refocus on the important bits.

"Someone came in here without our permission. That's unacceptable." I lift my chin. "But furthermore, we need to protect Wren."

"Agreed," Evan says.

"Yeah," Grant chimes in. "Obviously. I think we're all in agreement about that."

"Okay, so let's get these cameras installed." I slide one of the boxes to Grant and Sully. "That's for the front porch." Another to Taylor and Archer. "Back door." I keep one for me and shove the other at Evan. "That's an interior one."

"Let's do this." Archer claps.

"One more thing," I call out. "Wren's moving back into my room. Effective immediately."

I already moved her stuff out of that dinky closet. While I was in there, picking up her clothes and bedding, my stomach knotted with guilt. She's been sleeping on the floor, essentially. With nothing more than a few inches of blankets as cushion.

So, yeah. Before the game, I made sure no trace of Wren was left in that small space. She'll just have to deal with it.

And me.

The guys don't really balk at that, sharing some knowing smiles. I ignore them and take my camera, heading for the kitchen. Just in case the outside camera doesn't catch someone coming in, this is basically a backup.

I bought top-of-the-line shit. This one is tiny and practically undetectable.

In less than twenty minutes, the cameras are all set up and synced to our phones. We meet back in the kitchen, learning how to use the app, when Evan nudges me.

"I need to talk to you," he murmurs.

Great. "Okay…"

I follow him around the corner. As soon as we're out of sight, he fists the front of my shirt and shoves me up against the wall.

"Jesus. You gonna make out with me, E?"

"You have no fucking right to steamroll her," he growls. "You've hated her forever. And I get it, you didn't sign up for a project. Your best friend suddenly gets a little sister every few months who tags along with us. But you went from verbally sparring with her to *hating* her. Now this?"

"What do you want me to say?"

I know what he wants. He wants me to explain the shift. As much as I tried to hide it from him, after I was arrested, I just couldn't hold it together. Wren did a great job of avoiding me, scampering off in the hallways like I was going to eat her for breakfast.

And maybe that's why I didn't tell Evan—because she listened to me.

She stayed out of my way.

Telling him this, *now*, would just hurt him and Wren, and I won't do that.

"I want the truth."

I knock Evan's hands away from me. "There's no mysterious, all-encompassing truth. There's no magical explanation for me not liking your little sister. But I'm… I'm over it, okay?"

"There is an explanation."

Our heads whip around.

Wren stands at the top of the hall, wringing her hands together. Tears fill her eyes. "There is an explanation, Evan. And it's all my fault."

CHAPTER 21
WREN

"WREN, NO."

I stumble backward at Stone's rebuttal when I make the decision to tell Evan the truth. The sternness on his face throws me off balance because it's weird for him to suddenly act protective. Evan glances between Stone and me with a little crease on his forehead.

"Yes." I move toward them both.

The hallway isn't long by any means, but it feels never-ending with their eyes glued to me. The rest of my house-mates are in the kitchen, talking amongst themselves, so I lay it out in the open, rushing through something I've buried for years.

"The day he got arrested…" I start, leaning back on the wall with my arms crossed over my chest for protection. Protection from what? Evander hating me, I guess. "It was my fault."

"Wren."

Stone's tone sends shivers down my arms, but I refuse to look at those soul-sucking blue eyes that caressed every inch of my body last night.

"Stop it."

I ignore Stone and look at Evan. He's waiting patiently with his hands in his pockets, resting against the wall opposite of me. The space between us feels just as big as the wedge that I know is going to make a dent in our trust.

"How was it your fault?"

I gulp and look down at my shoes. My feet hurt from my shift, but I stay ramrod straight and suck in tears. "I knew the drug dogs were at school that day because when I went out to your car to take a nap, I saw them and freaked out." A shaky breath leaves me, and I'm pretty certain the entire house is listening, because you can hear a pin drop. "My dad gave me a package that morning, and though I didn't look, I knew it was drugs."

Shit. Why is this so hard to relive?

I run my hands down my face and continue to stare at my shoes. The memory is a broken record repeating itself over and over again. "I didn't want you to get in trouble, and I didn't want your parents to hate me. They were the only stable adults I had in my life." My voice breaks, and I try to move past the lump in my throat.

Stone steps forward and moves beside me. Our arms brush, and I glance at the touch.

"So she put the drugs underneath the carriage of my truck, knowing the dogs would sniff it out, and you'd be in the clear."

"What?" Evan's whisper is a slap against my cheek. He hates me. I know it.

"I'm sorry," I choke. "I just knew that Stone would get a slap on the wrist because of his dad. If I was the one caught, I'd lose my scholarship, and I couldn't fathom it. It was my only way out, and if you were the one who got caught, your parents would be buried in court fees and—"

"Stop."

My neck cracks when I look at Evan. Stone steps forward, like he's prepared to rescue me if Evan tells me to get out, but instead of Evan looking at me, he looks at Stone.

"So you knew? And you never told me?"

Stone shrugs but says nothing. He doesn't deny it, and he doesn't offer an explanation.

Evan moves his attention to me. "And that's why you let him bully you? Because you think you deserve it?"

"I do deserve it," I reply. "And if you want me to mov—"

"Did." Stone's hand wraps around my upper arm.

I inhale at his touch. It's sincere, and I have no idea what to do or how to act. Stone isn't a nice guy, especially to me.

"You *did* deserve my coldness, but I didn't know how bad it was. I didn't think things were so black and white or life and death. Now, though…"

Evan puts his hands on his hips and blows out an exasperated breath. He stares a hole at Stone's grip on my upper arm. "I never thought I'd see the day that you, Stone Foster, would put someone else before yourself."

"He's gone soft!" Archer yells from the kitchen, staying hidden behind the wall.

Stone scoffs and drops his hand from my arm.

Evan rolls his lips with hidden laughter, but I don't find anything amusing.

"You're not angry? I got your best friend locked away behind bars, hauled out of school in handcuffs."

"I'm not angry. No."

I am thankful, don't get me wrong, but there is a sickening part of me that wants Evan to be angry, because whether Stone and Evan agree, I *do* deserve it. I brought doom to Stone two years ago, and it was the entire reason he posted a stupid picture of me and let my father know of my whereabouts, and now, doom is coming for us all. Someone was in our house, in my stupid little nook of a bedroom.

"I put the tension in your friendship and caused so many fights between you two." I waft my hand out into the air, aware that I'm spiraling. "My past is coming to bite me in the ass, and you are all involved because I live here. Actually, you know what, I'm gonna move ou—"

Stone comes around and puts his hand over my mouth, silencing me. I try to elbow him, but he's too quick and dodges the blow.

"Be. Quiet."

I bite his palm. He hisses between his teeth, but his laughter fills my ear.

"I haven't gone soft despite what everyone in this house is currently thinking. I'll bite you back, Sticks."

He eventually drops my hand, and everyone is watching us go head to head. His glare is cold and hot at the same time, sending little shivers all over my body at the thought of his teeth skimming my skin.

There's a snicker of laughter from down the hall, and I cross my arms, leveling my housemates with a withering stare that they all laugh at. "I'm moving out."

"Over my dead fucking body." Stone's hands dip into his pockets, and he walks over to Evan, leaning on the same wall, waiting for my reaction.

"Over all our dead bodies," Grant adds.

"Ugh!" I yell and stomp down the hall to my room.

I hate myself for the feeling of relief, because I know I'm being selfish. My housemates are beefy and have too much testosterone, making them more lethal than most—*especially* on the ice—but they're nothing compared to guns. And that's exactly the type of weapon my father and his sick friends bring to every fight. There is no law they won't break to get what they want and, furthermore, to taste revenge on their tongues.

I fling open the door to the closet—*my room*—and stand in disbelief. There's bubbling laughter from the kitchen, and I bare my teeth. I spin, and Evan and Stone are both looking to the ceiling like the *Mona Lisa* is painted up there or something. Evan's lips are pulled into his mouth, and Stone's tongue is pressed to the inside of his cheek as he pretends nothing is unusual.

"Where the hell is my stuff?" I ask, staring directly at Stone because I know he's the only one who would do this.

He slowly lowers his head and serves me with one raised eyebrow. "Hm?"

"Stone," I bark. "What did I say about going into my room?"

"You mean the closet?" He shrugs. "The door is broken. You'll have to relocate until we fix it."

"Relocate?"

There is something familiar in his eye, and I'm beginning to read him very well. He walks over to me, and everyone else fades away.

"Yep," Stone says, gripping my chin. "You're staying with me now, Sticks."

No.

I open my mouth to protest, but suddenly, I'm flying through the air and end up dangling over his broad shoulder. "Stone!" I yell through the jostling. I look at my foster brother. "Evander! Do something."

"Sorry, sis." He grins. "But it's for your own good."

I'm shocked and unsure of how I feel about Evan and Stone no longer having their little disagreement over me. "Are you guys seriously tag-teaming me now?"

Stone's grip on me tightens when we reach the top of the stairs. "No one will be tag-teaming when it comes to you."

I roll my eyes. "I didn't mean it like that, Stone! Gross. He's my brother."

His chuckle vibrates against my chest, and eventually, I stop trying to escape and sway over his shoulder because what's the point? I can't even escape from him inside my head.

"Welcome to your new room." He drops me down onto

the bed and flicks his chin at my purple pillow. It's closest to the wall, right next to his. "That's your side."

I hear the lock of the bedroom door and stay quiet. He comes over and flops down beside me.

"And this side is mine."

Great.

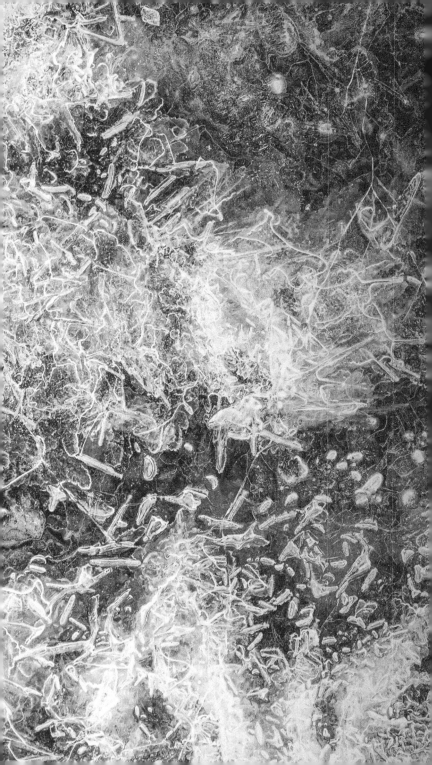

CHAPTER 22
STONE

I'VE GRADUATED to full-fledged stalker. Which, upon further examination, is probably not the *best* thing for Wren. She's already been traumatized enough by sharing her secrets. But after last night, lying beside her in the dark without touching her, I realized enough was enough.

This house is quickly turning into a family, and family protects each other through whatever means necessary.

I follow her from campus to Shadow's, waiting until she's clocked in and tied her apron around her waist before I head inside.

The hostess immediately smiles at me.

"Wren's section," I tell her.

"Are you flying solo tonight, Stone?"

It's kind of weird that she knows my name. Still, I nod at her and force a smile, then look over her shoulder and catch Wren's eye. Her head snaps toward me, her brow furrowing.

Tough luck.

The hostess leads me to a booth, and only a moment after she's gone, Wren is practically breathing down my neck.

"What are you doing here?" she whispers.

I glance around. "Why are you whispering?"

"Because—"

"Are you embarrassed?" I take the menu and tap it on the table. "I just wanted something to eat before practice…"

She glances at her watch, then back at me. "You're not getting my discount."

"Wouldn't have wanted it."

"And you have to tip me."

I lean toward her. "If you want my tip, *baby*, all you've got to do is ask."

Her lips part.

Goddamn, she's so fucking pretty. She tucks her dark hair behind her ear and straightens, the shock fading to mock-outrage. Because she's not really angry. She's doing her best to hide a smile.

"If you need a little mid-shift stress relief, I know just the thing."

"*Stone*." She clears her throat. "Do you want to order or…"

I roll my eyes and order a water and their spaghetti and meatballs. They're not a true Italian place, but they manage to keep the noodles al dente. Which is fine enough for me.

She makes a face and wanders away, and I pull out my homework. I spread it out on the table and go through it until she returns with the water and silverware.

"How long is your shift?"

She shrugs. "On a Monday? I'll probably get cut at seven."

It's dead quiet, and it's almost five-thirty.

"Great, do that. You can come with me to practice."

"No."

I give her my best offended expression. Judging by the purse of her lips, though, she doesn't fall for it.

"I think it would be in your best interest," I say slowly.

"No need to talk down to me, Stone."

"I could drag you there." I sit up straighter, the wicked thoughts of exactly what I would do to make her stay there running through my mind. "Have you ever been fucked in the penalty box, Sticks?"

She groans. "Oh my God."

"You mean, '*Oh my Stone.*' Better practice because that's what you'll be screaming later this evening…" I chuckle and grab her hand. "Get cut early and come to practice. Don't make me say please."

"Would you? Say please?"

I smirk. "Maybe…"

She sighs. "I'm going to check on my one other table."

As soon as she's gone, I slide out of the booth and approach the hostess. "Who's in charge of cutting waitresses for the night?"

The girl is too…I don't know, starstruck? She stares at me for a beat, and I'm reminded that I am into Wren because she doesn't have this insane reaction. I'm human. Just because I play hockey well doesn't mean girls need to throw themselves at my feet.

Garnering national attention for how I play is damaging to the ego enough as it is.

"Um, I do," she finally answers.

"Great." I flick through my wallet and pull out a fifty, pushing the bill into her hand. "Make sure Wren is off in the next hour."

She glances from me to the money, then back up. "Oh, um…"

"Thanks!" I leave her standing there before she can change her mind. People generally react better that way—when they think you expect something of them, and they don't have the chance to refute it.

Once my food is gone, my bill paid—and Wren tipped, as demanded—I catch the waitress's gaze and raise my eyebrow.

She sighs, nearly audible from across the room, then heads in Wren's direction.

They have a little chat, and Wren turns to glare at me. She

tears off her apron and disappears into the kitchen, reemerging with her bag only a minute later.

"Ready?" I ask at the front entrance.

"You're an ass."

I shift my bag higher on my shoulder, then tug hers from her grip. "Look at it this way, Sticks. It's just foreplay to see what I can do with *one* stick…"

She elbows me.

But almost two hours later, practice has concluded, and Wren Davis is still waiting for me.

Well, I hope she's waiting for me. She definitely doesn't seem to be paying any attention to Evan, who gives her a weird look before heading to the locker room.

"C'mere, Sticks," I call.

She scoffs.

I plant my hands on my hips. "Get on the ice, Wren."

She mouths something. It's a toss-up between *I can't hear you* and *Fuck off*.

"That won't work." I skate in a circle and come back. I point to the door that opens between the stands and penalty box. "Through there."

She throws up her hands. A moment later, she's moving down the rows toward the door. I meet her there, unlocking it from the inside and grabbing her hand, just to drag her through faster.

"Your coach literally just left the ice," she breathes. Her hand presses against my chest. "What are you doing?"

I catch the back of her head and lean down. Our lips collide, and although it takes her a second, she's suddenly just as *in* it as she was the other night.

Part of me thought it might be a fluke. That she was so out of her mind from the nightmare, from someone being in her room, from *fear*, that she just latched onto me because I was a willing distraction.

I pick her up and set her on the ledge next to the door for

the ice. She spreads her legs, letting me step up closer. I nip her lower lip. She groans in my mouth.

The sound goes right to my dick trapped behind the fucking cup. I release her with one hand and yank it out, tossing it on the bench behind us. I shift forward and press my hard-on between her legs.

"Tell me you want me to touch your pretty little pussy, Sticks," I say against her lips.

I drag my mouth down her jaw. She tilts her head, giving me more room to kiss and suck on her neck. The urge to leave a mark floods through me. Her hands skim along the waistband of my sweatpants.

It's driving me absolutely fucking wild.

I grip her hair and force her head back farther, biting her skin.

"Fuck," she groans. "We're in public."

"No one can see us," I say against her pulse point.

She whimpers again. My hands are all over her. I cup her breasts through her shirt, then slide down and into her pants. She makes a noise when my fingers brush her clit, and farther still to curl inside her.

"Someone's turned on." I lean back just enough to smirk at her.

She grabs my face and kisses me again. Her tongue stokes a fire under my skin that I can't fucking control. I undo the button of her pants and yank them down, dropping to my knees. I put her legs over my shoulders and wink at her.

"Stone—"

"Not now." I push aside the strip of her panties hiding her cunt from me.

"*Stone*—"

My mouth lands on her clit. I lick her, tasting her arousal, and my dick twitches. I'm going to come just from this alone.

Her hands thread through my hair, tugging like she has control. I ignore it and slide my finger inside her, pumping in and out in time with her ragged breaths. When I add a second finger, her hips jerk. One hand leaves my head to hold on to the ledge her ass is balanced on.

"Fuck me," she whispers. "Someone's going to see us."

"I don't fucking care. Do you?" I pull back and focus on her face. "Do you want me to stop before you've come?"

She growls.

I chuckle, still moving my fingers inside her. It's enough to make her shake her head.

"Good girl," I murmur.

She gets wetter.

"My girl likes praise?" I lick her slowly, from her slit to the top of her mound. "You taste so good, baby. I'm never going to need another meal again as long as you keep your cunt wet for me."

"Oh, I hate you," she says. Except, her eyes are closed, her head tipped back against the glass.

I avoid her clit and play with the rest of her pussy. Until her heels dig into my back and my scalp aches with how hard she's gripping my hair. Only then do I latch on, flicking and sucking until she's coming apart at the seams.

And when she does explode, clenching around my fingers and arching her back, she cries out *my* name. My blood sings.

My cock is throbbing so bad. I push my sweatpants down and rise, tilting her hips and sliding into her before she even seems to register what I'm doing. I hold her hair, keeping her head tipped back, and my gaze fixates on hers.

I pound into her with zero restraint. Her mouth is open, panting, and I lean down and claim her lips again. Our tongues dance together, while her nails scratch my back under my shirt. Forcing me closer.

Did I stop to even put on a freaking condom?

Nope.

Let's hope she doesn't kill me for that.

My balls tighten, and I pull out. I shove her shirt up and

pump my length once, twice. It's not the same as being inside her, but it does the trick. I come hard, spilling ropes across her abdomen and stomach.

"Damn," she whispers. "Well…"

I tuck myself back in my sweatpants and watch as she rights her panties. We didn't even take them off her. She looks down at the cum and wrinkles her nose, her shirt still shoved up to just under her tits.

"Do me a favor, Sticks."

Her eyebrow rises.

I drag my finger through the cum on her skin. "Leave my mark on you."

"You're awful."

"And you're mine." I shrug. "Fair's fair."

She adjusts her shirt, still seeming perturbed, and does up her pants.

I turn around, so my back faces her front, and squat a little. I grab the backs of her thighs.

"What are you doing?" she squeaks.

"Bringing you to the locker room," I say. "Obviously. Get on my back."

When she does, her arms wrapped around my chest, I step out onto the ice and glide across it toward the far opening. Her mouth touches the shell of my ear. Goosebumps rise along the backs of my arms.

"You can leave me alone for a moment, you know. And we're not on the ice—"

I roll my eyes and push through the locker room door.

As expected, we're alone.

She sighs and takes a seat while I get out of my skates. Something buzzes, and she pulls her phone out of her boot.

A neat trick.

I narrow my eyes as she answers it.

Silence.

Then—

"Why are you calling me from an unknown number, Brad?" Her brow is pinched.

I shoot to my feet, but she waves me off.

"No. I don't care that you're sorry. Don't call me again." She hits *end* and tosses her phone onto the bench beside her.

We stare at each other for a beat.

"Don't even think about it," she warns.

I raise my hands in surrender. "I wasn't thinking *anything*."

I definitely wasn't thinking that fucking *Brad* just got moved to the top of my shit list.

CHAPTER 23
WREN

"IS he going to come to every shift?" Ally, one of the new waitresses, stands with her elbows over the bar top.

I follow her line of sight, though I don't need to. I know who she's referring to.

Stone.

Only, tonight, it's all of my housemates. Even Evan is in on it.

It's like a sick joke they all have—watching my every move, following me around campus, forcing me to go to their stupid practices.

I try to act irritated by it, especially when Stone tries to grab my hand or tugs me close while walking me to my car after each of my classes, but the truth is, I like it.

Kind of.

My stomach flips, and something in my chest bubbles. The heat on my cheeks has nothing to do with the temperature, and I know he notices the way I blush every time he glances at my mouth.

"Hey, refill over here!"

And the blush turns to anger, just like that.

I snap my head in their direction and glare.

Ally slaps her hand over her mouth and mumbles, "Oh, I've gotta see this."

I grab the pitcher of beer and slowly approach their booth. "Excuse me?" I say as sweet as possible. "What was that?"

Stone leans back and rests his arms over the cracked leather. His gaze slips down to my mouth, but it doesn't matter because my face is already pinched with annoyance. "Were you talking about me over there?"

Ally snorts quietly, but I still hear it.

"Why would we waste our time talking about you?" I smile mischievously. "And if you guys would like a refill, I expect you to use your manners."

I glance at Evan. "I know for a fact that your mama taught you right."

He chuckles. "May I please have a refill, Your Highness?"

I roll my eyes playfully. "You may." I reach forward past Stone and start filling up Evan's cup. Goosebumps race to my arm when Stone's hot breath whooshes against my skin. It pokes a nerve right between my legs, and I slowly move my arm to the right, missing Evan's cup on purpose. Beer falls to Stone's lap, making it look like he's pissed himself.

"Fuck, Wren." His large hand envelops my wrist, pushing it away.

A soft laugh flies from me. Ally stifles a gasp and slaps a hand over her mouth, while my housemates snicker.

"You think you're funny, do you?" Stone raises an eyebrow, and he's so hot my mouth waters. His arrogance used to make me see red, but now, tingles race to my fingers in anticipation of what he'll do to retaliate.

"I am funny," I counter.

I spin on my heel, and Ally follows. She doesn't bust out laughing until we are safely tucked behind the bar.

"That was fucking gold." She's practically jumping with joy. All bright-eyed and bushy-tailed. "Stone is one of the most popular guys on campus, and no one has attempted to put him in his place. Most of the girls on campus are too nervous to even glance at him. But not you."

"That's because he doesn't scare me." *I have other scary people to deal with.*

"Orrrrrr," she uses a sing-song voice. "Is it because you two are sleeping together?"

I freeze. "Who said that?"

"Your blushing cheeks any time he is around." She pauses. "Or the way he watches you like he's afraid you're going to slip through his fingers. Or maybe the fact that he comes to every single shift of yours and walks with you around campus. Or—"

"Okay, okay!" I grab a rag and wipe the bar top to give myself something to do. "I get it! Are you following me around too?"

"No. Which is even worse because I still noticed."

I suck in my lip and glance at their table. Everyone is preoccupied, laughing and chatting, except Stone. He's staring directly at me like he can read my lips and knows what our conversation is about.

I look at Ally and drag my attention away from him. It feels wrong to do so, but I don't know why. It just *does*. "Do you want to go to the game with me tomorrow?"

Her eyebrows rise. "The hockey game?"

I nod, bundling up the damp rag in my hand. I haven't been to a single hockey game this season—or any of the seasons prior, for that matter—but I know for a fact that Stone is going to demand I go. Might as well beat him to the punch.

"Yeah, sure," Ally says, seeming to think it over. "Should we head to jock row after too? Or will your big, bad boyfriend lose his mind?"

I shoot her a glare, and she laughs at her joke.

"I'm kidding! I'll pick you up tomorrow at seven. Just text me your address."

"'K." I smile. "And I have just the thing for us to wear."

Ally wiggles her eyebrows but scurries off to tend to her tables a second later.

"What was that about?"

I slowly turn and see why she scurried off. *Traitor.* Stone is leaning over the bar top, and I reach on my tiptoes to see the wet spot on his pants. I laugh under my breath, and he growls.

"We're your last table, right?"

I peek around him. The guys have left, and the busboy is already putting their empty cups in his tub.

"Yep. Looks like I'm off."

"I'll pick you up at the back after you grab your things."

Stone turns and makes his way through the doors. I furrow my brow but go about my usual business, counting my tips and leaving some for the busboy. I clock out and wave to Ally before turning and heading for the employee entrance.

The hall is dark, except for a single light casting a dim glow over the bathroom door. I pull my purse up on my shoulder and suck in a screeching scream when the door flies open, and a familiar hand grabs onto my upper arm, pulling me into the bathroom.

Stone's palm is against my mouth, so my scream sounds muffled. He shakes his head at the same time his fingers skim down to my chin, holding my face close to his. "You need to be carrying Mace. I could have been anyone grabbing you."

I gulp because he's right, but there's a very unlikely chance I'll admit it out loud. "Who could grab me with you constantly lurking in the shadows to protect me?"

"Protect you?" he whispers. "This isn't me protecting you."

The porcelain sink cuts into my lower back when Stone presses into me.

"This is payback."

His wink seals the deal, because I'm putty in his hands.

My tongue darts out, and with the way his eyes glimmer beneath the dull bathroom light, I know he likes it.

"What were you and your little friend talking about?"

My fingers slip against the porcelain as I reach back and steady myself on the sink. I tilt my chin and give Stone access to his favorite spot. His teeth graze my thrumming pulse, and the beating increases.

"Hmm. None of your business," I tease.

Suddenly, I'm flipped around and staring at us in the dingy mirror. My head flies backward with Stone's finger hooked beneath my hair tie. My hair cascades down my shoulders, and I gasp in pleasure when he drops the black elastic in the sink.

"Everything about you is my business, baby."

"Stone," I say, stuck between excitement and annoyance.

"Wren," he replies, placing a kiss against my neck. "Tell me what you two were whispering about? Telling her how good I am in bed?"

His smile is a faint touch against my skin. I breathe out through my nose and have a hard time sucking the air back in. "I told her you were terrible in bed."

I smile at his sarcastic laugh, but the hard nudge against my backside drowns out the noise. I've never been one to mess around anywhere other than a bedroom with the door locked, but after he took me in the rink, I think it might be the biggest turn-on of all. "Do you think I'll be as terrible in this disgusting employee bathroom as I am in the bedroom?"

Let's find out.

I push back against him, enjoying his grunt. His hands fly to my waist, and he pushes me forward. I shiver at the dominance he yields and almost turn around and fall to my knees to show him that I'm at his mercy. I would never do such a thing, but I want to.

The way his hand caresses the curve of my butt has me

meeting his eye. He smirks at the sound of my jeans zipper, and I throw my head back at the air grazing my skin.

"Tell me what you two were talking about, or I'll pay you back far more than I plan to."

What does that mean?

A whimper creeps up my throat when his thumb brushes my clit. *Fuck him.*

"I asked her…" I grip the sink harder. "To go to the hockey game with me tomorrow."

Stone's hand stops moving, and he steps away, putting space between us. "What?"

"I… I asked if she wanted to watch the game with me tomorrow. In the stands."

His swallow is loud enough for me to hear. "You're coming to my game?"

"I figured you guys would play better if you didn't have to worry about me being alone at home."

"Fuck, Wren."

My panties fly down my legs, and Stone's hand splays out on my back. My ribs ache from the sink cutting into the bone, but the bite of pain only lasts a second when he fills me.

"That's too much for me to handle."

I reach up to my shoulder and grip his hand that keeps me steady. He pumps into me slowly, hissing between every breath and pulling pleasure out of me like it's his favorite pastime. I don't even think he stopped to put a condom on, and it feels too good for me to make him do it now, just like when we were in the rink and I was afraid someone was going to see us.

"You feel so good, and knowing you did something so I could play better is a fucking turn-on," he murmurs against my skin before biting onto my earlobe.

Sprinkles of pleasure race to my blood, and I whimper.

"That's a good girl, already squeezing my cock."

Fuck me.

I burst at the seams when he tilts my hips and slides in fast to hit the spot that I need. His mouth captures mine, and we both stop kissing as soon as my orgasm peaks.

"Fuck, your pussy is milking me, Sticks."

He leaves me empty as he pulls back and twists me around, hurriedly pulling up my jeans and spilling himself all over the front of them. My brows furrow at the act, and when he lets out a breath and calms his rising lungs, he sends me the cockiest look I have ever seen.

"Payback, remember?" His gaze falls to my pants that are now wet and sticky.

I'm too blind by the pleasure sweeping through my body to realize what he's referring to. Without so much as a flinch, I allow him to take my hand and press it to the mess he left against the denim. "Now you look like you've pissed yourself too."

My lips part, and he places a quick kiss to them before putting himself back together and opening the door. Cool air rushes in, and the fog on the mirror quickly disappears as he pulls me, leaving my hair tie in the sink as a little memento to what we'd just done.

I don't have to show Stone that I'm at his mercy.

He already knows.

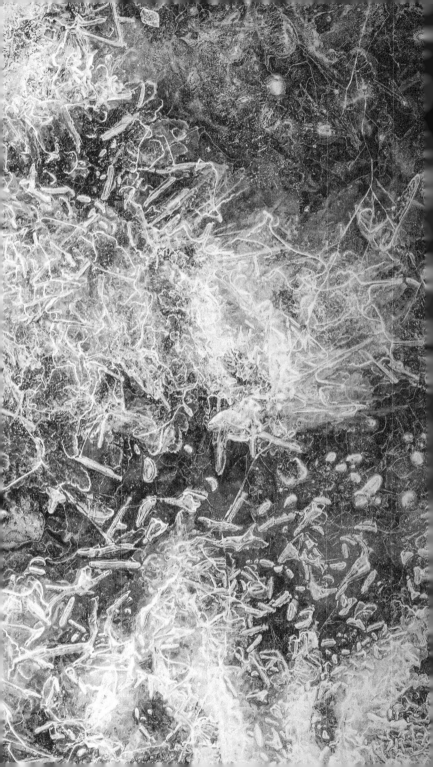

CHAPTER 24
STONE

MY OBSESSIVE INFATUATION with Wren is *fine*. It's not out of control. It's not taking over my life. I'm not constantly thinking about her.

I've got hockey to think about. Especially since she offered to come to the game tonight.

I close my laptop and pack my bag, then lean back and eye Wren four tables away. Her back is to me, hunched over her notebook. We're the only two people studying in the library. It's game day, and I think everyone *except* Sticks decided to sleep in.

As soon as she left this morning, climbing over me and getting dressed in the bathroom like a chicken, I hopped out and followed her.

Past Wren, at the reception desk, the sole student worker has her head buried in a book.

I hoist my bag over my shoulder and stalk up behind Wren. She's got earbuds in. Totally distracted.

"Ahh!" I yell, sliding my hands under her arms and yanking her backward out of the chair.

She full-on screams, flailing as I hoist her over my shoulder. She brings her legs up to her chest, her arms going everywhere. Her hand smacks into the side of my face, fingers digging into my mouth, and I can't withhold my laugh. I drop her back to her feet and spin her around.

As soon as she realizes it's me, her mouth drops open.

I burst out laughing. "Sorry, Sticks," I wheeze. "Is that your defense plan for when someone grabs you? *Flailing?*"

Her face is getting red. The flush creeps up her neck, and her mouth opens and closes. I wipe fucking tears from my eyes while she gets more pissed by the second.

The student worker glances over at us, but I ignore her.

"Come on, baby. Maybe you should take a self-defense class or two…"

"You—you *asshole*," she shouts, shoving me back a step.

I catch her wrists and drag her in. I kiss her before she can stop me, nipping at her lower lip. "Mmm," I whisper, "you should've just stayed in bed with me."

"I have to study," she grits out.

Yeah, yeah.

I release her wrists, and she straightens her shirt. She circles the table and rights the fallen chair, huffing hard enough that displaced strands of her dark hair float out in front of her face.

She's adorably out of sorts.

When she sits back down, I frown. I drop into the chair beside her.

"What are you doing?" she asks, her voice guarded.

"You're cute when you're pissed." I tuck her hair behind her ear and let my fingers trail down the side of her neck.

She puts her earbuds back in.

Pointedly.

I chuckle to myself and lean back, watching the side of her face. She goes back to reading something, her lips moving. Until her phone lights up between us, and her attention goes to the screen.

"Aren't you going to answer it?" I shift forward.

Unknown number.

Wren flips the phone upside down.

"Do you know who that is?"

She shrugs. "No. I don't know. Maybe."

"That sounds suspicious." I narrow my eyes. "Sticks?"

"Stop calling me that," she hisses. "And it's nothing."

I snatch her phone. She makes a noise of protest, but she doesn't stop me from using her face to unlock it and then going straight to her recent calls.

A half dozen *unknown number* calls from today and yesterday. Only one, the first, was answered. And she said it was her ex.

"Brad?" I force out.

She just shrugs.

I shake my head at her, then shoot off a text to Archer.

And a second one to Evan.

Twenty minutes later, both guys join us in the library. Archer has his school bag slung over his shoulder and two cups of coffee. He drops into the seat across from Wren.

She yanks out her earbuds again, glaring at me.

"What?" I raise my hands in surrender.

"I don't need to be *babysat*."

I scoff. "Archer is an excellent babysitter. E and I have some business to attend to."

Arch grins. "You don't want to hang out with me, Wren? I got you coffee…" He slides one of the cups toward her.

She pinches the bridge of her nose and takes a moment. Maybe reining in her temper. But she eventually drops her hand and points at him. "I need to *study*. No talking. No loud music. No distractions."

He lifts one shoulder. "That's fine, I've got an econ paper due on Wednesday."

She takes a sip of the coffee and nods. "This is bribery. But I accept."

"Perfect." I tug a lock of Wren's hair. "See ya later, baby."

Wren purses her lips, and I leave her with a smile. It falls from my lips once we're outside, and I glance at my best friend. Things have been a little awkward since…well, really, since Wren moved into the house. I sometimes catch him watching me with a weird expression. Like he's thinking something, or suspecting something, but then he brushes it off.

It was only made worse by Wren's confession. I didn't want Evan to know because it was my business with Wren. Tainting her relationship with her foster brother would've done no one any good.

We're a block away from the library when Evan finally speaks.

"Where are we going?" He makes a face. "Your text was a little vague. And freaking *early*. What's up with you and Wren anyway? Are you—"

I elbow him. "If you're about to ask me something you don't want to know the answer to, I suggest you shut up. Because I'll answer it. Explicitly."

He scowls. But then… "You didn't tell me about the drugs."

"What drugs?"

"At school. When you got hauled out of the lunchroom, *arrested*, and…you didn't tell me about the drugs planted on your car. All you said was that it was a misunderstanding." He stops.

I face him on the path and wave him off. "It *was* a misunderstanding. They thought I was a drug dealer, but…eh, whatever. Water under the bridge."

Minus the part where I threatened Wren to stay away from me.

He sighs and resumes walking.

I roll my eyes. "We're fine now. Me and her."

"She spilled beer on your lap less than twelve hours ago. And you're fine?"

Well, okay. I smirk. "I think hating me is her love language. It just means she cares. Anyway, this isn't about that. The soccer team practice is ending right about now."

Evan groans. "This isn't about *that*? But it's about the soccer team?"

In the time it took them to get to the library, I did some hunting. It was either that or continue to stare at Wren. And as alluring as she is, I'm not that dull.

Dad always said there was exactly one way to know one's enemy. Or, well, he used to say opponent. And he was definitely talking about prosecutors. But his advice can be applied toward the lowlife cheating scum of an ex-boyfriend.

That philosophy has also been hammered into me by hockey coaches since I was old enough to care. Watching game tapes, analyzing plays.

It shouldn't be a surprise at all that I spent my time wisely. And that is, hunting down all the information on social media platforms about our dear *Brad*. Even his name reeks of the garbage hiding under his skin.

"You do no research, do you? Even when Wren showed up at your door after their breakup? You didn't look into him?"

Evan has the good grace to seem a *little* ashamed.

I hold up my phone. More specifically, the cheating dickwad's social media page, which highlights him on the soccer team.

"He keeps calling her from a private number," I add.

"Excuse me?" Evan frowns.

I throw my hands up. "I know! As if Wren doesn't have enough things to worry about. I know we're watching her, and we've got her back, but honestly. When will it end? The nightmares have pretty much stopped. But she didn't bother to tell either of us about this caller—"

"How does she know it's him?" he questions.

"She answered the first call. Ignored the rest."

He grunts.

We arrive at the field just as the team is finishing their practice. I point out Brad, a tall, very average douchebag. We stand and watch for a long moment while my anger climbs slowly.

The more I analyze him, the more I know Wren was wasting her time. But that doesn't negate the fact that she trusted him, and he *cheated*.

The coach heads off with a few players, disappearing around the only permanent building for the practice field and heading in the direction of campus. Brad and another player are picking up small orange cones on the field.

I stride toward him, leaving Evan rushing after me.

"Do you have a plan here?" my best friend whisper-yells.

"Yep."

No time like the present to throw caution to the wind.

"*Stone*—"

"Hey," I call. "Tall, dark, and asshole."

Brad straightens. He recognizes me, and a split second later, he realizes what I said. It's obvious from the sheer annoyance that takes over his expression.

But here's the thing: guys like Brad whatever-his-last-name-is deserve to rot in Hell. How the fuck could he see someone like Wren Davis and think she's not worthy of all the love in the world? How could he look at anyone else when he had *her*? Much less *fuck* someone else.

"What's up, Foster?" Brad asks. "You seem like you have a stick up your ass."

I clench my teeth and ball my fists.

I'm ten feet away.

Then five.

Evan grabs for me, but his hands slide off my shoulder. "Stone, no—"

I punch Brad as hard as I can.

In the nose.

Pain radiates down my arm, familiar and new—not quite as masked by game-day adrenaline as during hockey fights. But it's worth it, because the slimeball folds like an accordion. There's blood coming out of his nose, and he otherwise doesn't move.

Evan stops beside me, belatedly gripping my arm.

And I didn't even get to warn him to not call Wren anymore.

We stare down at him, and the soccer teammates start yelling from across the field.

I glance at Evan and shrug. "Too late."

Ah, well. Brad didn't stand a fucking chance.

CHAPTER 25
WREN

WELL, studying was a bust.

I slam the front door, and Archer grunts a moment later.

He walks inside and pouts. "Come on, Wrenny. Don't be mad at me. I was just doing the guys a favor."

I cross my arms over my huffing chest after dropping my backpack to the floor. "And where *are* the guys?"

"We're right here, baby." Stone's arms wrap around me.

I'm on edge.

I crane my neck and stare up at his jawline, wondering why he is being so...*nice*. My brows furrow, and I glance around at the rest of my housemates.

Evan won't meet my eye, and that's how I know he's up to something.

Stone's arms fall away when I arch my back and shove my butt into him. He wheezes, and my housemates laugh.

"What did you do?"

He can't talk. He's too busy gasping for air and cupping his balls. Evan is staring at the ceiling again with his hands in his pockets.

"Evan..."

"Oh, no you don't." He shakes his head. "You two are not putting me in the middle of this."

"So you didn't approve?" Stone asks through sharp breaths.

Evan half shrugs.

I zero in on Stone's hands, which are still cupping his balls.

"Why are your knuckles red?"

"I hit some jackass."

I rush forward and grab his hand, rubbing my fingers over the swelling. "You have a game later! Why would you do th—"

There isn't a noise to be heard when my phone starts vibrating in my bag. Everyone's attention is on it.

Before I step forward, I press on Stone's red knuckles. "Stay put."

His mouth twitches.

When I pull my phone out, I'm confused. But only for a moment.

"You hit Brad, didn't you?"

"Is that him calling?" Stone's eyes widen.

I put my hand up. "Don't you dare, Stone Foster!"

There is no use in trying to find some privacy in this house, not after the guys decided that I needed a bodyguard at all times, so I put the phone up to my ear and say, "Hello?"

"What the fuck, Wren?"

"Speaker, now," Stone whisper-snaps.

I give him the finger, and Evan snickers.

Brad's voice disgusts me.

"Did you seriously sic your psycho boyfriend on me for calling you one *fucking* time?"

Why did I ever like him again?

"He better watch the way he fucking talks to you."

I shuffle backward so Stone can stop using his supersonic hearing and listening to the conversation.

"One time?" I ask. "I have multiple calls a day from *Unknown*, Brad."

"Well, it isn't me!" he argues.

"And you want me to believe you? You cheated on me for months and lied right to my face. How could I ever believe a thing you say?"

"Fucking bastard."

"Maybe we should all take turns punching him?"

"Fuck yeah."

I glare at the guys, who are all staring at me with their arms crossed. They're each sharing a scowl, and I scoff. I don't need them to fight my battles for me. I was doing just fine fending Brad off myself.

"Well, believe what you want. I called one time, and the only reason I blocked my number was because I didn't think you'd answer if you knew it was me."

"Well, you thought right. Don't call me again."

"Don't even think about her again," Stone says.

I push Stone back, and he goes willingly, smirking the whole time.

Brad curses in my ear. "Tell your psychotic little hockey player boyfriend that if he ever touches me again, he'll be done for."

I hang up and stare at Stone from across the hall. "You are unbelievable!"

Stone's hand stretches forward, and I think he's going to pull me in to try and put a damper on my frustrations, but instead, he grabs my phone. Everyone is leaning over his shoulder as he flips through my missed calls.

"You're changing your number," he mutters.

His finger continues to scroll.

"Sure are," Evan says.

"If it isn't Brad calling, who is it?" Grant asks.

I try to laugh, but it dies on the edge of my lips when I see that they are all sincere. "You can't be serious. You want me to change my number? I can't do that."

"Why can't you?" Stone flicks his head to the guys.

They head upstairs. I wait until they're out of sight before ripping my phone out of his hand.

"Because..." The word lingers in between us. "I can't afford to just get a new number. I've already been there, done that. I can't keep changing my number."

His eye roll is more of a dismissal. "I'll take care of it."

I stomp like a toddler. "No."

"Wren." His tone is borderline angry.

My lip pops out. I'm crushed to his body next, and he tilts my chin to meet his face.

"I know you're used to being independent, but you're going to have to get used to me taking care of you."

I say nothing and let him press his lips to mine. It soothes me for a second before he lets go of me and heads up the stairs.

"Oh." He glances over the banister, and I'm leery of his smile. "I put a tracker on your phone, so if you decide to try and pay me back for hitting your ex, and not show up to my game, I'll be able to find you."

My mouth drops as I stare at the device in my hand. "You are unbe—"

"*Unbelievable*," he finishes for me. "I know. I'll show you later how unbelievable I really am."

I ignore how my belly drops with his sexual innuendo.

I am more than happy to show up to his game, but I'm still going to pay him back and show him that he can't just come into my life and control everything.

———

"WOW, SO THIS IS WHAT IT LOOKS LIKE TO LIVE WITH A BUNCH OF hunky hockey players."

I shut the front door behind Ally but not before glancing to the left and right, making sure there aren't any suspicious cars hiding out in plain sight. The moon is peeking out, and I really wanted to get to the arena before sunset.

I refuse to say anything to the guys, but I'm a little uneasy after figuring out that Brad isn't the one calling me multiple times a day. I know who's behind it, but if I don't say it aloud, then I don't have to face it.

"Hunky hockey players?" I bristle at her compliment. "Don't say that in front of them. They'll try to get into your pants."

She laughs. "Except Stone. I heard he likes to get into only one person's pants…in the employee bathroom."

I trip up the stairs. Ally busts out a laugh before grabbing onto my arm and saving me from face-planting, which wouldn't be the worst thing in the world because then I could blame my red face on the floor instead of embarrassment.

"Oh my God. Who told you that?"

We walk into my room, and she glances around. The covers are messy, and Stone's school stuff is sitting beside mine on the desk. My clothes are on the floor, and right beside my t-shirt lays Stones.

"Wait, you're rooming with him too? Wow, you two are the real deal."

"Who told you about the employee bathroom?" I pray it wasn't my boss. The last thing I need is to be fired from my job.

"Relax." She waves her hand into the air. "I saw you guys leaving. No one else knows, and your secret is safe with me."

I shake my fingers out. "Whew. Thanks."

She nods and takes her hair down, running her fingers through the golden strands. "But just a warning, that man is obsessed with you."

"He is not," I argue before working on my own hair. My brown strands weave in between my fingers as I pull them into a high pony, fluffing the ends of it for a little volume. I think about Stone and how he put a tracker on my phone. Okay, *fine*. "He's possessive. Not obsessed."

Ally stops putting on her lipstick. "I don't see the difference."

My lips twitch because she's kind of right. Then we both laugh, and I have to admit, it feels nice to have a girlfriend again. I've had a few acquaintances here and there, most of them girlfriends of Brad's friends, so none that amounted to anything. I still talk to Jasmin at least once a week, but she doesn't attend Shadow Valley, so it isn't very often that we get together.

"Want to be naughty with me?" I ask Ally.

I smile to myself as I head for the bedroom door.

"Does this involve pissing Stone off? Because after watching his reaction after you dumped beer on his lap the other night, I am totally down."

"Mmm-hmm." I skip over to Archer's room.

I nod to Evan's door. "Go in there and grab Evan's away jersey. You're gonna wear it tonight."

Ally pauses. "And you're wearing...not Stone's? I'm assuming with the way you're smiling."

I snap. "Correct. I'm going to teach him a little lesson."

We meet out in the hall with the jerseys in our hands and laugh like little schoolgirls. I start to strip, but Ally puts her hand on my arm.

"Wait, why is there a camera in the corner?"

I'm standing in nothing but my jeans and bra when the blood drains from my face. "What?" I look in the direction she's pointing and pull the jersey on before grabbing her by the hand and disappearing into my room.

We both look in the corners and come up empty-handed. I rush for my phone but pause when I see a text on the screen. Ally is looking over my shoulder, and the rumble of her silent laugher vibrates against my back.

STONE

That better be my jersey you're wearing.

"Oh my God!" My jaw flies open. *Did he put cameras up?*
"See." Ally is clearly amused. "Obsessed."
My fingers fly over the screen with anger.

Are you kidding me? You're spying on me now? That is totally uncalled for and inappropriate!

I rip open the door to our room and let it slam against the wall. My back is to the camera in the corner, and I peek over my shoulder and wink before walking back into my room.

Ally rolls her lips. "This is so entertaining."
"He is unbelievable. I swear to God."

STONE

Take it off. Now.

You're not the boss of me.

You'll regret saying that.

I shove my phone in my back pocket, and Ally follows me around the house as I hunt for the rest of the cameras. I snag us both a beer out of the fridge, and we drink them without saying a word. Part of me wants to take the cameras down and crush them with a baseball bat, but the other part of me feels a little better knowing that if someone else were to break in, we'd have it on camera. I have no idea if the rest of the guys are in on this, but it doesn't matter. What matters is that Stone kept it to himself, and that pisses me off. He's treating me like a child, and I don't like it.

"Are you going to take the jersey off?" Ally throws our beer bottles into the trash.

I meet her eye and smile. "Absolutely *not*."

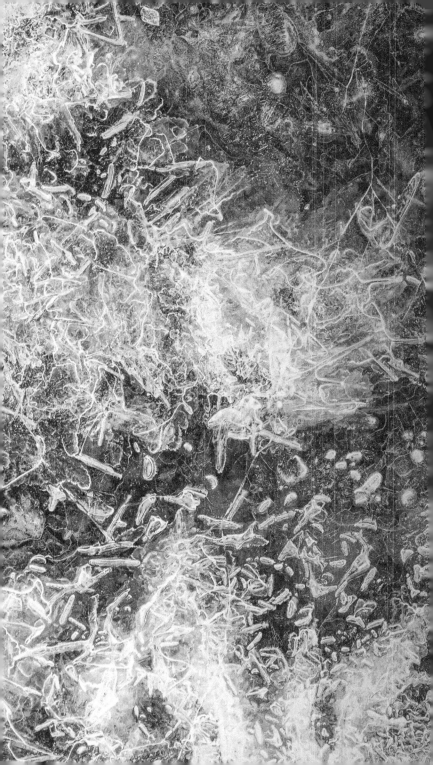

CHAPTER 26
STONE

I'M PRETTY sure I hate her.

The image of Wren putting on *Archer's* jersey, with his last name blazed across her shoulders, is burned in my mind. I mean, it's like she wants me to be unable to concentrate.

It takes a few hard hits to get my head in the game. But as soon as I'm still, catching my breath on the bench, I find myself scouring the stands for her. Or, alternatively, glaring at Archer.

Poor asshole has no idea why I'm giving him the stink eye.

Evan drops into the spot beside me. "Dude."

I glance at him, then back to the players on the ice.

"Channel all this rage into the game." He elbows me. "It's the least you can do."

I take a breath. He's right. I have an outlet that I haven't been using. I focus on the way Wren makes me feel—in a word, *pissed*—and get up without responding. I move down the line to stand in the door. When our other left wing skates to the wall, I seamlessly take his spot on the ice.

Evan's idea works. I skate faster, play harder. I chase after the puck with single-minded fury, beating out my opponent time and again. I hop over a player's stick and pass to Sully, who gives it right back to me. My attention is already on the goalie, who flexes and drifts forward to meet me.

I snap the puck forward. It rebounds off the goalie's arm block, flying toward Grant. Grant to Sully, back to Grant. Across to Evan, who rejoined us at the last change. A D-man for the other team is right on me, and I shove him back. He pushes into me again. I grunt out a swear and inch in front of him, just as Evan slips the puck to me.

And without thinking, I take the shot.

Instinct and drills, along with countless hours of practice, has created muscle memory that I can rely on without a thought. So when the puck sails under the goalie's knee a second before he drops it, and the light behind the goal flashes red to signal a goal, I'm not really *surprised*.

But I do let it be a momentary balm to my anger.

I raise my hands and am immediately swarmed by my teammates. The celebration feels distant. I'm happy, but not really. I just want to bash in the goalie's face or the guy who keeps getting in my space.

Evan pats my helmet. "Way to channel."

I roll my eyes.

The game restarts, and I'm hot. My blood is singing. The other team gets the puck and heads toward our goal. I target the player who has possession and slam him into the boards. The hit is fucking jarring, the plastic mouthguard saving my teeth from clacking.

"What the fuck is your problem, Foster?"

The D-man grabs the back of my jersey, keeping me from chasing after the puck. It's long gone anyway. It slung around behind the goal. Taylor takes it up away from danger, away from Archer in the crease.

I whip around and shove the asshole off me. "My only problem is you, dickhead."

He pushes me back. A sharp jab of his hands and stick

across my chest. I rock back on my skates. He wants a fight? Me, too. I ditch my stick, my gloves, and he mirrors me. We circle each other, and I sneer at him.

"Fucking coward," I call. "Don't start something you can't finish."

He lunges at me. We grapple, and I distantly hear another whistle being blown. The roar of the crowd blends with the blood rushing in my ears. He knocks my helmet off, and I do the same to him. I drag him closer and hit him square in the mouth.

His head snaps back, eyes going wide with anger.

When he hits back, it's like a fucking hammer across my cheekbone. I let the momentum shift my weight, and I use him to keep me upright. We trade shots like that until blood fills my mouth. I think it's coming from my nose. Either way, he tires before I do, and with one heavy twist, I slam him down on the ice. I land on top of him, but hands immediately grab for me, pulling me up and away. I spit blood and run my hand under my nose.

"Penalty box," the ref yells in my ears. "Now."

My nose smarts, and my eyes water. I glance back at the other guy, smirking as he climbs back to his feet. He scowls in my direction.

Distantly, the crowd's approval seeps in. I'm escorted into the penalty box and sit heavily, only registering the fans clapping and cheering around me once the official closes us in.

My teammates return my items. Stick, helmet, gloves. I fist-bump Evan, who hides his smile with a quick shake of his head. My old coach used to say, "If you're going to fight, don't embarrass me by losing one-on-one." I'd like to think I made him proud.

I look across the announcers' booth to the other penalty box, where the other guy sits. His hands are running through his hair, and he seems a little stressed out, to be honest.

"First fight, Mary?" I yell over to him. "You hit like a virgin."

He ignores me.

I lean back in my seat and smile.

Who knew a fight would take the edge off?

———

THE GIRLS—WREN AND HER NEW WAITRESS FRIEND—WAIT FOR US in the atrium outside the locker room with some others.

Our team pulled off the win, six to three. I've been bestowed with a gold Burger King crown, courtesy of the guys for my hat trick. Evan scored one, and I have no idea who scored the other two.

A win is a win. Another saying my old coach had. No matter if it's by one or by five, you stay fucking humble.

So when the congratulations pour in from the fans, aka college girls wanting to get in our pants, I shrug it off.

I've only got eyes for Wren and the blasted jersey she's wearing anyway.

When I finally get up next to her, she barely looks at me.

Game on.

I run my knuckles up her arm, across her shoulder and under her hair. She shivers when I grip the back of her neck lightly.

"Excuse us," I interrupt Abby. Ally. Whatever her name is.

She frowns at me. Wren does, too. But I ignore both and use the pressure on Wren's neck to steer her away from the crowd.

"Stone—"

"Don't talk."

We round the corner, and I yank open the first door I see. Storage closet.

Whatever.

I push Wren in ahead of me and close us in, flipping the

lock with my free hand. She clicks the light on, a single bulb over our heads. It buzzes a little, angry with disuse.

"Listen…" She sounds nervous. There's a flutter in her voice that wasn't there before. That's not usually there. She licks her lips. "You seem mad."

"That was your intention, wasn't it?"

I'm glad I ditched the cup in my pants as soon as I got back to the locker room. My hair is damp, but I'm clean. I changed into a t-shirt, sweatshirt, and jeans. And now, my cock is stiffening in my pants before we've even done anything.

Pure anticipation.

Because I thought about how I might like to make Wren Davis pay me back, and there's only one acceptable answer.

I step forward, and she goes backward. A game of cat and mouse in a tight cage. It doesn't take long to trap her against the back wall, kicking aside a mop bucket and cleaning supplies.

"Wasn't it, baby?"

She swallows…then nods.

I grasp her hips. She makes a noise in the back of her throat, but she doesn't stop me from running my fingers up under the hem of Archer's jersey. I push it up, up, up. Exposing her pale stomach and the cropped tank she put on under it. Over her breasts, barely concealed by the thin top and her lacy bra, until I get it over her head. I throw it toward the mop bucket, smirking at the splash of it hitting dirty water.

"No girl of mine is going to wear another guy's jersey," I say quietly. I run my finger across her collarbone.

"Well, the good news is—I'm not your girl."

I stop.

She stares at me with wide eyes. I'm casting her in shadow like this, blocking out the pretty green and brown of her eyes.

"You're mine, Wren Davis. What more do I need to do to

prove it? Fuck you in front of Evan? Get my name tattooed on your skin?" I cup her jaw, forcing her head up. "Or your name on me? Now that sounds tempting…"

"Stone—"

"Where do you want your name, Sticks?" I adjust myself. Jesus, talking about marking myself for her has me harder than ever. "On my dick? Across my chest? My knuckles, maybe?"

"You're talking crazy." She steps forward. "You can't just do whatever you please and declare that I'm yours. That's not how this works."

"Turn around," I order.

Her eyes narrow. "Why?"

Because I'm done playing games. Without warning, I spin her to face the wall. She lets out a gasp, and I yank her hips back toward me.

"Enough fucking questions, Wren. Hands on the wall."

She complies, and it gives me another rush.

I take my time dragging her pants down. I get them to her ankles, and I run my hands up the outsides of her smooth legs. To her panties.

"Don't—"

I rip them off.

With my teeth.

She groans as the fabric slides out from between her thighs, and I drop it from my mouth. I can smell her arousal. And a quick check, slipping my finger through her center, confirms it.

I stand back up and finally undo my jeans. My dick twitches as it's unleashed, and I cup her butt cheek.

"When I fuck you in this dirty storage closet, Sticks, there's exactly one name you're going to be screaming."

"Archer's?" she sasses.

Smack.

My palm connects with her ass, and she nearly jumps a

foot. I grip her hips and slide into her a moment later, and we both groan.

"Keep your hands on the wall," I bite out.

She has to lean forward to reach, and I go with her. Bending over her like an animal. Her muscles squeeze at my dick, and I run my hands up her back. I unclip her bra and wrap my arm around her, palming her breast. My other hand fists her hair. I tug until her head comes back and her gaze is on the ceiling.

"Fuck," she groans.

"Shut. Up." Each word is punctuated by a thrust, by a twist of my fingers on her nipple.

She's so fucking wet I have no problem sliding in even deeper, hitting a new angle. I take out my anger, my frustration, my loathing of this hold she has on me, on her cunt.

Just because she's mine, and I'm hers, doesn't mean I don't hate her for it.

"I'm close," she pants. She pushes harder against me, her hips bucking.

I bite her shoulder. My hands are everywhere. Breasts, throat, hair, my fingers sliding into her mouth. I'm fucking possessed, and her sharp cries only egg me on faster.

She might be close—but I'm closer. And I make no move to touch her clit to help her along. My balls tighten, and I grind to a halt inside her. Pleasure detonates up my dick, up my spine, when I come hard.

After a minute, my vision returns to normal. I slowly remove my fingers from her jaw. I guess I covered her mouth. And now she's breathing heavily, just like me. The nape of her neck is damp, her short dark hairs curling there. I push the rest of her hair over her shoulder and run my finger down her spine.

Just to see her shiver.

I pull out slowly and turn her around.

"I didn't come," she says.

I smile. I kneel in front of her and tug her pants back up. Before I get them all the way secure, I slip my finger into her. She makes some noise, choking it off, and my smile widens.

"I know," I say simply.

And then I've got her pants buttoned and her tank top mostly righted. It still bares her stomach, and her bra is painfully visible.

I shed my sweatshirt and shove it at her. It has my name on it, at the very fucking least.

"Archer's jersey—"

"He'll pay the fine to get a new one." I wave my hand. "Or you will. Either way."

I pick up my fallen cardboard crown, planting it back on my head.

She glowers at me. "And not letting me finish? Is that punishment?"

I unlock and open the door, letting much more light flood into the small room. As small as it is, it's bigger than the space she was sleeping in. Good thing she's never going back there.

I steal a kiss from her lips as she moves past me. "Now you're getting it."

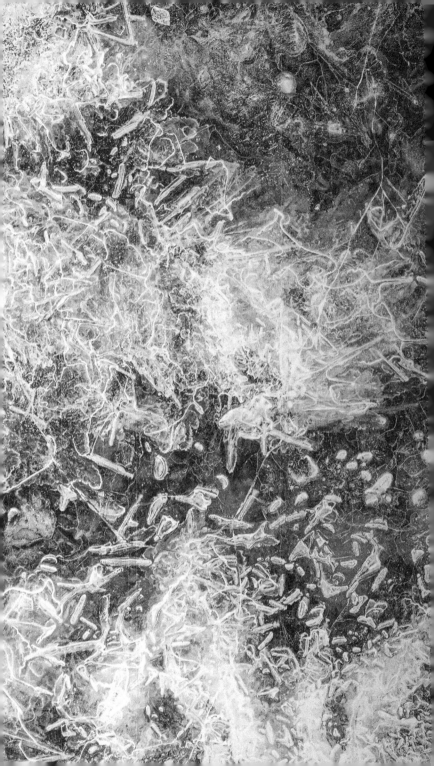

CHAPTER 27
STONE

THE AFTER-PARTY IS KILLER. A few puck bunnies were wrangled, thanks to Taylor or Grant, to set up our house. The doors to all our bedrooms upstairs are locked. The downstairs is almost unrecognizable. The furniture is shoved to the far edges of the rooms, a bar set up in the kitchen, a keg out on the back porch.

We were nearly the last to arrive, and I must've forgotten to mention those plans, because the glower Wren gave me to discover a massive amount of people in and around our house... well, it was enough to make me want to drag her around the side and repeat our storage closet adventure.

I didn't, though, because as soon as they caught sight of us, we were dragged into the thick of the party. More congratulations, more cheers and high fives, and echoes of how Shadow Valley is going places this year. All the way to the playoffs.

Wren has been plastered to my side since we arrived, even going so far as to pull me out on the makeshift dance floor and grind on me until my dick woke up. *Again*. Payback, I suspect, although I kept that thought to myself.

We've been served a steady stream of drinks into her waiting hand and mine.

Tomorrow is a day of rest. We've got it off from practice, there are no classes, and my homework is miraculously caught up. If I wanted to do absolutely nothing but watch the 1980 Olympic hockey final, then I could.

Now, I'm drunk in a warm way. My face has stopped throbbing, although one of the girls pouring the drinks informed me of the nasty bruises making an appearance. More tequila was the solution to that one. I feel like I'm floating in one of those pools that makes you feel like you're in a womb.

Wren's on my lap, grinding against my groin and sucking on my neck. I palm her ass and close my eyes, wanting to just exist for a moment.

Her teeth graze my skin. She does it again, then giggles. She's drunk, too.

I crack one eye open. "What?"

Shit, my speech is slurring.

"Your dick twitches every time I do that." She cups me through my jeans.

We're in the living room. The lights are low, and the party has devolved into debauchery. The only ones left are pairs in various levels of undress. If she was wearing a skirt, it would be easy to just…slide into her. Fuck her here.

"Well, my dick likes you." I frown. "Obviously."

She giggles again.

I don't think I've heard her giggle. It's so fucking freeing, my heart gives an erratic thump. And anything that happens with my heart in relation to Wren Davis is concerning. But with the tequila in my system, it's easy to brush it off. To not think it means anything, even though it obviously does.

Catching feelings for my best friend's sister wasn't on my to-do list, and yet…

I mean, I declared her mine. To her. In a storage closet.

But now I'm doing it more publicly, keeping us out in the open. I danced with her. I made out with her. I ignored seething looks from Evan and dodged Archer's questions about the jersey she may or may not have had on earlier.

I was wrong earlier. I have a feeling I'm going to end up paying for Archer's replacement.

The simple truth of the matter is that Wren is sexy as fuck, no matter what she's doing. Straddling my lap is a prime example, but even watching her walk across the house is enough to want to chase her.

It's an obsession. An unhealthy one.

I watch her on the cameras. I follow her around school.

And yes, obviously it's because I'm worried that her psycho dad is going to do something from prison, like send someone to threaten her or something. We had that break-in that wasn't really a break-in and nothing else since.

It's been quiet, which has really just given me an excuse to watch Wren more. To drift away from looking for the danger around her to just looking at her. The way she flips her hair off her shoulder before she puts on her backpack, or pats her pockets to check for her keys, phone, and whatever else. The way she smiles at her friends.

Her lips return to my ear, catching the lobe with her tongue, then her teeth. It's a zing that goes straight to my groin, and I suppress the urge to fuck her for the billionth time.

"Maybe we should take this upstairs," she whispers in my ear.

"Maybe," I reply. "Or maybe I enjoy torturing both of us."

She huffs.

"Tell me, Sticks. Is my cum still between your legs?" I slip my hand into her pants. "Oh, hmm, my girl is wet."

She bites her lip. "What are you going to do about it?"

I move my hand lower, thrusting one finger into her. Then two. My smile feels wicked. "I'm going to watch you get yourself off, baby."

Her eyes widen, and she glances over her shoulder. Her lips are swollen from kisses, her eye makeup a little smudged. What I really want is to put her on the floor between my legs and watch her suck me off, but this is a close second. Her orgasm face is one of my favorites.

"There are people," she whispers.

"I know." I raise my eyebrow. "So…promise to never wear another one of my teammates' jerseys, and I'll let you come right here. Otherwise, I'll make sure you don't come until Tuesday."

She gives me a baleful look, then nods. "I promise never to wear one of your teammates' jerseys," she parrots. "And now…"

"Now go to town." I curl my fingers inside her, and her body shudders.

She wriggles. Her hands come up onto my shoulders. And slowly, she sets a pace. She grinds her clit against the rough heel of my palm, and I scratch the *itch* deep inside her. Her head tips back, but her gaze stays locked on mine.

I lean forward and pull her tank and bra cup down, exposing her breast.

She squeaks in surprise.

I press my palm to her back, keeping her steady, keeping her on my lap and not shooting through the ceiling, and lick around her nipple.

It pebbles under my attention. Her hips move faster, her muscles squeezing my fingers. I suck it into my mouth, flicking my tongue against the sensitive nub. I graze it with my teeth, the same as she did to my neck, and she moans.

Her hands slide from my shoulders up into my hair. She tugs me closer while her hips roll faster. Fuck being in the living room. Fuck having an audience. I pull my hand out abruptly and lift her, keeping her bare breast hidden against my chest. I carry her to the bathroom, the only door not locked, and set her on the counter.

"The door," she mumbles.

"Fuck it." I yank her pants down.

I'm inside her in an instant, and we both groan. God, she feels too fucking good. The best elixir. I lean her back and bite her breast, and she bucks. Her legs wrap around my hips, heels digging into my ass and pressing me closer.

"Just like that," she groans. "Fuck me harder."

I like her drunk and mouthy. I like her sober and mouthy, too.

"Right there. *Fuck*, Stone. Yes. *Yes.*"

She falls over the edge fast. I grab her wrist belatedly, yanking it away from her clit as she comes. She laughs as she trembles, her pleasure making her expression hazy. Dreamy.

"Too fucking perfect," I growl.

My movements become frantic, chasing the high, and it doesn't take me long to come inside her for the second time tonight. But with her body wrapped around mine, it's ten times better.

"Jesus Christ."

We both look toward the door.

The open bathroom door.

Evan stands there with his hand over his eyes. "What the fuck are you two doing?"

I grin and slide out of Wren, tucking myself away. She's slower to regroup, touching her head and going for her pants —sans panties, which I ripped away earlier—before realizing her tit is still out. She tugs her bra back into place, her face flushing.

"I'm sorry you had to see that," Wren mumbles.

I raise my eyebrow. "I think everyone knew what was going on here, Sticks."

Evan's face slowly turns red.

"What?" I continue to Wren, rolling my eyes. "It's not like you weren't yelling, *'Yes, Stone, fuck me harder!'* about two seconds ago."

And that's how I end up getting punched by my best friend.

CHAPTER 28
WREN

HIS BRUISE IS STILL ANGRY-LOOKING, even days later, but Stone deserved it. That doesn't mean I'm not totally and irrevocably consumed by him, though. Because I am. I say I hate him every other day, but I also find myself thinking about him in every empty space within my thoughts.

It's a sickness, and it's not one that I want a cure for.

"Don't be inappropriate, guys." I place my hands on my hips. The house smells of popcorn, and one bag is already down, with three more lined up on the coffee table.

The living room, typically only a place for my housemates to play video games, is filled with blankets, pillows, and five beefy hockey players in sweatpants and hoodies.

Evan huffs. "Don't be inappropriate? Are you fucking kidding?"

"Watch it." Stone's tone is lazy, but we all know better.

"You fucked her so hard I heard her screaming your name, and then I find out the door is open. *That's* inappropriate."

Archer snorts, and Grant chokes on a piece of popcorn.

I sigh.

I feel bad.

I do.

But I don't regret it—something Stone recognizes as he smirks at me from the loveseat.

The knock on the door pulls my attention away. "There's Ally. Seriously…" I eye them. "She's not coming over for a gang bang, okay? She's my friend. Leave her alone." Before I make it to the door, I say over my shoulder, "She already thinks you guys are crazy with all the cameras around the house."

"That was Stone's idea."

"Oh, *please*," I whisper.

My fingers wrap around the doorknob, but I stumble backward when Stone's hands fall to my hips.

"What are you doing?" I ask.

Stone pulls open the door at the same time he shoves me behind him. Once Ally speaks, I pop out while shooting him a dirty look. *What the hell?*

"Come in." I smile and brush Stone away.

"I brought dessert." Ally whooshes forward like she owns the place, and by the looks on my housemates' faces—besides Stone's—she is about to own all of them.

"We love you." Taylor stands and pulls her into the kitchen.

They come back a few seconds later with bowls, spoons, and the containers of ice cream.

The guys pile their bowls to the top. Ally and I are a little more respectful and scoop a proper amount before settling into the couches. Stone's lips brush my ear. He smells like chocolate and cherries, and my mouth waters.

"I always knew you were a vanilla girl."

I snort after licking my spoon clean. "Vanilla girl? I'm with you, aren't I?" I raise an eyebrow, and his eyes drift to my lips. "*Absolutely not,*" I whisper. "And what was that earlier? You practically levitated to open the door."

Stone pulls back, and I notice the shadows along his jaw flicking back and forth. There's a loud commotion on the TV from the movie, so he leans in closer. "Wanted to make sure it was Ally."

"Oh," I tease, snuggling back into his chest. "Acting chivalrous now, are we?"

His arms wrap around my torso, and the soft kiss he places on my hair turns my stomach into mush.

"Shut up and watch the movie."

Before I know it, the movie is almost over, and half the guys are asleep, along with Ally. Her head is resting against Taylor's shoulder, and her legs are draped over Archer's lap. Stone's breathing is even—something I'm not used to. He's always so *angry* or tense. Worried too. But right now, he's relaxed. His fingers continue to roam against my lower belly, like they've been doing the entire movie, but he's been on his best behavior. Chills covered me at one point when his finger swooped down low, but he pulled it away—like he had lost control for a second.

"You want to go to bed?" I peer through my sleepy eyes.

Stone nods. We both look over at Ally. *She'll be fine.* I don't have to worry about her, and even though the guys have been talking about how hot she is, they would never cross a line. They're annoying, but they're still good guys.

I stand first and then grab Stone's hand. He towers over me for a second, dropping his gaze to my mouth, but then he follows me up the stairs after checking the lock on the front door.

It's cute.

His need to be protective is alluring.

"What?" he asks, closing the bedroom door.

His quick glance is worrisome, and it leaves me confused. *What is with him?*

I panic, and words fumble out of my mouth. "Why are you being so nice and protective? You're on your best behavior, and I—"

"You what?" Stone tilts his head. "You don't like it?"

I have butterflies. Like, full-on rapidly flying butterflies. "No. I do." In fact, it has me thinking dangerous things—like how I don't want to live without him. "I just...don't understand."

Stone laughs. His head falls, and I can't read him like usual.

"Sticks, what don't you understand?"

"Wh—"

"Baby, I'm fucking obsessed with you." His deep voice is hot. "I can't sleep if you're not beside me. I can't eat if you're at work and I'm not sitting there in a booth, watching your hips sway with your tray. Even during my practices and games, if I don't know where you are at all times, I fuck up and nearly fall on the ice."

My throat constricts. Stone's honesty sucks up all the oxygen in our shared bedroom.

"Tell me you feel the same."

This isn't a time for jokes. I would usually have some snarky rebuttal and say something like, "*Or what?*" but I can't find it in me to shut him down, because if this is Stone's version of pouring his heart out to me, I'll take it and run.

"I do," I whisper.

"Then get over here so you can prove it."

His words move me toward him, even though the independence I have possessed since a young age is begging me to stay put.

I can't say no to him.

Once his hands find my cheeks, he tugs me in close. Our chests rub together, and his heart is beating just as hard as mine is. I sigh when his tongue dips into my mouth, but for the first time, his kiss isn't urgent. It's slow and sensual, and I fall into it like a honey trap.

There isn't a word spoken between us. Stone shoves my shirt up over my head and drops it to the floor beside my feet. My leggings are pulled down past my hips, and the brush of his fingers over my skin sends a chill down my spine.

"Stone," I rasp. I dig my nails into his shoulders.

He stays kneeled below and places a soft kiss against my panties before standing back up and undressing himself.

He doesn't have a single flaw.

Strong, toned muscles line his stomach, and they flicker with his grip around himself. My mouth parts, and a soft sigh falls in between us as I watch him stroke back and forth. He wiggles his finger at me and tells me to come closer...so I do.

Our eyes are locked, and he pushes a finger into me achingly slow. I'm already ready—something he clearly appreciates. I fall to the bed, and he's in between my legs, taking his time with me.

I arch when he pulls out and then goes in again. This time is different.

His touches are gentle, like he's trying to memorize every last curve, and his intense gaze stays glued to me with every last thrust. It's hotter than when he's touching me like he wants to hate me. He's touching me like he loves me, and I feel it digging into my bones.

I'll forever be branded by him.

"I'm close," I pant, gripping the blankets for dear life.

The orgasm builds faster than I expect, and my stomach hollows. Stone tilts his hips and hits the spot that no one has touched before. I fall into a bliss, mesmerized by his deep kiss. I'd give him my entire soul in this moment if he asked me for it, and knowing Stone, he will eventually.

"Fuck," he moans. He steals his mouth away from mine and buries his face into my sweaty neck.

His body stills, and I spread my tingling legs wider, letting him fill me to the brim. Stone has been careless, and I've been letting him come inside me as if there is no other way. Thank God I'm on birth control—something he has never inquired about.

Once Stone climbs off me, he hurries back with a towel. The moonlight shines a glow on him, and my breath is stolen the moment he cleans me between my legs. Typically, he says something crass and wants his cum to stay there, but right now, he's taking care of me.

My lip wobbles, and it's something he notices.

"Wren?" His brow furrows. "Out of all the times we've fucked, I didn't think this one would hurt."

I swallow roughly. "I'm not hurt."

"Okay…" The bed dips, and he brings me close. Our naked bodies are wrapped around one another. "Then why are you crying?"

A shaky breath clamors from my lips. "I'm not used to someone taking care of me."

His chest expands beneath my head, and the steady release of air tickles my neck. I sigh at the soft kiss on my temple.

"Sleep, baby."

I shut my eyes to hold back the tears, knowing I'll sleep better than I ever have before.

CHAPTER 29
WREN

I REACH my hand back and slap the nightstand. Except, instead of hitting the wood, I slap Stone instead.

"What the fuck, Sticks," he mumbles.

I'm pulled backward and sigh at his warmth.

"Should I slap you back?" His voice is sleepy.

His teeth graze my ear, and I have no idea how it makes my body twist, but it does. My cheeks heat, but then the vibrating of my phone starts up again. I shove his arm off my hip and sit up, pulling the blankets up to hide my naked chest.

"Really? Hiding your tits from me? They were in my mouth no less than three hours ago."

The sun is peeking through the window, and exhaustion has set in. My body hurts, and there's a soreness between my legs that wasn't there before I fell asleep last night. After Stone told me to sleep, I drifted off, only to be woken up again to his fingers trailing my thighs. He went back for seconds *and* thirds.

"Who's calling you?" he asks, moving the blanket down.

I lean over him, and he flicks his tongue onto my nipple.

"Stone!" I chide.

My phone slips into his hand with his catlike reflexes, and he presses it up to his ear. "Hello?"

There's a pause, and I sit back while dragging the blanket up to my neck again. I wait and stare at his strong profile.

His throat moves with a swallow, and then he snaps, "Who's asking for Wren?" Stone's angry brow unfurrows. He takes the phone and turns it on to speaker. "Here she is."

I don't recognize the number, but I'm grateful it doesn't say *unknown*.

"Um, hello?"

"Wren?

"Yes?" I answer with a question because I don't recognize the voice.

"It's Mary-Lou."

I sit back. I only know one Mary-Lou, but I question her anyway. "Mary-Lou Anderson?" *My old social worker.* She wasn't a bad one. She did her best, always stealing me away from my father the moment he slipped up and placing me with Evan's parents.

"Yes, it's me."

Stone sits up and rests against his headboard, letting the sheet fall to his hips. I'm too concerned to stare at the thick outline below it.

"Oh...um, hi?" *Why is she calling me?* I haven't spoken to her since my eighteenth birthday, because once you're out of the system, you're *out* of the system.

Stone's hands jut outward.

"My old social worker," I mouth.

"Wren, someone broke into my office last night."

"Okay..." My response lingers, and I'm conflicted. "Do you think it was me...?"

Her light laugh floats out of the speaker, but her humor doesn't last long. "Of course not."

My heart beats erratically, and I'm no longer concerned about the blanket covering me. Stone brushes my hair off my shoulder, and I know he can see how fast my chest is heaving. The longer I sit on the phone, the more anxious I become.

"Your file is missing."

My file.

My thick, depressing fucking file.

"The whole place was trashed and…"

There's more?

"Calm down," Stone says, not caring that Mary-Lou can hear him.

It's hard to focus on his hand rubbing up and down my spine. *My file.* Does it have an updated address? I chastise myself. Someone has already broken in here once. They know where I am. What do they want with my file?

"And what, Mary? Are you okay?"

"I'm in the hospital."

I pop forward and try to move off the bed. Stone catches me by the waist, all while holding the phone steady. He keeps me pinned in his lap and buries his face into my neck.

"What happened?" I shut my eyes like it's going to help. *This is my fault.* "Did they say who they were?"

There's a faint beeping in the background, and all I can picture is a beaten and bleeding Mary-Lou on a hospital bed. *It's all my fault.* Trouble follows me *everywhere.*

"I caught them in there. I have an alarm. Once I confronted them and asked why they were tearing apart my filing cabinets, they said your name. I tried to fend them off, but…"

But you can't bring a knife to a gun fight.

"I didn't get the chance to stop them, and after they left and the police showed up, it was confirmed that the only thing missing was—"

"My file." A tear falls down my cheek, but Stone is quick to sweep it away. I suck in my emotions, a sob knocking inside my chest. "I…I am so sorry."

"It isn't your fault, sweetie."

"No, it isn't." Stone spins us around and places me on the bed.

He moves to find my clothes and dresses me as I stay still, listening to Mary-Lou's labored breathing.

"It's part of my job. This isn't the first time someone has broken in and stolen files or confronted me. It is the first time it's been *this* physical, but…" Her voice shakes. "Wren, I'm worried about you. Are you okay? What's going on? Is it your dad—"

"Wren is safe." Stone takes the phone off speaker and places it up to his ear.

My legs are trembling, and my teeth sink into my bottom lip. Blood fills my mouth, and I'm in a daze. I'm not sure how much time has passed, but at one point, I watch Stone stalk over to our bedroom door. He shouts for Evan. They talk through the door. I can't make out what they're saying through the ringing in my ears.

I remain unmoving, even after Stone bends down in front of me again.

"Tell me what you're thinking." His blue eyes are difficult to pull away from.

I try but fail. "I'm scared."

A sob escapes my throat, and Stone stumbles backward. His face falls, and he looks like I've just cut him.

My face is pushed into his chest with force.

"I would kill anyone if they tried touching you, Wren. You have nothing to be afraid of."

I try to get away, but his arm tightens against me, and he refuses to let me curl in the other direction.

"Don't you dare shut me out."

Another cry rips from me, and it pisses me off. I grip the sheets and squeeze my eyes shut. "I hate him. Why can't he just fucking let me go?"

"He won't touch you."

"You don't know him!" I shout. I meet Stone's angry brow

and steely jaw. "You have no fucking idea what he is capable of."

"No, baby," Stone growls. "You have no idea what *I'm* capable of. Especially when it comes to you."

I listen to his words, but I don't believe them. Hatred runs deeper than love, and it's obvious that Stone no longer hates me. And if it wasn't clear in my childhood, it is now. My father doesn't have a loving bone in his fucking body.

I'm not safe, even with him in prison.

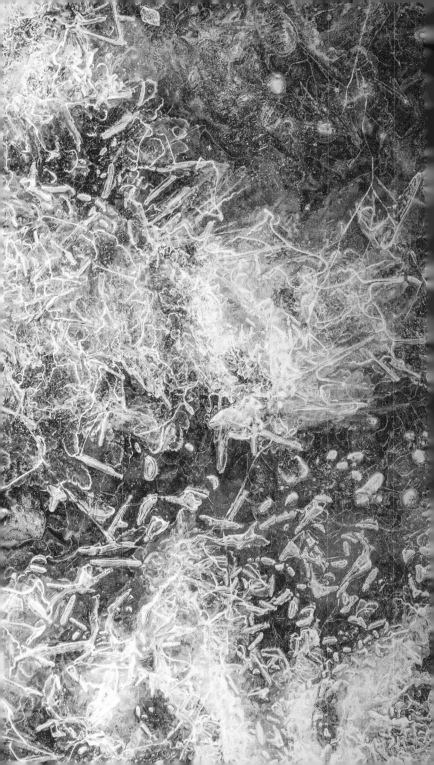

CHAPTER 30
STONE

"WHAT DO you know about a Mary-Lou Anderson?"

Evan flinches.

Flinches.

"What?" I demand, dropping into the seat across from him.

Wren is with Taylor, on her way to campus for one of her ungodly science classes.

My best friend frowns. "Look, man, I appreciate you wanting to do what's best for Wren. Protect her and all that shit. But rooting around in her past isn't going to endear her to you—"

"I know she's the social worker," I interrupt. "And she called Wren last night."

Evan frowns. "Why?"

I reach across the table and close his textbook for him. "She was assaulted."

"Holy—"

"It gets worse," I interrupt. "She was assaulted in her office as someone was going through it. And when the cops showed up, they discovered one thing missing—Wren's file."

He blows out a breath. "Fucking hell."

"We've got zero leads," I hiss. "We've got nothing on the cameras. No more break-ins, or people lurking around Wren, or—"

"Stop." He flattens his hands to the table. "You're going to freak yourself out if you keep going like this."

"I am freaked out." Something I'd never fucking admit to Wren, but it's true. There's a chill lodged in my bones, and I can't shake it no matter how many precautions I take. "So just tell me what I need to know about this social worker."

Over the next hour, Evan fills me in on every interaction he's had with the social worker, every story Wren's told him over the years. And it slowly dawns on me—because I'm apparently a fucking idiot—that Evan has a whole-ass relationship with Wren that I've never wanted to know about.

I mean, obviously she lived in his house. He cares about her. But he also *knows* her.

God, I hate the jealousy that twists my gut.

But the more he talks, the more I recognize that Wren's social worker was a saving grace in her life. Swooping in whenever things with her dad got particularly sticky, figuring out her next safe haven. Which was almost always Evan's family.

"What could've been in the file that her dad would want?"

He blinks at me.

"Come on. It was obviously some of her dad's guys." I glower at him. "Unless you think it was some other stalker?"

"Well, it definitely wasn't Brad," Evan mutters. "I heard he started dating a cheerleader. And Wren's conversation with him sounded...honest, actually. I believe that he only called her once."

"And the rest...?"

Her dad. Or someone close.

I straighten suddenly. "We need to go on the offensive. Burying our heads in the sand isn't working."

Evan grabs his computer from his bag.

"What are you doing?"

"Pulling up the public records for her dad's arrest."

I grin and come around the table, dropping into the chair beside him. I lean over while he types, opening up a web page that gives bare details about his sentencing. Drug possession with intent to distribute is the top charge, among others. Weapons, extortion, other drug charges.

But there's a note. A little flag on the file.

Appeal ongoing.

Evan and I exchange a glance.

"Who's his lawyer?" I ask. "Some shady fucker?"

I lean farther in and scan the page.

And then I spot it.

Evan inhales sharply a split second later.

"What the fuck is your dad's name doing on these records?" Evan asks in a low voice.

Great question. "Beats me."

My father is Wren's dad's lawyer. Evan and I stare at the screen while I try to wrap my head around this. My dad is a good defense lawyer. One of the best in our town. But...I don't know, I guess I had it in my head that he only defended wealthy white-collar assholes and innocent people. Not drug dealers.

Not her *dad*.

"Okay." I clear my throat. "If this is true—"

"I don't think we can rule it out," Evan interrupts.

I grit my teeth. "Fine. But I can't just up and ask my dad. There's attorney-client privilege and all that shit. He used to say that anytime I was curious about his cases growing up."

There's an uncomfortable pit in my stomach.

The kind that comes along with the realization that your dad might not be a good guy.

And *yeah*, I know some people, like Wren, have been living with this all their lives. But I idolized my father. I wanted to be him when I grew up. That was before the shit with my mom, before he married the step-monster, and before I discovered I could have a future in hockey.

I have no doubt in my mind that Jessie Davis is guilty of everything he was charged with. So where does that put my father?

Is he a good guy like I always thought? Defender of the innocent?

Or is he just…a lawyer who will do anything to get the job done? Who will fight the law, and exploit all its loopholes, and get his guilty clients set free?

"Fuck," I murmur, pinching the bridge of my nose. "My head hurts."

Evan grunts his acknowledgement. He can't really talk, though. Besides sympathizing secondhand with Wren, and me when Dad became hyper-fixated on a case and spent all his days and nights at his office or taking work home with him, he can't really relate.

His parents are *wonderful*.

"What are you going to do?"

I glance at Evan.

What am *I* going to do, not we.

"I guess I need to confront him…somehow. Without triggering his auto-response. Or raising his suspicions." I pause. "Do you think he knew who the drugs belonged to when he got me out of being arrested on that drug possession charge in high school?"

He ponders that. Then, "Well, you knew right away. And it wouldn't be a stretch for your dad to know the Davises. We made it no secret that Wren stayed with us, and you were over at my house all the time."

"Yeah…" Except my father and I didn't really talk about that kind of thing. I had my truck, he had work, and at the time, I was doing everything in my power to avoid the house. I hated living there. I hated Martha.

As long as I was staying out of trouble and keeping my

grades up, Dad only vaguely knew that I was often at Evan Mitchell's house. Another hockey player whose face would be somewhat familiar. He'd be able to pick out my best friend in a lineup if we put him at gunpoint.

Maybe.

I clear my throat. "I just need to talk to him in person. Appeal to his…"

"What does he care about?"

Isn't that a great question? I suck my lower lip between my teeth and consider it.

"His image." I hold up my index finger. "Being the world's best defense attorney has always been high on his list of achievements."

"Naturally," Evan agrees.

"Um, the step-monster. He loves her, which is rather unfortunate." I wrinkle my nose.

"You can't call her that." Evan groans. "You're going to say it to her face one of these days."

I smile. "Pretty sure I accidentally did on the phone one time. I played it off…I think."

"Ass."

"Third, as much as I hate to admit it, he does care about me."

"You could've just said family," Evan mutters. "That's it, then? His image, which is essentially work, and family? The two most basic things *ever*?"

I raise my hands. "I don't know."

"Okay, okay. So we appeal to both." He considers me, his eyes narrowing.

"What?"

"There's something you're probably forgetting. An opportunity…"

What the fuck. I grab my phone and click on the unread messages from Martha, which have come in over the past two months. Reminders of his birthday party. Asking me to RSVP.

Telling me it's okay if I bring a friend. I can stay the night in my old room. On and on…

"Shit." I drop the phone. "His birthday is next week."

Evan straightens. "You seriously are the worst son ever. When's the party?"

"How do you know there's a party?"

He rolls his eyes. "When does Martha *not* go all out for your dad?"

That's true. I scan her texts again and shrug. Then close out of her thread, which is ninety-nine percent one-sided. Then exit the messaging app entirely. I toss my phone on the table and lean back in my chair, balancing it on the back two legs.

"There's got to be another way," I reason.

"Stone."

"I'll consider it."

Evan turns back to his laptop, scanning the records again. Not that it's going to yield any more information. I think we hit our quota of good luck for the night.

The door bangs open. Evan slams the laptop shut as Wren coasts into the kitchen, dropping her bag on the chair. She looks a bit like a hurricane, all fierce and sharp-eyed. Not spooked or scared like before.

And it's kind of irritating how much I've missed her, while she was just a few blocks away.

She plants her hands on her hips. "I've been thinking."

Taylor comes in behind her and sighs. "They're not gonna go for it, Wren."

"I'm going to go see Mary-Lou," she continues. "And it's not up for debate. I want to know what was in my file that could harm me."

Evan and I exchange a glance. I reach for Wren, running my hands down her sides before pulling her into my lap.

My first instinct is to say no. That it's not necessary, that she shouldn't put herself through that. That her social worker probably wouldn't want Wren to see her like that.

But as I bury my face in her hair, inhaling her scent, I consider something else. The possibility that there *was* something damaging in the file.

Something that, if we know about it, could help keep Wren safe.

So, in the end, I suppose she's right. Especially with what we know now about the appeal. And the possibility of her dad getting out on parole.

Two things I need to tell her—but not yet.

"Okay," I readily agree. "But I'm going with you."

CHAPTER 31
WREN

STONE'S FINGERS stay intertwined with mine the entire drive to Camwell, the little town right outside of Maysville. Evan opted to stay in Shadow Valley, knowing if his parents found out we were this close to home, they'd be upset that we didn't stop by.

If we went to visit, they'd want to know why we made the drive for just an evening. I refuse to tell Rebecca and Stephen what's going on. They are no longer my foster parents, and they are the last people I want to drag into this mess.

I smile when Stone's lips brush against the back of my hand. He parks the car and turns it off, but neither of us rush to get out. I peek at the sky, watching the gray clouds disappear.

"What are you thinking?"

His voice is soothing but not enough to ease my dread. I shrug instead of saying anything. Stone tugs on my hand, and somehow, I end up straddling his lap in the driver's seat. My knee digs into the seatbelt when Stone slowly slides his seat backward.

My hair is a curtain around us, shielding the way he's

looking up at me like he wants to pull every last thought out of my head.

"What's on your mind, Sticks?"

My lips part, and his eyebrow rises.

There is no point in hiding things from him. Stone recognizes all my defense mechanisms now, and he's starting to know all my secrets too.

I sigh. "I'm nervous. There, I said it. I'm nervous to see her."

I fail at my attempt to climb off Stone's lap. His fingers dig into my hip bones, keeping me hostage. His blue eyes look darker than normal against my shadow, yet I can't stop falling into them like they're some sort of trap.

"You're nervous?" he asks, leaning back farther against his leather seat.

My lip is sore from all the nibbling I've been doing during the drive. I don't even realize I'm doing it again until Stone reaches out and pops it free from my teeth.

"I can help with that," he whispers. He drags his finger across my lower belly.

"Stone," I chastise.

My stomach clenches, and I swing my gaze around to see if anyone is looking through the windows.

"They're tinted."

Not only is he starting to know my secrets, but he can suddenly read my mind too.

"We shouldn't." I hear the strain in my voice.

Stone smirks.

"We should." His neck works with a slow swallow, and my thighs squeeze around him. "Let me calm you down."

I laugh. "This is the opposite of calming me down." My heart is thumping wildly with thoughts of his touch, and it only gets worse when he tilts his hips to meet the throbbing between my legs.

I am not someone who likes public displays. *Unless I'm with Stone.*

"Shit." I arch my back when his finger slips in the front of my pants. "*Stone.*"

He shushes me and creeps past my panties.

"You'll be calmer after I make you come, so don't hold out on me."

I gasp and thrust my hips forward. His finger dips inside, and he curses. My cheeks flush when his nostrils flare.

"Your cunt is always so wet for me, and I fucking love it."

God. I move against him, and it doesn't take long for me to crave the rough heel of his hand scraping against my clit.

"That's it," he encourages, moving his fingers in and out of me, playing with my pussy like he owns it.

I dig my nails into the leather seat behind his head and work my body, chasing the high. *He is right. This is a total distraction.*

"Fuck," he groans.

My nipple puckers when air brushes against it, and Stone's hot tongue flicks it before he tugs the bud into his mouth.

"I want to fuck you."

"Do it," I whisper. "I'm yours."

My words are lazy with pleasure, and my eyes start to close. I rock my hips, and my hair tumbles down my back.

"Then I couldn't watch you come all over my hand like you're my own dirty little slut."

His words send me over the edge, and I break. The tugging of my hair burns my scalp, and Stone hooks his fingers inside even farther, sending another bout of pleasure down my body.

"Oh my God," I cry, still grinding against his hand until my high fades.

Stone's breathing is labored, and when he pulls his hand out of my pants, I'm slightly mortified at how wet his fingers are. His eyes harden when he puts his fingers in his mouth, and the hollow parts of his cheeks deepen right before he pops them out.

"Fucking delicious."

I am a total fucking goner for him.

"Feel better?"

I nod, and it takes me a minute to remember where we are.

"Then let's go see this Mary-Lou woman and figure out who's trying to get information on my girl." He buttons my jeans and taps my leg, flicking his head to the passenger seat.

I climb over the center console, flushed and sweaty and completely dazed.

Stone opens his door and is on my side before I can even step out onto the pavement.

His damp finger lands on my chin, and he tilts my face. "It's not your fault."

"What isn't?" I rasp.

"Mary-Lou being assaulted."

I go to argue, because it *is* my fault, but he pushes me against the side of his car and presses his hard length into my stomach. "But this…"

My hand is suddenly cupping him.

"Is." He winks and pulls me forward, leading us to the hospital entrance. "Just think of your reward for later."

A smile plays against my lips, and that's when I notice my belly isn't full of nerves anymore but something else entirely.

Stone knows me better than I know myself.

———

IT IS WORSE THAN I THOUGHT. STONE'S HAND LANDS ON MY lower back when we step into her room, because he knows that I need stability even if I refuse to admit it.

Mary-Lou's blackened face peeks up over her book, and she freezes. "Wren? What are you doing here, sweetie?"

Sweetie. If I were her, I'd hate me.

The gray-blue shade beneath her eyes is the first thing I see. My mouth opens but quickly snaps closed when I see her wince. She's climbing out of her bed, and she's in front of me before I can even fathom a word.

"I'm sor—"

Stone's hand never leaves my back, even as I'm wrapped in Mary-Lou's familiar embrace.

"It's not your fault, Wren."

"That's what I keep telling her." Stone's smooth voice commands the room.

Mary-Lou smiles at him. "Stone Foster."

"That's me," he answers, leading me to the chair off to the side.

Mary-Lou slowly walks back to her bed and sits on the edge.

"How do you know Stone?" I ask.

"I know his father. I've seen him command a courtroom like no other."

Stone's growl isn't noticeable to her, but it is to me.

"Please tell me you didn't come all this way to tell me sorry, Wren."

I open my mouth, prepared to apologize once more, but Stone stretches his legs out in front of himself and drops the bomb.

"We came to figure out what was in her file."

What wasn't in my file is the real question.

Mary-Lou nods. We all stay silent as a nurse waltzes into the room and has her sign some paperwork. She's being discharged, which is a relief to me.

As soon as the door clicks shut, Mary-Lou goes into social-worker mode and asks the same questions she used to ask when I was in her care, but I stop her.

"My dad is still in prison, but I'm certain this has something to do with him."

Even through the swelling along her face, I see the hesitation. I squint, and Stone stiffens beside me. *Wait.*

"What do you two know that I don't?" I bounce my attention back and forth between them. My pulse thrums violently.

Stone won't look at me.

"He's appealing his conviction."

The room spins. It takes Stone's palm on my thigh to bring me back. "H-how? No. Is he out?" I turn to Mary-Lou. "Was he the one who assaulted you?"

"No, not that I would be surprised if he did. I've taken you away from him too many times to count." Her soft laugh is sarcastic.

I can't muster up the energy to match it.

"Did they take the entire file?" Stone asks. His hand stays on my thigh as it bounces up and down.

She winces with the shake of her head. "No. They took one sheet. The rest was thrown at me."

Thrown at her.

I picture her bleeding and crumpled on the floor of her office with papers covering her bloody body. I tremble, and Stone briefly looks at me with his heavy brow and disapproving scowl.

Mary-Lou interrupts our moment. "They took the sheet that had your previous foster parents' information on it. I suspect he's looking for your address, thinking you're still living with the Mitchells."

Stone and I know that can't be accurate. My dad knows exactly where I am, and the same men who broke into her office were probably the same ones who ransacked my bedroom.

The rest of the time spent with Mary-Lou is a blur. She asks me about school and makes an obvious effort to avoid bringing up my father. He may be the reason I'm face to face with my old social worker again, but she's never been one to spend much time talking about the negative.

After giving her a gentle hug and apologizing for the hundredth time, which she and Stone reprimand me for, Stone leads me to his car. I sit in the seat and stay silent, focusing on the revving of his motor.

"Did you know?" My voice is a rasp.

"What kind of boyfriend would I be if I didn't?"

I suck in a breath. *Boyfriend? Is that what he is?* I'm well aware of how concerning it is for me to smile, but I do it anyway. I only let the slip in my emotions last a second.

I wait until he presses on the gas to mumble, "A lying one, I guess."

His neck snaps. I fly forward when his foot hits the brake, halting us in the middle of the parking lot.

"What did you just say?"

"Don't hide stuff from me, Stone. I don't like it."

He stares at me with his soul-sucking blue eyes and then smiles like the devil. "But you like it when I call myself your boyfriend, don't you?"

"No."

"Now who's lying?"

I cross my arms in defeat, and he presses on the gas, flinging me backward.

"Don't worry, baby. I fully plan on making you admit how much you *love* the idea of me being your boyfriend later."

I press my lips together at the same time my thighs clench.

Boyfriend or not, I kind of hate him.

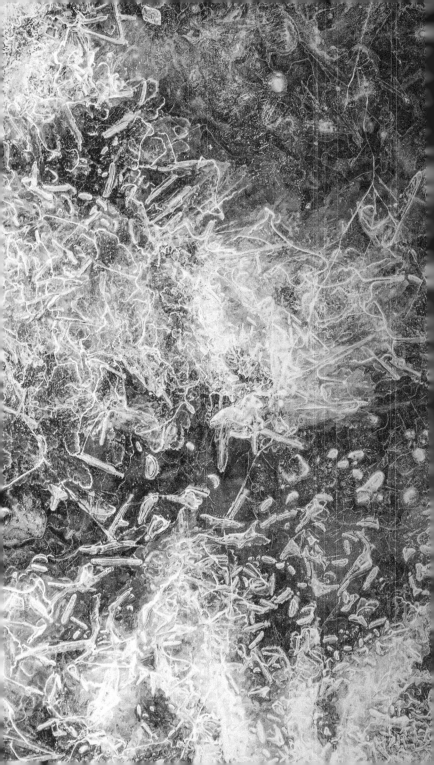

CHAPTER 32

STONE

STEP-MONSTER

Stone!!! Please call me!!!

I STARE at the text from a week ago. I didn't answer it. Didn't bother coming up with an excuse. I have no doubt it's about my father's birthday party, which is probably coming up soon.

Actually.

Before I can think better of it, I dial her number.

"Oh my gosh, Stone!" Her voice is sugar-sweet. Enough to give me a mouthful of cavities. "I was just thinking about you. I expected your call a few days ago."

She's polite enough not to say a week ago. Or more. Since I've been dodging her texts and calls since the start of the school year.

"Sorry." I clear my throat. "It's been busy. Adjusting to a new school and team, all that…"

"Of course, of course. So, are you able to make it?"

"To the party?" I put her on speaker and scroll through the texts. She never mentions a date. "When is it, again?"

She makes a tsking noise. "It's tonight. Starts at six. And

you know you're welcome to spend the night before returning to school."

Fucking hell.

"I'm bringing a guest," I tell her. "I, uh, just wanted to make sure that was fine."

"Of course! Is it Evan?"

"No…"

She gasps. "A girl?"

"Yeah, my girlfriend."

I set my phone down on the kitchen counter and turn to open the fridge. As she continues gushing about how great a girlfriend will be for me, and how I've been single for too long, with too much of a focus on hockey, I contemplate slamming the door shut on my head.

Beer is out of the question. It's eight o'clock, everyone else is asleep, and I can't get drunk first thing in the morning. As much as this conversation is driving me to do so.

"Hey," I interrupt, "it's at the house, right?"

"The party? Yes, of course. We have caterers…" She keeps talking.

I shake my head and grab my phone, bringing it with me back to my room. I take her off speaker and set the water bottle I don't really remember grabbing on the nightstand. Wren's still asleep, and she looks too fucking peaceful like this. She's star-fished in my absence, her hair spread across the pillows. She's left no room for me…except on top of her.

I pull the blankets down, pinching the phone between my ear and shoulder, and drag off her panties. It's amazing she even got them back on after last night, but she must've gotten up to go to the bathroom while I slept.

Either way.

They get tossed behind me, and I kick off my shorts, too. It doesn't matter what my stepmother is yammering on about— something about the decorations now—I'm already hard as a rock for Wren Davis.

I climb over her and notch my dick at her warm entrance. She's already wet, even asleep, and I hope that she's been dreaming good things. About me.

"Martha."

Wren's eyes snap open, and I quickly cover her mouth. Her eyes narrow into slits, but they widen when I push into her.

"Sorry," the step-monster breathes. "I get carried away. I know you don't really care about all of that."

Wren feels too fucking good.

"I just wanted to say thanks for letting me bring a guest tonight. And I've got to get going…"

"Okay. Oh! Don't forget, it's formal. Black tie, long dresses only."

"Of course."

Wren's teeth scrape my palm, and I grin at her. I pull out and thrust back in, and I very nearly groan. She does, the sound reverberating against my hand, and I smirk at her.

"Well, we'll see you tonight!" Martha says.

"Great. Bye." I hang up and throw my phone onto the floor.

Wren shakes off my hand. "What was that? And why are you—?"

I kiss her. My teeth catch her lower lip. She kisses me back harder, winding her arms around my neck. She moves across my jaw, nipping my earlobe.

"Are you trying to distract me?" she whispers.

"I'm trying to distract myself."

"From what?"

I shake my head and shift to the side, slipping my hand between our bodies. I find her clit and play a familiar tune. One that has her writhing in minutes, while I continue to fuck her slowly.

As soon as she comes, her body trembling and her expression blissed, I slip out of her and flip her onto her stomach.

She makes a little squeak. I shove a pillow under her hips and keep her legs together, straddling the backs of her thighs.

"What are you—?"

I slide back into her. It's tighter and hits a new, deeper angle. It steals my breath, and judging from the way she abruptly stops talking, it takes her by surprise too.

"Fuck," she groans. "What the fuck?"

I pick up speed. She braces her hands against the head-board, her nails digging into the wood while I take what I need from her.

It doesn't take me long to come. *Hard*. I see stars, and I don't bother pulling out of her. I just collapse on top of her, rolling us to the side so I don't crush her. But my dick stays semi-hard inside her, and I band my arm across her waist to keep her from shifting away.

"Stay," I order. "We get to sleep for a little while."

And then I'll break the news about the party. And my father.

———

"Where'd you go?"

I tilt my head. "What?"

"You left before I got out of the shower." Wren leans on the doorway into the kitchen, her arms crossed.

She and Evan had some sibling bonding lunch or something. They were going to talk to his parents and make sure everything seemed okay with them. And she's right—I had shit to do, so I left while she was taking an extra-long shower.

I close my laptop and hop up from the table. "I've got something to show you."

"Okaaaay." She narrows her eyes and follows me upstairs. "Is it a surprise that requires being naked?"

I chuckle. "I mean...kind of."

"I like those surprises."

Pretty sure she's not going to love this one.

I stop outside our room, with my hand on the knob, and face her. "We've got to go to a party."

"Right."

"My father's birthday party."

Wren sucks her lower lip between her teeth, contemplating. Like she has a choice in the matter. She doesn't—I already know I have to be there, and I don't think I can go through with asking my dad the questions I have to without her by my side.

"And that's tonight?"

"Yeah."

"You just found out about it?"

"Something like that," I hedge. I don't want to admit that I've been dodging calls left and right.

She nods carefully. "And you want me to meet your parents?"

"My dad and stepmom," I correct. I take her hand and squeeze. "Plus, a million other people will be there, so it won't be weird. I mean, maybe Martha will make it weird—"

"She's who you were talking to this morning."

My face is getting hot. "Yeah. Just RSVPing."

"Uh-huh."

I open the door and lead her in. I point to the black garment bag hanging on the back of the closet. "This is for you."

"Oh. Stone." She turns from it to me. "I don't think I can—"

"Please don't make up some excuse out of fear." I force a laugh. "It's just a party. Okay? Can you just try it on…"

"Fine," she whispers.

"Great. I'm ninety-eight percent sure it'll fit. And you've got three hours to get ready." I steal a kiss from her lips and backpedal before she can hit me. "See you later."

"Stone!"

I slam the door and hurry away. The dress I got her is formal, one the step-monster would approve of, black and glittery with a halter top and plunging neckline. Oh, and it's backless.

Ally shows up less than twenty minutes later, glaring at me as she sweeps by and up the stairs. I chuckle to myself. I showered earlier, and my tux is in Evan's room.

I hit play on the latest game tape—this one of a recent game between Bexley Wolves and Crown Point Hawks, who we're playing next weekend—and settle in on the couch to pass the time.

Three hours later, I'm dressed and ready, and I wait for Wren at the bottom of the stairs.

In a way, I feel more nervous for this than I did for my high school prom. Of course, Wren was also there, haunting that moment. I took some girl who followed around the hockey team—I don't even remember her name, except that one of the guys set me up with her. That was inconsequential.

This feels much more serious.

"I can't believe you're taking Wren to meet your parents," Taylor says from the couch. "It's ballsy, for sure."

I flip him off.

It *is* ballsy, especially since my dad will probably take one look at her and know exactly who her father is. I can't imagine he's represented Jessie Davis all this time and not known about his daughter. The daughter who was fostered with my best friend's family.

Jesus.

It's all sorts of fucked up.

"What's she doing up there?" Taylor asks.

"Getting ready." I shift. "I don't fucking know."

"You're fancy as fuck, dude."

I glance over my shoulder. Evan and Grant drop their bags in the living room, grinning at me like they've never seen me wear a freaking tuxedo.

Okay, yeah, I had to go rent one when I picked up Wren's dress. I've got suit jackets for the away games, but nothing that would qualify as black tie.

The sacrifices we make.

I sigh and shoo them away.

Upstairs, a timer goes off. I hide my smile at Wren's distant, "*Shit*!"

I pace the foyer until she appears at the top of the stairs. The skirt of her gown is in her hand, keeping her feet clear to go down the stairs. First her sparkling, strappy, silver heels come into view, then her toned legs. Then the glittering gown that fits her like a glove. She paired it with gold jewelry. Earrings, bracelets, a few slim necklaces that dangle down between her tits.

God.

I fold my hands over my groin and will myself not to get fucking turned on like a teenager at the sight of her.

Her hair is up in some sort of elaborate bun, with pieces pulled out and curled to frame her face. Dark-red lipstick, dark eyeshadow with gold on the lids.

She gets down to me, and she's a good deal taller than she usually is. Not as tall as me, but still.

"You look perfect." I kiss her cheek. Her skin is warm under my lips.

"Thank Ally," she murmurs. "She was a magician."

I glance up at Ally, who's coming down the stairs slower with her supplies.

"Thank you, Ally."

She grins.

I hold out my arm to Wren. "We've got a drive ahead of us. Ready?"

My girl nods. "Yep."

CHAPTER 33
WREN

I'M FLUSHED AND NERVOUS. Stone's teasing hand on my leg during the drive didn't help matters either. His head kept turning every few minutes with a longing stare, and each time I tried to catch him, his jaw would flex.

"You seem tense," I whisper. I lengthen my spine and hold my chin up high, pretending to be someone we both know I'm not. "Are you sure I look okay?"

He bought the dress for me, something I was—and still am—less than thrilled about. I found the price tag in the bathroom trash. The amount he spent on a stupid dress for his father's birthday party confirms that we are *not* the same.

His teeth snag my ear as he places tender kisses against my jawline. We're outside of his house, and it's bigger than I remember.

"You look *too* good," he says.

I roll my eyes. "Whatever."

I gasp when he grabs my hips and presses me flush with his body. My bare back hits the front of his perfectly fitted tux, and my thighs clench with how hard he is.

"I'm going to fuck you so hard after this."

I'm counting on it.

"And you're keeping the heels on."

I shake my head at his demand and refuse, but we both know that Stone has a way of getting what he wants.

"Ready?" he asks, slipping his hand into mine.

I let him help me up the cobblestone steps like a child. *Why am I so nervous?* I have met his father before. It was a brief introduction. Stone's dad was always in a rush, never having the time for a full conversation with Evan's parents. He was married to his job—something that Stephen mentioned a time or two. He also mentioned that Daniel Foster was one of the top defense lawyers in the United States, and after taking in the pristine entryway of his home, I would guess he is one of the wealthiest too.

"Good evening, Stone." A butler appears out of thin air.

People actually have butlers?

"Hello, Gerald. It's good to see you."

The older man smiles, and I almost trip after seeing Stone return the favor with his own smile.

"Your father's party is out back."

"Thank you."

My heels click against the shiny marble when Stone drags me forward. I'm still in awe over his genuine smile. He doesn't smile nearly enough.

"Wow."

Stone stops, but the closer we get to the party, the more tense he becomes. "What? You've never been to a fancy party before?"

"Well, no. But that's not why I said wow."

His eyebrow rises, and I'm half tempted to run my hand through his gelled-back hair. He is too handsome for his own good.

"I just didn't know you were capable of smiling."

I giggle at his glare, and suddenly, I'm crushed into his chest. His hand cups the side of my cheek, and he smiles again, only this time it's directed at me. It takes my breath away.

"I love it when you laugh."

Butterflies fill me, and I know my cheeks are pink.

"Let's go. The sooner we get through this, the sooner I can strip you out of that dress."

My teeth sink into my bottom lip, and I flush harder, but all thoughts of Stone undressing me leave when we make it through the open archway. It's beyond clear that we had *very* different childhoods.

The backyard is as big as the trailer park I grew up in, but instead of half-broken, flickering street lamps lighting up the area, there are string lights hanging from every tree, casting the prettiest glow over everyone. Waiters come from every direction, holding their shimmery silver trays filled with champagne glasses, bubbling with a golden liquid, and enough food to feed a village.

My jaw unhinges when my head sways to the left and then the right. Although the party takes place in a backyard, it isn't your typical *backyard party*. It's lavishly decorated, dripping with gold and glittering decorations that steal my attention.

I glance down to my dress, and I'm suddenly thankful that Stone made me wear it. We fit right in.

"This is..." My sentence trails off.

"Absolutely ridiculous and over the top?" Stone mumbles.

He places his hand at the small of my back, and I laugh.

"I was going to say extravagant."

"Martha knows no limits when it comes to party plan-ning." He pauses. "Especially when she has my father's Amex." His shoulders bunch up for a moment before his lips flatten. "Speaking of the step-monster..."

"Stone," I warn.

It's hard not to feel slightly resentful with his digs toward his parents. I understand that he didn't have the most loving or attentive father, but what I would have given to grow up with privilege instead of poverty. At least Stone's dad isn't a junkie.

"There you are!" Martha makes a beeline for Stone with open arms and a slightly dazed smile.

Her pretty blue eyes are glossy, and I choke on air when she shoves me into her chest, crushing me with a soul-sucking hug.

Stone grunts with humor. I shoot him a glare, and he rolls his eyes.

"When Stone told me he was bringing his *girlfriend* I almost fell out of my chair."

Stone whispers behind me, and I'm thankful Martha didn't hear. *"It was probably all the cocktails."*

"The party is beautiful," I say, complimenting her. "Stone told me that he wishes you'd throw him a party like this one day."

I smirk.

Stone steals a flute of champagne off a butler's tray and chugs it.

"Oh, I wish he'd let me!" Martha's excitement is obvious with the high-pitched noise she makes. "Oh, just wait! Maybe I'll be planning your wedding one day."

Stone wraps his arm around my waist. "Oh, look, time to go."

He starts to back us away, but Martha's hand falls to my shoulder.

"Wait! Here comes your father. Make sure you tell him happy birthday."

My heart skips a beat, and suddenly, I feel anxious. Stone stiffens, and his arm falls from my hip. He reaches his hand out and shakes his father's. Daniel Foster is just as tall as Stone and just as intimidating too.

"Good to see you, son."

Stone keeps their handshake short. "Happy birthday."

I inhale a short breath and smile. Daniel is clearly unaware that it is impolite not to thank someone who has wished you a happy birthday, but I smile, nonetheless.

"Dad, this is Wren Da—"

Daniel's cheek lifts, and his hands find their way into his pockets. "Wren Davis. Yes, I know who she is."

It didn't sound like a good thing, but I'm used to that.

"Happy birthday, Mr. Foster." I fake a smile and shift closer to Stone. A strange sense of protectiveness flies through me, and just like that, I'm ready to leave.

"Thank you."

He nods, and it's polite, but I'm not fooled by his feigned charisma or handsome face. Daniel Foster isn't a good man.

"Can you excuse us for a moment? I have someone here that wants to chat with Stone."

Stone steps forward. "She can come."

It's painfully obvious that his dad doesn't trust me, and I'd rather not go through the embarrassment of him making up an excuse.

"No, it's okay. I'm going to use the restroom." I smile at Stone, but he can see right through me. "I'll come find you in a few."

I turn and head for the main house.

I don't breathe again until I'm safely tucked inside and directed to the bathroom.

———

I never imagined what Stone's childhood bedroom looked like, but now that I'm standing in the middle of it, it's hard to imagine him growing up here.

There isn't a single thing in this room that tells me it's his other than a photo of him with our high school hockey team celebrating the championship our senior year. I run my finger along intricate markings on the frame before I tiptoe over to the window overlooking the party. It's still in full effect. Ritzy-looking couples are slinging back flutes of champagne and laughing about something other equally ritzy couples have said.

I find Stone's dad immediately. Martha is beside him, doting on him as she straightens his tie. I don't see Stone anywhere.

"Don't you know the upstairs is off limits?"

I smile but keep my back to him. "Is it? I wasn't aware."

The door latch catches my attention, and before I know it, Stone's arms are wrapped around my torso, and his hot breath is on my neck.

"Liar."

I shrug. "I like to break the rules sometimes."

I feel his cheeky grin against my neck, but it disappears quickly. His loud swallow catches my attention, and I crane my neck back to look at him. The only light is from the party down below, but even so, I see that he is on edge.

"What's wrong?" I ask, spinning around in his arms. I trap him with mine around his neck.

His jaw flexes. "I hate it here."

I nod. "I know."

"I'm sorry he was an asshole to you."

I roll my eyes and brush him off. "You think that's bad?" A sarcastic laugh lingers in between us. "My dad is a junkie, and he let his thug friends touch me. Your dad is nothing compared to him, Stone."

His throat moves with a slow swallow as he stares down at me. I push away a strand of his gelled hair as soon as it falls against his forehead.

"You know, I've never fucked a girlfriend in here."

I squint. "That's because you've never had a girlfriend, Stone."

He crushes me to his strong chest. "Until you."

My mouth opens a second before he pounces. Stone's

tongue swipes inside as he deepens the kiss, flinging me backward so fast I crash into the wall beside the window. His hand flies to my neck, and I break our kiss, tipping my head backward.

"Are you asking to fuck me in your childhood bedroom, Stone?"

"I'm not asking."

I shake at the urgency in his tone.

A gasp escapes me when his fingers bite into my thigh, spreading me wide. I hook my leg around his back and wait for him to notice that I'm not wearing any panties. I suck in a breath when his fingers touch me. He pulls back and tightens his grip around my neck, gently pressing his palm against my windpipe.

"Are you trying to kill me?"

My teeth sink into my bottom lip, and I smile. He growls when he plunges his fingers into me. *Fuck.* Stone's eyes roll into the back of his head, but he rips his hand away.

"Hands over your head."

I do as he says because I'm too drunk on lust. The zipper at my back is loud with the tugging. He strips me out of my dress.

"Fuck." He drags his shadowed gaze down my body.

I'm completely naked except for my silver heels. Stone undoes his pants.

"On your knees, Sticks."

I swallow and do as I'm told because I'm pretty sure I want this more than he does.

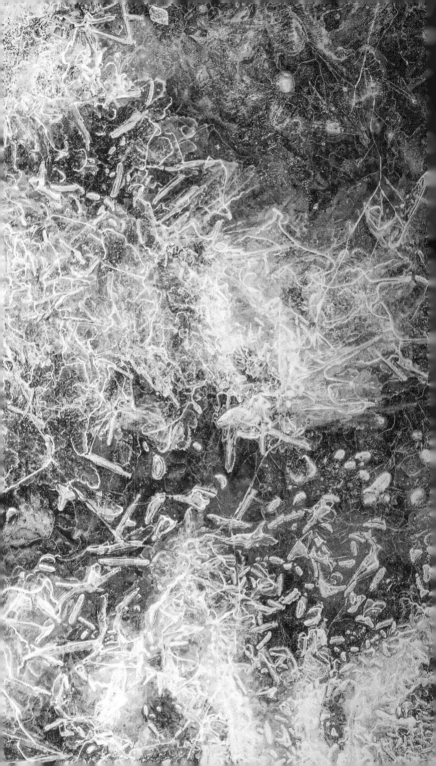

CHAPTER 34
STONE

THE SIGHT of her on her knees in front of me is too much. I run my fingers through her hair, not giving a shit that she spent hours on it. She helps me, pulling out hidden pins until her long, dark hair is loose around her shoulders.

Now she's naked except for those silver heels, as undone as I feel on the inside.

I move both hands through her hair again, tipping her head back, and her eyes flutter. She stares up at me with those big hazel eyes. My heart gives a weird little thump, and I know in my bones I want to do more than just make her choke on my dick.

I want to marry her too.

"Stop looking at me like that." Her voice is husky.

Her gaze drops back to my pants, at the obvious bulge there. Because she could just smirk at me and my body reacts. She undoes my belt. Untucks my shirt, her hands skimming my abdomen for a moment.

I flex for her, smirking at the way the pads of her fingers trip over my abs.

Wordlessly, she unzips my pants and shoves them down.

She frees my cock and grips it immediately, squeezing the base before sliding her hand up.

I groan at the contact.

"Suck me off, Sticks," I order.

She smirks a little, and my dick twitches. As expected.

I don't expect her to blow me without some sass, but her movements seem almost eager as she leans forward and licks me. She takes me in her mouth, and I watch in awe. Her tongue swirls around me, and I groan when the tip touches the back of her throat.

She pulls her lips off me and meets my gaze. Her pupils are dilated, her lips wet.

"Fuck my mouth," she whispers.

I twist her hair in my fingers and drag her back on my dick. She goes willingly, her hands going to my ass and squeezing.

Damn.

I rock my hips forward and slide deeper into her mouth. I'm lost in pleasure, in the noises she makes deep in her throat. And when she gags around me, I get harder.

Abruptly, I pull out. I yank her back to her feet and push her against the wall. She stares up at me until I hoist her up.

"Dig those heels into my ass, baby, because you're in for a ride."

Her mouth pops open. She complies, wrapping her legs around me, and a second later, I'm sliding into her.

"Much better," I murmur, kissing her neck.

"My blowing skills aren't up to your standards?"

"They were too good," I reply. "But I'd rather fill your cunt with cum than your mouth."

She tips her head to the side, giving me more room to mark her. My teeth graze her skin, and I suck on the area. Making sure to leave a hickey that'll stand out like a claiming beacon to anyone and everyone.

"Enjoy this, baby," I say in her ear. "And remember it later tonight."

She inhales. Confused, maybe. It'll make sense when she realizes my true motivation for coming here. And bringing her with me.

But right now, I can't get enough of her. I ram into her hard enough for her body to hit the wall. If there wasn't a party going on, it would be clear from the sound what we're up to. As it is, she's barely containing her moans. She meets my thrusts, our bodies slapping together.

"Touch yourself," I manage. "Come with me."

She wordlessly slips her hand between us. I palm her breast, rolling her nipple in my fingers and pinching it while she brings herself to the edge.

"I'm going to—"

"Good," I growl. My balls are tight, and it only takes her shuddering orgasm contracting around me to trigger mine.

I close my eyes and bury my face in her neck, my movements only slowing as I fill her. And we stay like that for a long moment, her draped around me, until my mind returns.

We just had sex in my childhood bedroom.

The room I lived in up until I left for college.

I set her feet back on the floor and go for the adjoining bathroom. She's still standing there when I approach her with a damp washcloth. I clean up her thighs, but I don't touch her pussy.

"Do me a favor, Sticks?"

She eyes me.

I wipe my dick clean and tuck it away, righting my pants and shirt. It's a lot easier to pull myself together. I barely got undressed.

"Leave me between your legs."

Her mouth opens and closes. Her eyes heat, but she otherwise doesn't say anything.

I turn in a slow circle. "My room used to be a lot more."

Not sure why I'm telling her this.

"What do you mean?"

I clear my throat. "Well, I don't know. It was just…"

After Mom left, I begged Dad to move. There were two options: keep the house like a shrine and remind ourselves every day that she left both of us, or start over again.

Instead, he scrubbed our home free from any trace of her. Leaving it distinctly…antiseptic.

Until the step-monster came along anyway.

But removing Mom from the house meant getting rid of the mural she painted on my wall. And donating the quilt she crocheted for me as a kid. All the pictures, save the one on my dresser, were put in a bin and hidden away in the attic.

All the memories of her are collecting dust.

"Stone," Wren murmurs.

I shake my head. "Sorry. You can stay up here if you want. If you're not enjoying the party. I've just got to talk to my dad."

She twirls her hair around her finger. "Tempting…"

I kiss her. I meant it to be a quick thing, but there's no such thing as *quick* around Wren. I'm sucked in, leaning down into her, as her lips slide against mine. Her tongue skims the seam of my lips, and I open for her. Letting her wind her arms around my neck, pressing her bare breasts to my chest.

She's going to be the death of me.

And I think I love her for it.

———

Now or never.

I finally tore myself away from Wren, promising to be quick. She could hide in my room and then meet me at the car, or we could stay… But staying would lead to more conversations in the morning, and I'm not convinced my dad won't tell me to get out as soon as I broach the subject.

The party's on its last legs. My father is drunk, sitting in his favorite wing-backed chair on the back patio with a glass of whiskey in one hand and a cigar dangling from the fingers of his other. The drink is neat, per usual. Ice is practically sacrilegious.

The chair is normally inside, as it's his favorite. But I guess Martha decided to take all the good indoor furniture outside for this ridiculous party. It kind of gives him a regal appearance.

A king on his throne.

His eyes are tired, tracking his guests as some make their way to the exit. A few men are left, with cigars in their hands, chatting amongst themselves.

"Stone," Dad calls, spotting me. "I thought you had slipped out without saying goodnight."

"I figured we should talk." I take the seat beside him. "Tonight was a whirlwind."

He lifts the cigar to his mouth, sucking in a mouthful of smoke and slowly exhaling it. "Indeed. Martha goes all out. What did you do with that girl of yours?"

"She's upstairs."

"I'm right here." Wren comes around the corner, her hair loose around her shoulders. The dress is back in place, molded to her perfect body.

I drag my gaze away from her tits and lock on her face. She sits on my lap.

I frown. Her weight settles on me, and I automatically put my hand on her bare back. She shivers slightly, goosebumps rising on her skin. I let my thumb trace just under the edge of her dress. I've been touching her all night, but this feels different. A little more dangerous.

This is in front of my father.

"I'm right here," she repeats. "Wren Davis."

Dad purses his lips.

"She was fostered by Evan's parents, Dad." My mouth is dry.

I have no fucking idea how I'm going to ask my questions with Wren on my lap. Because as soon as I start talking, she's going to know I lied to her.

Well.

Omitted.

But it's the same thing, isn't it? At the end of the day…

"Ah, yes. The Mitchells. How is Evan?" Dad's polite, his voice even, but his gaze is not on us anymore. He's checking out of this conversation.

"Maybe in danger, since Wren's dad had guys beat up her social worker and steal the file with his parents' address on it."

Dad's attention flicks back to me. Like a shark scenting blood, his gaze sharpens.

Wren shifts.

"Be honest with me, Dad. How could you represent him?"

She stiffens.

I tighten my grip on her waist, keeping her from bolting. Because I know her as well as I know myself. Maybe even better. And right now, she'd love nothing more than to rush away and get the wrong idea.

Or maybe she'd have the right idea.

"I can't discuss ongoing cases," my father says, waving his hand.

"This is different," I argue. "Wren's life is in danger."

"Stone—" Wren says.

"Quiet," I murmur. To my dad, I continue, "Please. We know you're appealing his conviction. We just need to know if there's a chance of him getting out—"

"Well, it's much too late for that." Dad sighs. He stubs out his cigar and finishes off his drink, then stands. "The appellate court heard our case this week."

I put Wren on her feet and stand too. "And?"

"And…" Dad shrugs. "As of yesterday, Jessie Davis is a free man."

Well…fuck.

And *that's* when Wren bolts.

CHAPTER 35
WREN

MY WORLD STOPS.

As of yesterday, Jessie Davis is a free man.

I'm gone.

I turn, and for someone who rarely wears heels, I make a pretty good escape with them strapped to my ankles.

"Wren!"

Stone's voice booms from behind, but I pick up the pace. I know the streets like the back of my hand. I grew up on them. A tree branch slashes at my bare arm, but I keep running.

My chest heaves, and I feel sick. I wrap my arms around my tight stomach, and my hair sticks to the sweat on my forehead.

The only house I've ever considered a home appears up ahead, but I don't run to it. The last thing I want is for Rebecca and Stephen to see me like this.

I'm a mess. Stricken with fear and weighed down with betrayal.

How dare Stone get me all dazzled up in this stupidly expensive dress, tell me how beautiful I am, drag me to his father's house, and then drop a fucking bomb on me?

The little hut that Evan and I used to hang out in is a

beacon in the night. The slit in my dress parts when I dip down. My knees drag over the damp grass, and I crawl inside to hide.

A sob wants to rip out my body, but I keep that shit under lock and key.

Instead, slow tears drip down my cheeks and land on my pretty dress. They don't stop even when I shut my eyes and rest my head along the splintered wood.

My dad is out of prison. His threat is vastly more dangerous now.

He'll come for me, and I'm going to have to figure out a way to keep him from destroying everything I've worked for.

How could his case get appealed?

Stone Foster's father. That's how.

He is the most successful defense lawyer in the United States, and he's proven to be worthy to a criminal like my father.

The creaking of a stick catches my attention, and I stiffen.

An old beer bottle that Evan and I left behind rolls over crispy leaves, and when Stone's shiny black shoe appears, I build my wall and clamp my lips shut. I wipe my eyes before his face appears in the small opening.

How did he find me?

"Come out."

I don't speak. My silence is an answer in itself.

"Wren. It's cold out. I can see mud covering your heels and knees, so I know you're wet. Let's go."

I'm afraid of what will come out of my mouth if I open it. There's a wedge in my throat that makes it hard to breathe, and I am hardly keeping it together as it is.

"I will drag you out."

Go for it.

His large hand falls to my ankle, and I suck in a breath when he forcefully pulls on my leg. My fingers dig into the soft ground, and I kick him.

He grunts.

"Are you fucking kidding? I know you're mad—"

"Mad?" I shout, coming out the rest of the way. I stand on shaky legs. "I'm more than mad."

I'm *everything*.

The trees sway, and the moon shows through, giving way to the red mark on his jaw. He rubs the spot I kicked and scowls. "Well, you can tell me all about it in the car. Let's go."

I silently refuse, and his jaw tics.

"Do you really think I won't pick you up and carry you to my car, Sticks? Because I will."

I huff because I know he's right. I bump into his shoulder and move past him. Surprisingly, he doesn't touch me, and after I see his car parked near the curb, I fling open the door and settle in the passenger seat.

Filth covers me. The heels are ruined, and my knees are stained with dirt.

"How did you know where I was?"

I feel his stare, but I keep my attention out the window, watching the blurring lights. His car revs, and we speed toward the interstate.

"I always know where you are."

"Evan and I are the only ones who know about it."

Stone shifts and picks up the speed. "You think I didn't watch your every move when we were in high school?"

Whatever.

"I always knew where you were in a crowded room, Sticks. Just like I do now. I know you a lot better than you think."

I glare at his strong profile. His jaw hinges back and forth, and his fingers tighten on the shifter.

"I know how pissed you are about my dad, and I know you're afraid out of your mind because of yours being a free man."

I bite my tongue.

He shifts again, and I fly into the back of the seat.

"I know you just bit your tongue because you hate that I'm right."

He's right. He does know me.

I don't give him the satisfaction of being right, and I refuse to run to him because I'm scared.

The rest of the ride home, I perfect my walls, placing every last brick in place to shut him out.

As soon as the car comes to a stop, I open the door and run inside.

I'm halfway up the stairs when Evan pops up from the couch. "Wren?"

I turn and stare at him over the banister. His brows are furrowed, and he moves his attention from me to Stone. He's casual with his tie loose and his shirt undone.

Fuck him for looking hot.

"What's going on?"

"Did you know too?" My stomach drops when I see the guilt on Evan's face.

Ouch.

"Neither of you talk to me right now."

"What's going on?" Taylor asks. He walks down the hall with a bowl of cereal in his hand.

"Taylor, mind if I stay in your room tonight? I would rather not lie in bed with a liar."

Stone slams the front door, and Taylor makes a quick exit.

"Knock it off, Wren. I get that you're mad, but stop being stupid."

"You know what's stupid?" I seethe. "Thinking that I'd be able to trust you." I shake my head. "I never should have let you in."

"Wren," Evan starts but stops at the sight of my face.

"And you! I expected more from you."

"We were—"

I hold my hand in the air. "Keeping shit from me isn't

protecting me. It's making me ignorant! Were you even going to tell me if I didn't happen to walk in on the conversation?"

"Tell you what?" Evan asks. "Did you tell her that your dad is appealing the case?"

"Appealing?" I laugh. "Try putting that word in the past tense."

Evan's face falls, and Stone pinches the bridge of his nose.

"He's out, Evan."

I turn and rush up the stairs, holding back tears of anger and fear. I gather my blankets and pillow, because I wasn't kidding when I said I wasn't sleeping beside a liar. My entire body is trembling, but I still tiptoe over to the window and glance down into the street.

I wouldn't be surprised if I saw my dad standing on the sidewalk, waiting to welcome me home with open arms.

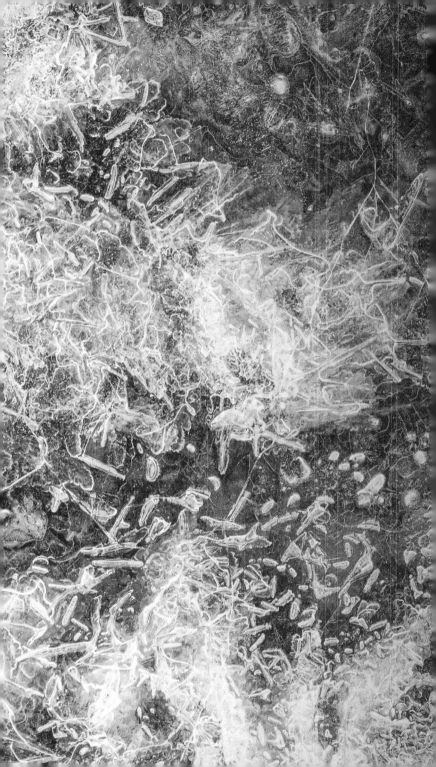

CHAPTER 36
STONE

I THINK I underestimated how long Wren would stay pissed at me.

After she tried to hide—a pathetic attempt if I've ever seen one, in which she gave a startlingly accurate impression of a disgruntled cat, claws and all—she then thought sleeping in the Harry Potter closet was her best option.

Needless to say, that didn't fly.

But it's been five days of *nothing*, and I'm about at my breaking point. She's given me blank stares—if she deigns to look at me at all. Otherwise, she avoids me until she climbs into our bed at night, and then she spends the next hour avoiding my touch.

Like now, she's asleep next to me, so far away her arm is touching the wall. And I'm nearly on the opposite edge, trying to be nice and respect her boundaries.

Sort of.

I heave a sigh, and she responds by elbowing me in the ribs.

"I thought you were sleeping."

"Your silence is so loud it woke me up," she replies.

Ouch.

She pushes the blankets off her legs and shimmies to the end of the bed. I watch her move around the dim room, gathering clothes off the floor and out of her dresser. And I stay where I am as she gets dressed robotically. There's no expression on her face.

As soon as her shoes are on, she's out the door.

The bathroom door closes down the hall with a little *snick*, and I throw my arm over my face for a moment. A moment to allow my frustration to bubble up, to nearly choke me.

But a moment is all I get. On the next inhale, I force myself up and down the hall to Grant's room. I knock twice and enter.

His room is darker than mine, the blackout shades he installed over the windows pulled down into place. He's flopped in the middle of the bed, and there's a girl curled into his side.

Naked.

Lovely.

"Grant," I call.

Nothing. Ah, well, I tried. I grab the glass of water on his nightstand. I don't feel the slightest bit bad for dumping it on his head.

He and the girl both wake up almost instantly. He roars, swinging, and I leap out of range. His soaked hair is plastered to his head, and he looks ridiculous. I burst out laughing before I can stop myself.

"Fuck, Foster," Grant snaps groggily. "What the hell are you doing?"

The girl is barely covering her tits with the sheet. Not that I care for her tits. They're not Wren's, so I ignore her and focus on my housemate.

"Wren's going to class early. You need to go with her."

We stare at each other for a long minute.

"*Fine,*" he grumbles. "Just because you somehow fucked up with her…"

I wave him off. "Better get dressed. Pretty sure the university has some policy about shoes and a shirt."

He waggles his middle finger at me. "Get out."

"Gladly. I'm going back to bed."

That's kind of a lie. I hurry back to bed before Wren gets out of the bathroom, hoping she'll come back in. But she doesn't. She breezes down the stairs, and a second later, Grant's heavier footsteps follow.

Good.

The front door closes, and I'm back out of bed. I get ready for the day and wake Evan up. Luckily, he rolls over as soon as I say his name. No water over the head necessary.

"Is there a reason you're waking me up at the crack of dawn?"

I huff. "It's seven. The sun is up."

Okay, maybe it's six-thirty. And the sun was rising, last I checked…

"Whatever." I kick his leg. "We've got shit to do."

Evan eyes me. But he's a better sport than Grant in more ways than one, and he only takes five minutes to brush his teeth and pull on fresh clothes. He meets me in the kitchen, where I slide him a toasted bagel and the tub of cream cheese.

"Uh-oh. Are you trying to…well, fuck, the butter pun would've worked better if you didn't offer me cream cheese."

"Coffee." I snap my fingers. "That'll make you make sense."

He agrees.

I pour us cups and sit across from him, then take out my phone. I set it down. Pick it up. Set it down again.

"What?" Evan finally asks.

"You talked to your parents, right?"

I mean, it's been five days. I overheard Wren and Ally talking about it at the restaurant in hushed tones, whispering about the worry she has for her foster family.

He nods. "They know about the break-in, that someone has their address. That her dad is out."

Out. That was definitely a bomb my father dropped last weekend. And I didn't even have a chance to prepare Wren. How the hell was I supposed to break that to her, though? And then force her to make small talk with rich strangers until we could interrogate my father?

"I didn't want to have that conversation in front of her," I admit. "And then she was there, and I couldn't stop it."

Evan eyes me. While I've taken the brunt of Wren's cold shoulder, she hasn't been speaking much to any of the guys. Especially Evan.

"Okay, okay." I guess we're going for honesty. Maybe that will make me feel better. "I didn't want to stop him. It was either that or he would've reverted to a wall."

Kind of like how Wren is right now.

I rub my face. "You should've seen the look on her face. And then I dragged her out of that little hut in your parents' backyard…"

He winces.

"I *know.* It was your safe place. And I know you only told me about it because I snuck in there that one time…"

Oh, man, I had never seen Evan so mad. Sputtering, red-faced. He said it was private, which obviously meant it was something between him and Sticks. I kind of hated their relationship when I was fourteen. Everything was changing. We started high school, a new hockey team, Wren was flitting back in and out of the Mitchells' lives. Evan's attention was being pulled away, and selfishly, I just wanted him to be my friend while everything else was rocky.

And she was just so…*irritating.* I couldn't help but watch her. Where she was. What she was doing. All cataloged and filed away for later, like the stupid tree fort that never made it off the ground.

It's *later* now.

I pick up my phone again.

Set it down.

Fuck.

"What?" Evan snatches it up.

"Don't—"

He unlocks it and stares at the screen.

At the app that tracks Wren's phone.

It currently shows her in class, for the record.

"What the fuck, Stone?"

I grind my teeth together.

Evan sighs. "I know you're doing this to protect her, but—"

"There's no but," I snap. "There's no second chance here, man. If her father gets his hands on her, I think that's it. No coming back from it. I just have this feeling he's going to do something terrible to her."

That's my fear realized.

Out loud.

And suddenly I want to take it back. Snatch the words out of the air and stuff them back down my throat, erasing the shocked expression from Evan's face and dulling the spike of adrenaline crashing through my chest.

I don't want to be afraid. It's a stupid, useless emotion.

What I need to do is channel it into something productive —like figuring out where Wren's dad is and what his plans are.

The only problem is, we haven't fucking seen anyone.

"They have to be watching, don't you think?" I glower at my phone in Evan's hand. "They were in her room."

"Well…" He shifts.

"What?"

Guilt crosses his face. "You know me. I'm the first to believe Wren. But she can be a little paranoid, and…"

I narrow my eyes.

"And she accused me of going through her stuff once.

When we were, like, thirteen." He looks away. "I didn't. No one did as far as my parents could tell. But she had a melt-down anyway, insisting that someone had. That they left her an obscure little note in one of her books."

Well...fuck.

"What happened?"

"She showed us the page, and it was nothing. A drawing of a freaking pumpkin in pencil. And not a very good one. If she hadn't said that's what it was, I would've guessed an apple." He sighs. "I just... I'm not sure if she's so wound up, she's more likely to cry wolf."

Interesting.

"Well, there's one way to find out, right?" I shove back from the table and head upstairs.

Evan trails me to my room, and we both stop and stare at the disaster.

"Okay, it's messy," I mumble.

And it's kind of killing me. I like neat and orderly, and ever since Wren moved in, it's been chaos. Wordlessly, I start cleaning. Picking up dirty clothes—hers, mine, doesn't matter—and tossing them in the bigger of the two hampers. I pile up textbooks, trying to keep them separate, on opposite ends of the desk.

"I'm gonna leave you to this," Evan says on a laugh.

I wave him off.

Once the floor is clean, I move to the bed, changing the sheets, acting like an actual human being.

An hour later, my phone chirps that Wren's leaving campus—a feature of the location-sharing app I didn't think I'd need but now insanely appreciate. My room—no, *our* room—is spotless. And all that's left is...

I move to the stack of notebooks and flip through them one by one. Looking for anything that's not Wren's bubbly handwriting.

How girls have such neat, *cute* handwriting is beyond me.

I'm on my fifth notebook when I find it. And my blood runs cold.

Your father says thank you for all of your help, Pumpkin.

"What are you doing?"

I slam the notebook closed just as Wren reaches me. She yanks it out of my hand, tossing it on the floor like it's burning her.

"You can't just go through my stuff," she scolds.

I scoff. "No? Why didn't you tell me about your father's henchman's little note? This could've been helping our case. Instead, you hid it."

She flinches.

I stare at her. Her hair is up in a bun. She's not wearing a speck of makeup. There are dark circles under her eyes, and she's too fucking pale.

"Why are you scared of me, Sticks?" My voice is so low. I don't want to scare her off. I just want her to understand that I am going to do anything and everything to protect her.

How she wormed her way into my heart is a fucking mystery.

Taylor bangs on our open door, popping his head into the room. "Why aren't you ready, Foster? We're leaving for the bus in twenty."

Fuck.

I nod without tearing my gaze away from Wren. We're locked in a staring contest, and I don't know what will happen to the loser.

"Did you not believe me?"

It's my turn to wince. "Sticks..."

"Don't," she whispers. "Don't act like you care when you

thought I was crazy. I knew someone was in my room. And you needed *proof*?"

"No—"

"God, stop *LYING!*"

I jerk back. "I hate you so much it's going to kill me."

"The feeling is mutual," she bites out.

"I know." I stalk forward.

She goes back, bumping up against the wall. Her breathing hitches, and she tilts her head back to keep her gaze on mine. She's so angry she's practically vibrating with it.

"All this fury," I murmur, tracing her jaw. "So fucking beautiful."

She smacks my hand away.

This has gone on for too long. She's been icing me out, but inside she's been burning up.

I grab her wrist and drag her closer until she collides with my chest. "Show me how you really feel, Sticks."

Her fingers curl in my shirt. Instead of shoving me away, she moves her hand up to the back of my neck. Her nails dig into my skin, and she pulls my head down to hers.

Finally.

CHAPTER 37

WREN

I HATE HIM.

I hate him so much, and I think it's because I love him.

"Fucking finally."

His mouth leaves mine for a second, and I grow angrier, so I shush him.

"Don't talk."

My shirt flies off, and he grips my chin fiercely. I know he wants to say something. I can read him like the back of my hand.

Stone and I are always neck and neck.

Insult to insult.

Instead of saying anything, he clams up. He picks me up and throws me on the bed and rips my jeans off in one single whoosh.

"Spread," he demands.

Stone stands over me like a predator with my jeans still in his grasp. He drops them to the floor, and he goes next.

My panties rip, and I want to kick him, but when his hot mouth sucks on my clit, a moan leaves me.

"Fuck."

My orgasm builds quickly. I should be embarrassed at

how needy I am, but I've been giving him the cold shoulder for so long that my body is desperate for anything.

"You can say you hate me, but your cunt doesn't."

Asshole.

He's always right, and it's irritating.

Before I let go and come for him like I know he wants, I scramble away and replace his mouth with my hand.

His lips are glistening from burying his face between my legs, and it's so hot that it forces me to use both hands to work myself like he was.

His eyes narrow, and I tingle. My eyes close with pleasure, and I moan.

I'm coming so hard that I don't realize Stone has pinned my hands above my head with one of his while the other has three fingers inside me. I squeeze and ride his hand.

"I want to tear you to pieces." He bites on my ear lobe.

I spread my legs, and he positions himself.

I'm too turned on to shove him away again.

I've missed him too much, even if I won't admit it.

"Ditto," I reply, spreading myself wider.

He grunts beside my ear.

Oh my God.

I stretch, and our hands are everywhere.

His kisses are hot and sloppy, and when his teeth sink down onto my lip, I taste blood right away.

I lean back, and his face is red with determination. He licks my blood off his mouth and pounds into me even harder.

"You can hate me all you want." He bends down, and his tongue swipes against mine.

I kiss him back and bite his lip the same way he bit mine.

"But this pussy is mine, Sticks."

Another orgasm builds, and I yell out his name. I know the entire house can hear us.

But I don't care.

"Say it." Stone's grip is hard on my face.

My lips form a pout, but he squeezes my cheeks.

"Say it while you show me how much you fucking hate me, baby."

He spins us without breaking stride. I'm on top, and his fingers pinch my waist with delicious pressure.

There's a smack on the door. "Stone, we have to fucking go!"

"Leave without me." His voice is eerily calm, even though he has sweat dripping down his face and a red flush creeping up his neck. "Do what you want with me, Wren. Get that hatred out of your fucking system, because I'm done giving you space."

I move above him and try to focus on my own needs, but instead, I'm moving in the way that I know he likes and letting him touch every inch of my body.

"Fuck," he hisses between his teeth.

I curve my hips, dragging my clit over his dick with the angle.

"You're even more desirable with the look of hatred in your eye."

His abs flex, and we move in sync. He thrusts into me as I come down on him.

"I love it when you hate me."

I don't hate him.

I wish I did, but I don't.

That's why I've pulled away all week. I'm not angry. I'm hurt.

I whimper when he pinches my nipple. I throw my head back when another wave of pleasure works down my spine.

Stone stills beneath me, and hot pressure fills me at the same time that he kisses me feverishly, like he's afraid it's the last time.

"Stone! You have one fucking minute, and you're driving yourself."

"Fucking hell," he says against my mouth. He shoots an angry gaze at our bedroom door.

I try to climb off him, but he doesn't let me. His palms clamp to my hips, and he keeps me still.

"What are you doing?" I'm out of breath, so it comes out as a whisper.

"Waiting."

"For what?" I try to get up again.

He's going to be late.

I have never seen him look so sincere. His hardened gaze is nowhere to be found, and instead, his blue eyes are pleading.

"For you to stop hating me."

I suck in my lip, and he finally lets me go this time. I stand on shaky legs and wrap the blanket around me and watch him hastily move around the room to get dressed. His bag is slung over his shoulder, and his tie is loose around his neck. My heart pounds harder with each second that goes by.

"I don't hate you." I glance away. "But I wish I did."

My chest squeezes. I stomp my foot and clench my teeth. I pull the blanket tighter around my body.

His finger is soft when it lands on my cheek. My blurry eyes betray me, and a tear slips down, but Stone swipes it away before it has a chance to fall to the floor.

"I don't hate you either," he says, bouncing his gaze back and forth between mine.

"I'm still mad at you," I say.

"I don't care," he replies.

"Stone! Let's fucking go."

He doesn't even glance at the door.

"You hurt me." I push at his chest. He can't be late for the bus. His coach will murder him.

"I'm sorry." He looks away.

"Go." I nod toward the door.

"I can't."

My brows furrow.

His blue eyes snap to mine, like something just clicked into place. He grips my blanket and cups my cheek.

"I can't go without telling you that I love you."

My world stops.

My heart skips a beat.

I want to bang my fists on his chest and say, *How dare you love me!*

Because I love him too, and all love does is make you vulnerable.

But sure enough, I reach up on my tiptoes and whisper against his mouth, "I love you too."

He kisses me, but the door flies open and interrupts us a second later. Taylor is standing in the doorway, and he's furious.

"Oh my God. We're all just fucking *elated* that you two have made up, but we can celebrate later. We're going to be late!"

Stone grimaces.

I smile. "Good luck, boys."

Stone makes it halfway down the hall. "Ally will be here in ten minutes. I'll see you in the stands, baby."

My jaw drops. "What?"

He chuckles along with the rest of our housemates. "As if we'd let you stay here alone."

The front door latches, and I rush over to the bedroom window and pry it open. All their heads swivel to me.

"I have homework!" I shout. "And a huge chemistry test! I can't come to the game!"

"Study on the way!" Evan yells.

He's such a traitor.

Archer nods. "It's not safe for you to be alone."

Stone angles his chiseled jaw in my direction. "Do it in the stands, Sticks. Or do it on the way. Either way, your ass better be there."

I shove the window shut, and they haul ass down the road.

A Taylor Swift song catches my attention, and I know that it's Ally.

There's a defiant part of me that wants to stay home, just to irritate Stone. But at the end of the day, it really isn't safe.

My father could be anywhere, and chances are, he's closer than I think.

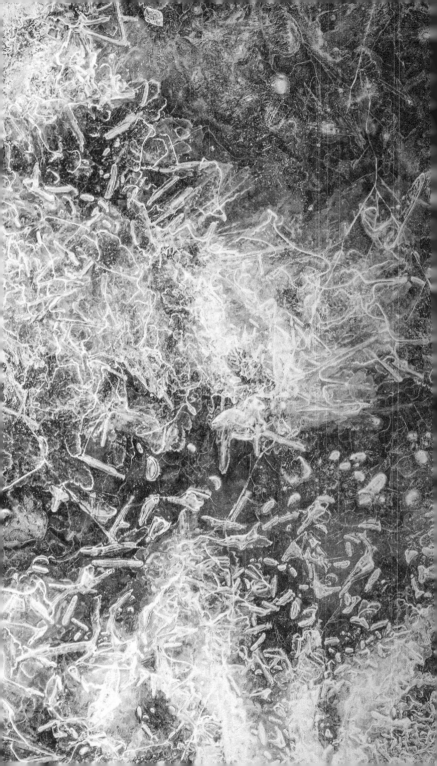

CHAPTER 38
STONE

I TOLD her I loved her, and then I fucking bailed. After *hate sex*, no less. But she said it back. And it wasn't really hate sex in the end, was it? Just…angry sex.

Because she loves me too.

I turn over her words the whole bus ride to Crown Point. While Shadow Valley has played here before, I haven't. There's a strong rivalry between the two schools, which are only a few hours apart. The tension on the bus seems to ramp up the closer we get.

Music—currently "Kryptonite" by Three Doors Down, a fucking masterpiece and somewhat ironic given Wren's status as my kryptonite—blasts in my ears. Music is how I've always mentally slipped into the zone for hockey, but now…

Well, all thoughts point to Wren Davis.

I pick at a loose thread on the seat next to me. Over the music, the guys' booming conversation filters in. They're discussing plays, girls, the latest NHL games.

Funny how I've been here for only a few short months, and these guys are more like family than my old team ever was.

And with a ride to the New York Guardians sitting in my back pocket, I can't help but feel like this is a time to savor.

Evan drops into the seat beside me and plucks out my earbud. "Hey."

"What's up?"

"You're rich enough to afford your own place."

I eye him. "Is that so?"

"With the trust fund and hockey contract and all."

I snort.

"What I'm saying is, having screaming sex with my sister at all hours of the day—"

"That was a one-off." I wave him away.

"Well, maybe you should consider getting a space for yourselves. Just the two of you." His face is red, and he rubs the back of his neck. "The guys and I took a little vote—"

"Oh, for fuck's sake."

"We're not kicking you out immediately. Just, you know, when this shit with Wren's dad gets resolved and things settle down a bit."

I consider that. Wren and me in a space of our own, like a one-bedroom apartment that we can make a home. It's a good idea. And it dawns on me that she's never really had a place that was truly hers. The hockey house is a shared space—even the bedroom, we go back and forth over who puts shit where—and before that, Evan's house.

She didn't sleep when she was at home with her dad. Didn't eat either. That couldn't have been considered a home.

So the idea of giving her that, of letting her decorate a whole apartment and doing anything to make her smile—and fucking her on every surface, in every room—lifts a little weight off my shoulders.

I want that. And I wouldn't have thought of it with-outEvan.

I slap his shoulder. "You're totally right."

He grins. "Yeah. Okay, good."

When he returns to his seat, I slip my earbuds back in and restart the music. This time, "All Apologies" by Nirvana. I close my eyes and try to recenter myself on the upcoming game. We reviewed tapes of CPU earlier this week, and I know what to watch for. I know that Steele O'Brien is an asshole of a D-man, and Greyson Devereux can skate circles around half the guys on our team. And their goalie, Miles Whiteshaw, is quick.

But there are ways to beat them and cracks in their defense, and I plan on exploiting that to the best of my abilities.

The bus rumbles to a stop. We all take a few minutes to straighten our nice outfits, fix our ties, and then we're off, grabbing our bags from under the bus and heading into the arena.

The hairs on the back of my neck rise, and I glance around. There's not much here—a half-empty parking lot with a backdrop of tree-covered mountains. Not much else besides our managers unloading from the bus.

Taylor claps me on the back. "You good?"

"Peachy," I reply.

I shake it off and follow him inside. Coach gives us the rundown, then basically says we're on our own for the next hour. I pull out my phone and call Wren.

"Hello?" Her voice is breathy and hesitant.

"Are you on your way?"

"With Ally," she replies.

"Okay, good." I swallow. "Yeah. I just wanted to make sure."

"Are you regretting what you said?"

I scowl. "Not in the slightest. Are…are you?"

"No." She lets out a laugh. "And now Ally is looking at me like I've stabbed her in the back."

"Well, I'll let you explain to her that you're hopelessly in love with me." Holy shit, I'm *teasing* her about this. Love always felt like one of those untouchable subjects. And here I am, poking fun at Wren.

But then again, when *don't* Wren and I poke fun at each other?

"You said it first," she mumbles.

"Oh my God," Ally yells in the background. "You said it?"

I laugh. "Bye, baby. Text me when you're here."

Evan and Grant sit across from me, and they trade a look.

Then Grant says, "Okay, so...you made up?"

I smirk. "Yeah."

"Great," Evan mutters. "More sex."

"The reprieve was kind of nice," Grant agrees.

I pick up a pad and chuck it at them. "Shut up, you assholes."

My phone goes off. I glance at it, and my blood runs cold. I try to hide my expression, running my hand over my mouth. When I glance up, Evan and Grant have switched their attention to Archer, who's doing some funky stretching in the corner.

I stand quickly and step past them. They don't question where I'm going, although I make a vague motion at my phone anyway.

There are other Knights in the hallway, kicking a soccer ball around. They call to me, but I shake my head and lift my phone again.

Sweat pricks at the back of my neck.

I shove out the heavy metal doors and exit onto the sidewalk, taking a deep breath. Then I scan the text on my phone again.

STEP-MONSTER

Your dad is in the hospital. Please call me.

My chest is tight. I brace my hand on the wall as the ground tilts. It must be serious—Martha never sends a text without an exclamation point. And there's no trying to ease the blow.

Simple, straight to the point.

Stupid.

I grip my phone tighter. Do I just leave? I'm hours away—

"Hello, Stone."

I straighten and spin around.

A man stands in front of me. He's got a black coat on over jeans and a black knit cap over dark, kind of longish hair. He's about my height. Thick, although it's hard to tell if it's muscle or fat. He's vaguely familiar. Something about the shape of his face...

He smiles. "I need you to come with me."

I start. "No—my dad—"

"Your father is fine." He holds up a phone. "Easy to clone a number nowadays. Technology at its finest. My name is Jessie Davis. And I know... I didn't expect to be meeting my pumpkin's first love this way either."

His gaze flicks over my shoulder, and he nods slightly.

My reaction time is pretty good. But even I'm not quick enough to dodge the blow that comes from the man behind me.

Pain bursts across my head, and my vision goes dark.

The last thing I remember is hands grabbing me before I hit the pavement.

CHAPTER 39
WREN

I SLAM my notebook closed and settle into the passenger seat. "Done."

Ally takes her eyes off the road for a second. "Wren. You're a freaking brainiac."

My face falls. "What? No, I'm not."

She focuses on the school's parking lot. It's busy, and there are people tailgating next to their vehicles, downing beer out of funnels like they're only there to party.

"Those were no ordinary equations. You just made whatever the hell math that was seem like second-grade addition problems."

I don't bother correcting her to tell her that I was actually working on chemistry and not math, because to the normal eye, it is all the same.

"Where did you get your brains from? What do your parents do?"

My body heats, and the quick memory of my mother fades. It's sad that the only one I have of her is one with a needle hanging from her arm. "Well…" I shift in my seat and watch Ally park. "My mom isn't in the picture anymore." I decide to leave that up to her imagination. It's less awkward

312 S. MASSERY & S.J. SYLVIS

that way. "And my dad…" I think about how to say it deli-
cately. "Let's just say he used his brains for the wrong
reasons."

Jessie Davis is actually a highly intelligent man. I got my
love for chemistry from him. We are both impeccable when it
comes to working out equations, and he taught me everything I know.

Except right from wrong.

That, he wasn't so good at.

"What do you mean?" Ally turns to me.

I nibble on my lip. I have no idea how to dig myself out of
the hole. "He's a convicted felon," I blurt. "Makes meth for a
living."

Silence fills the car, all except Taylor Swift singing about
being a vigilante, which is honestly quite fitting.

Ally's laughter fills the awkward space.

I turn to her and smile hesitantly. "Um…" *Why is she
laughing?*

"I'm sorry!" she sputters. Her attempt to collect herself
fails. "It's just…" More laughter. "I thought I was the only
one who had a fucked-up childhood."

I snort. "Fucked up is putting it mildly."

Considering Jessie Davis is a free man and is likely on his
way to me so I can make him that *good* shit. No one made
meth like I did—which is not something I'm proud of, nor do
I plan to tell Ally.

"Let's go," Ally says, finally ending her laughter.

I don't ask about her childhood, because if she wanted me
to know, she'd tell me. I am well-versed in keeping secrets—
especially if they're painful.

Ally and I find our seats right before the game starts.
We're not far from center ice, and I eye the Knights' side
down below. I watch for Stone because he's all I have eyes for.

I told him I loved him.

And I don't regret it.

"There they are."

I follow Ally's line of sight and watch our team fly into the rink. The crowd goes wild, and I find myself cheering too.

I see Evan first.

Then Archer.

Taylor is next.

I quickly dart down the line and back before grabbing my phone.

My brows pinch. Stone always sends me one last text before the game. Sometimes it's a dirty text, and sometimes it's a *I'll score one for you, baby* text.

I have none.

"Where is Stone?" I whisper.

Ally doesn't hear me. She's too busy clapping and yelling for the team.

The buzzer is about to sound, and I panic.

Relax. He's fine.

Evan's head is tilting in my direction, and I swear, time stops. He whips his helmet off and mouths, "Where is Stone?"

My stomach empties.

How would I know where Stone is?

Better question, why isn't he on the ice with his teammates?

I don't say anything to Ally when I turn and edge my way down the aisle. My feet hit the cement stairs, and I jog up them like I know where I'm going.

It's deserted out in the lobby area, a few lines of fans getting last-minute beer and popcorn, but I can see the hall that leads to the locker rooms.

I ignore the sign that says *Keep Out* and put one foot in front of the other. My fingers fly over my phone, and I pray he answers.

Knowing Stone, he probably did this on purpose. A way

to lure me to the locker room for a quickie before taking the ice.

Ugh, answer the phone.

My chest gets tighter, and my heartbeat is deafening.

I pause when the ringing stops halfway through. "Stone Foster," I reprimand. "Where the hell—"

"Hi, Pumpkin. It's so nice of you to finally call me back."

The hallway narrows.

Words are nonexistent, but I move into action right away, flinging myself out a door that says *Emergency Exit Only*.

The last thing I need is Ally following me.

"Where is Stone?" My voice is calm, but I feel the complete opposite on the inside. There's chaos. So much chaos.

"Waiting for you."

I turn at the sound of my deranged father's voice and lower the phone. He mimics me and does the same. The only difference between us is that he is wearing a sinister smile, and I'm hardly keeping my shit together.

I'm afraid.

I feel sick.

But most of all, I'm desperate.

"Where is he?"

My father's head tilts as he draws closer. "That's not the Wrenny-girl I know, showing all her worries firsthand." He tsks and reaches out to tuck my hair behind my ear. "Seems you need a wake-up call."

My chin is stern when I move away. "Nothing is more of a wake-up call than you kidnapping my boyfriend."

He can tell by the sound of my voice that I'm willing to do anything he wants in order to get Stone back.

That's why I don't run.

I'm not running anywhere unless it's into Stone's arms.

"Where is he, Jessie?"

His lips flatten. "Jessie? You're refusing to call me Dad now?"

Anger surges, and I want to kill him. My hands shake, and my legs are wobbly. I'm both angry and afraid, and it's an unsettling feeling.

Fuck, where is Stone?

"Where is he?" I ask again.

A pleased smile creeps onto his sunken face, and I instantly feel like a child again, fearful for what version of him I'm about to see.

"Why don't we take a ride, Pumpkin."

There is no use in refusing.

Omar is off to the left, resting his shoulder along a tree with his gun tucked into the back of his pants, and Kerrigan is prowling the perimeter with his ravenous eye creeping in my direction.

Vomit hits the back of my throat when I look at his hands. I remember the way they felt like it was yesterday.

"Okay," I say. My dad jerks me toward a van, and I stumble over my own feet.

I'm not as afraid as I should be.

But that's only because I know I'm headed toward Stone, and one way or another, I'm getting us out of there.

This entire time, he thought he needed to protect me. But it turns out, I'm the one who has to protect him.

CHAPTER 40
STONE

IT'S GOING *to be okay.*
   It's going to be okay.
   It's going to be okay.
   I resurface slowly. Kind of like swimming up from a great depth. My head throbs, but I crack my eyes open without moving the rest of my body.
   Survival instinct maybe?
   "It's going to be okay."
   I blink rapidly, focusing on the girl a mere ten feet from me. Her attention is on the glass beakers in front of her, a counter full of equipment I don't understand. She's wearing one of those white lab coats and plastic glasses. But even obscured, it's obviously Wren.
   And she's talking to herself. Over and over, saying, "It's going to be okay."
   I lick my lips. My mouth is dry. The base of my skull feels like there's a knife in it, scraping away at my brain. But before I call out to her, I take stock of the rest of myself. My hands are hung over my head, my wrists taped together and attached to a pipe. I'm sitting on an ugly, tiled floor.
   There's a sink directly to my left, and a toilet on my right.

I'm wedged between the two, the bathroom door wide open and giving me a view of the rest of the small place. A trailer, maybe? Judging from the size, a double-wide.

I shift my weight and wince at the ache. My muscles fucking kill, but my head is the worst.

I test the tape, but it holds fast. The pipe groans, though, and Wren's head snaps in my direction.

"Stone," she whispers.

It feels loud in this otherwise silent space.

"Are you okay?" I ask. "Did he—?"

Her eyes fill with tears, but she shakes her head quickly.

I sag against the wall. *Good.* If he had touched her, I would kill him. No contest. No hesitation. I glance around the tiny bathroom, but there's not even a window in here.

"I'm sorry," Wren continues. "I'm going to fix this. I'm going to—"

"Now, now." Her father steps into the trailer. "Are you making promises you know you won't be able to keep?"

A chill sweeps down my spine.

She stiffens, turning sharply away from me and back to the chemicals at hand.

Meth. Fuck. It dawns on me that she cooked for him, and that's what she's doing now.

She's trembling, holding onto the counter, as he steps into her space and runs his knuckles down her cheek.

And I lose it.

"Get your hands off her!" I yank on my arms to no avail.

Her father chuckles, moving past Wren and entering the bathroom. He pulls a gun from the waistband of his jeans and shoves the barrel against my stomach. I go completely still. But I still give him my best withering glare.

He chuckles. "Awful way to die. Shot in the stomach. All those nasty acids and bile mixing up in your abdomen. The pain...and the blood." He digs the gun in harder. "Don't tempt me, boy."

Fuck.

After a long moment, he rises and heads back toward Wren. She's stopped what she's doing and faces us. Her skin is nearly the same color as her white coat.

Her dad smiles. "You know, I had planned to take your foster brother. You loved him, so it seemed like the best course of action to use him to make you comply."

Another man enters the trailer. A bigger guy—maybe the one who knocked me out, I don't know. Either way, Wren's posture turns defensive. Her shoulders hunch, and she sidles closer to the counter. Her fingers wrap around the neck of one of the beakers.

"Get him up," Wren's dad orders.

The big guy comes for me, a knife suddenly in his fist. He reaches over my body and slices through the tape, then hauls me up. My legs are fucking jelly, my vision spotting white. He gets me in front of him, my arms behind my back in his vise grip.

Jessie stops in front of me.

"Wrenny," he calls. "Are you going to stand there all day or fucking *make something*?"

His fist smashes into my jaw. My head whips to the side, and I would've fallen if the guy behind me didn't keep me upright. He lands another punch to my gut, knocking the wind out of me. I gasp, bending forward, and he grips the top of my head by my hair. He pulls my face up, stepping out of the way so I can see Wren.

She's a shaking mess.

But I'm okay.

I'm wheezing, and there's blood in my mouth, but I'm *okay*. And I try to will that toward her, so she knows. Those hazel eyes of hers are going distant.

"I'll do it," she whispers. "I just—"

"Just nothing," her dad spits. "Every moment of inaction gets taken out on your precious boyfriend."

I grit my teeth.

The big guy drags me back into the bathroom. Jessie tosses him the tape, and he re-secures me to the pipe.

"Get to work." Jessie leaves.

The bigger guy stops just behind Wren, and he fucking sniffs the top of her head.

"Don't fucking touch her," I growl.

He laughs. "Or what? You'll come over here and stop me?"

"Kerrigan!" Jessie hollers from outside.

I note his name. And the shiver of disgust that rolls down Wren's back once he finally moves off. Without a doubt, I imagine he was the source of some of her nightmares.

The thought kills me. Because after this, how could she not go down that path again? How will the nightmares ever let her go?

There's only one way this can end—and it has to be with Jessie Davis's death.

———

I watch Wren make meth.

She does calculations in her head and carefully pours and mixes under a giant glass hood that I hadn't really registered until now. But it comes down around the counter, protecting her—and I suppose me—from the fumes.

"Wren," I whisper. My throat hurts.

She ignores me.

"*Wren*," I try again.

Her head snaps toward me. "Shut up, Stone."

I press my lips together.

For the past hour, her father or one of his goonies has periodically come in to check on Wren's progress. When the big guy Kerrigan enters, Wren freezes up. And after he goes, she dashes away tears.

While I just clench my jaw and stay silent.

They're smoking outside, the trailer door left open.

"It's going to be okay," she whispers.

Again. Like some sort of comfort—except, now I think she means it solely for me.

"I'm going to save you, Stone."

"Don't do anything stupid, baby."

She ignores me.

I turn my attention back to my wrists. They're raw, but I keep picking at the tape, trying to unravel it or at least rip it. I lean up and bite it, and it *finally* tears a bit.

Just as Jessie Davis returns.

"Are you being a good girl, Pumpkin?"

I hate his fucking voice.

Wren clears her throat. "It's almost done. Do you want to see?"

He steps in closer. She pours something into a beaker and quickly steps away. One foot, then two. She glances at me and mouths, "I'm sorry."

Why?

Too late, I know my answer. Jessie yells, the beaker smoking—and then it explodes.

A wall of fiery heat blasts outward, knocking Jessie and Wren against the far wall. My head ricochets off the tiles. The walls of the trailer tremble from the force, and the smell of smoke reaches me first.

The trailer is on fire. It's caught on the walls, climbing toward the ceiling.

I ignore the wetness on the back of my neck and lean up, biting and tearing through the tape. I get out of it and rush into the room. The air is thick, hot and smoky. I choke, pulling my sweatshirt up over my nose and mouth, and find Wren on the floor.

She's not moving.

My heart stops. But my feet don't. I stumble-run to her,

staying under the heaviest of the smoke. I drop to her side and brush her hair back. My hand comes away wet with blood.

Her dad lies a few feet away, in a similar state. Except, burns blacken the front of his shirt.

Ignoring him, I haul Wren into my arms and hurtle toward the open door. The floor tilts, and I lose my balance on the stairs.

We hit the ground hard. I roll just as hands grab for me and Wren. My foot kicks out on reflex, nailing Kerrigan in the balls.

Good.

He doubles over, gritting his teeth and curling his hand in the front of my sweatshirt.

My ears are ringing, and even as the asshole's mouth starts moving, I can't hear shit.

His head lifts. Something in the distance has caught his attention—but it doesn't last. Suddenly, he's focused back on me, and a sneer creeps across his face.

The first sound to filter in is the sirens.

And then his voice as he says, "Wren belongs with us."

The glint of the knife in his hand—the one that he used to slice through the tape earlier—now draws my focus. Almost in slow motion, he slides it into my stomach.

But the pain...that's delayed.

"What are you doing?" a voice shouts. "We need to get the fuck out..."

Kerrigan rips the knife from my stomach. That's when the agony lances through my abdomen. He rises and hurries away with the other guy.

I press my hand to my stomach, letting out a hiss of breath, and roll onto my hands and knees. I crawl toward Wren's prone form. She's lying on her side where she fell.

The blue and red lights from the cop cars flash across the house, followed by a fire truck and ambulance.

"Wake up, baby." My arms are shaking too badly. I fall to my side behind her, dragging her limp body against mine.

If she's dead, I don't know what I will do.

Tears fill my eyes. "Wake up, Wren."

I can't keep up with the pain. My head. My stomach. I hold onto her shirt. But I can't hold onto consciousness.

CHAPTER 41
WREN

EVERYTHING HURTS.

Especially my head when I think too hard about the beeping noise in the background.

I think of Stone.

Beep.

I think of my father.

Beep.

I think of Kerrigan and his disgusting sniffs.

Beep.

I think of the equations I did and what happened after.

My eyes open, and I blink rapidly, trying to adjust to the stark whiteness of the room. Mouthfuls of air do nothing to relax my lungs as they scream in agony with anxiety.

It's going to be okay.

"Oh! You're awake." A pretty nurse flies in the room in blue scrubs.

I squint, trying to piece together how I got here.

My head cranes to the IV pole near my bed, and I follow the clear tube all the way to the crook of my elbow.

"Where—" My voice is more of a creak. "Where is Stone?" Pain scratches at my throat, and I don't sound like myself.

Her nose scrunches, even though she's busying herself with the bag of liquid draining into my arm. "I'm sorry, sweetie. I can't give you any information on anyone who isn't a family member."

That's absurd.

I want to yell at her and plead my case on why I deserve to know where he is, or if he's okay, but I'm too afraid I'll taste blood in my throat.

"Is he okay?" I whisper, refusing to give up.

There's a knock on the door, and I sit up, wincing at the pain radiating through my skull.

"Can we have a minute?" A man wearing a shiny badge with a gun strapped to his side slips in the room.

The nurse nods once before checking my IV site.

Her whisper is hardly audible, but I hear her.

"He's in surgery."

Surgery?

The beeping ramps up, causing the law enforcement to shift his attention to the heart monitor.

"Hey, it's okay." He tries to reassure me and takes a seat in the only available chair. "You're not in trouble."

The nurse pats my leg gently and scurries away. He clears his throat, then dives headfirst into the last few hours.

I appreciate it, though.

The sooner he leaves, the sooner I can find Stone.

"Wren Davis," he announces.

I nod slowly, knowing my head will scream if I move too quickly.

"Jessie Davis's daughter."

I hate the sound of that.

"I think we've pieced together what happened, but if at any time I'm wrong, I need you to correct me. Okay?"

I barely manage a nod.

His brow furrows, and he rubs his hand over his five o'clock shadow.

"Before you start," I rasp. "I need to know if he's dead."

His lips flatten, like he's hesitant to tell me. I keep my mouth shut, but what he doesn't understand is that I *want* Jessie Davis dead, even if he is my father.

There is no way I'll ever feel safe again if he's still alive and roaming the streets.

"Your father is dead. Yes."

I sigh, and my heart rate slows—something he notices.

"And you are pardoned due to self-defense." He pauses. "It was self-defense, correct? I can't honestly think you willingly went to that trailer with those men."

A tear slips down my cheek, completely uninvited.

It's going to be okay.

"He didn't give me a choice."

He had Stone.

I stay quiet for the remainder of our conversation. I'm hardly present. I don't jump for glee when he informs me that my father's junkie right-hand men were caught and arrested, and I don't mention how Kerrigan is a borderline pedophile —known from experience.

I just want him gone.

As soon as he leaves the room, making sure to tell me how my act of self-defense was one that will be spoken of for decades, I slide out of bed.

Black dots dance in my vision, but I rip the heart monitor off my finger and grab onto the shiny IV pole, trailing it behind me like a shadow.

Stone.

It's a one-track thought.

My body hurts.

My pulse races with fear.

Surgery for what?

He's alive, but how serious is it?

I drag a breath out of my tight lungs and peek around the corner, making sure the police officer is out of sight.

The hallway is desolate, so I wind farther down, taking baby steps so I don't fall over and blow my cover.

I feel a cough coming, and I know it's going to hurt, so I wince before I let it out. The smell of smoke fills my senses, and I realize that I probably inhaled it when the blast occurred.

Jessie Davis is a fool for trusting me, and he's an even bigger fool for underestimating my knowledge of chemicals and their reactions.

I cough again, and this time, I have to put my hand on the wall to steady myself.

Shit, I probably have injuries.

I didn't think to assess myself before climbing out of bed in search of Stone—something he would absolutely lose his mind over.

I keep moving anyway.

My skull throbs with each slow step, and my throat is even more raw than it was when I first woke up.

"Where are you?" I ignore the tear falling over my cheek. *Fuck, where is he?*

I don't know how I'll survive if he doesn't make it. The thought is too much to handle, and the fear is unbearable.

I place my hand on the wall again.

There's a faint voice that catches my attention, and I turn toward it and take off at full speed with my pole in tow.

"What do you mean she woke up and now you can't find her?"

The nurse is standing in front of Evan, who is red-faced and beady-eyed. His hair is standing up in a million different directions, and I know it's because he has pulled on the ends of it out of frustration.

"Evander," I croak.

He doesn't hear me, but Archer starts running full speed.

"What the fuck are you doing?"

"Where is he?" I cry, clinging onto his shirt. My fingers bundle in the material, and I take a minute to read the scene.

They're all here. Every one of my housemates.

And they all look like they came straight here after the game, wearing the suits they traveled in.

"Stone," I demand, bringing everyone's attention to me.

Evan takes me from Archer's grasp, and the nurse is guiding us toward a chair.

"You weren't supposed to come down to the surgery hall!" She is flustered and checking my pulse and eye dilation.

"Is he going to be okay?" My chin is quivering.

Evan stares at it but then shuts his eyes.

My head is buried in his chest a breath later, and he kisses my temple softly. "I don't know, sis. I don't know."

An earth-shattering cry scrapes against my raw throat, and I shut out the pained faces of everyone staring at me.

I don't stop myself from yelling out his name, even if it comes out as a broken whisper.

Stone may not hear me, but I know he'll feel me.

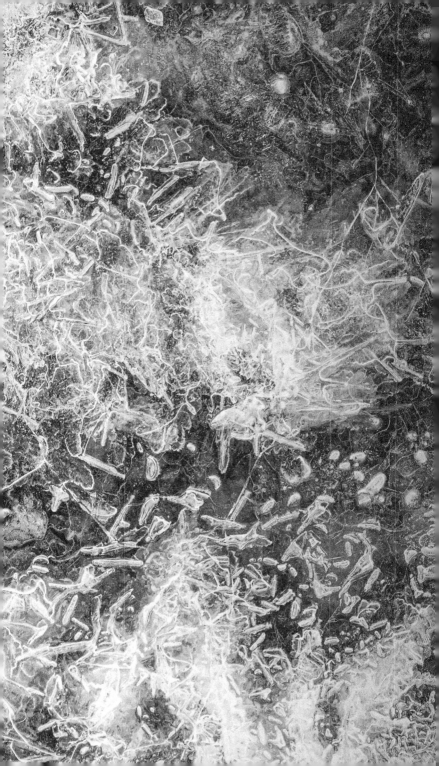

CHAPTER 42
STONE

"HERE WE ARE." I park the car at the curb and glance over at Wren.

She's pale, with dark circles under her eyes, and I fear we're a matching pair in that regard. Neither of us have gotten out in the sunshine lately, and we're running on a major lack of sleep. But she nods slowly and climbs out of the car, keeping her hand pressed to her ribs.

I meet her on the sidewalk, and together, we start up the walkway to the small house. The owners keep the yard neatly maintained, with cleaned-out flower boxes in the front windows and two rocking chairs on the porch.

When I pull out a key and unlock the front door, Wren's brows furrow. She follows me without comment, until we're standing in the empty living room. Or what I imagine will eventually be the living room.

"I'm not sure I understand…"

I take her hand.

"Waking up in the hospital to you lying next to me—" I swallow. The memory is still fresh, as the last thing I remembered prior to that was passing out with Wren's unconscious body in my arms. And then to have her next to me in the hospital bed... I didn't have a chance to question if she was okay. She was already waiting for me. "It meant a lot, Wren."

She squeezes my fingers.

"Anyway. It's about time the guys stopped eavesdropping on our loud sex, right?"

It's supposed to make her laugh. She cracks a smile, which I settle for, and I wave my hand at the space.

"This is for us," I say.

Silence. She seems to be processing it. Blinking and staring at me.

Then, "Wait..."

It's been a week since I got out of the hospital. Wren was discharged the day after we were brought in, but I was kept for a few days under observation. Turns out the knife nicked my intestines, so surgery was required. It was a lot of medical terms I didn't quite understand, but the short story of it is that I'll recover just fine.

Except for the bruises across my stomach and the surgical scar, and the concussion from being hit in the back of the head —along with a goose egg—I'm okay. The headaches are slowly going away, and Coach said I'd be cleared to play after the holidays.

Since we got the news that Wren's dad died... I don't know. I guess I was combating my own guilt and trying to fend off hers. After all, it was both of our actions that led to his death.

"Stop that," Wren murmurs. She touches my face. "Come back to me."

I blink.

"You had that haunted look in your eye again."

I turn my head and kiss her palm. "I just want this to be good."

"It *is* good. It's more than..."

I shoo her away. "Go explore."

She shakes her head and steps back, staring at me for a long moment before going to check out the rest of the house.

I let out a slow breath. Midterms are next week and then Thanksgiving break. After that, we've got a quick few weeks until winter break. And I don't know about her, but I'm ready to get out of Shadow Valley for a few weeks.

"How are we going to afford this?" Wren finally asks, returning to my side. "I mean… Don't get me wrong, I love it. But isn't it bigger than what we need?"

I shrug. "We need to have a space for Evan to come to dinner, and his parents might want to stay if they come to visit. Better here than the hockey house. Besides, I want a space just for us. For *you*."

She blinks rapidly. "Oh."

A lump forms in my throat. "Baby," I whisper. "You've never had a place to make your own. You had your dad's house, and you lived with the Mitchells. Even the hockey house, as much as I love the guys, wasn't really ours. But this whole space *is*. I want you to experience that."

With a little nudge from Evan. But he was right.

And watching her look around again, this time with a more analytical expression, has my heart thumping harder against my ribs.

"Our space," she repeats.

"Exactly."

I get a true smile from her now. The darkness that's been lingering lifts, and she jumps into my arms. I catch her automatically, swinging her around with a burst of laughter.

"Thank you," she whispers in my ear. "I love you."

"I love you too." I carry her through the living room and into the kitchen, setting her ass on the edge of the counter. I trail my fingers down her sides to the waistband of her leggings. "Let me show you how much…"

EPILOGUE

WREN

I SIT in the stands and wait for his text, like always.

It's been more than enough time—five years, to be exact—and I still have some lingering PTSD when it comes to Stone's *I'll score one for you, baby* texts.

The last time he missed sending a text like that, my father had him tied up and held captive in a nasty, meth-cooking trailer.

To say that I'm jaded is an understatement.

My phone buzzes, and my heart winds up.

STONE

I'll score one for you, baby.

I smile and send my usual response.

You'll score later too. ;)

He doesn't text back, but I know he is sporting his coy smirk.

A sneaky little grin slides onto my face, and Ally nudges my shoulder.

"You two are ridiculous. *Still.*"

My smile deepens.

Ally and I went in different directions after graduating. I went on to graduate school to further my love of biochemistry, whereas she said she'd rather stick a pencil in her eyeball than do any more schooling after her BA.

I have a goal of being a lead chemist in the development of vaccines, something that Stone and the rest of my friends and family support.

No matter where Stone's NHL career has taken him, we always find a way to be the constant in each other's lives, which is something I have never really had until him.

"There they are," Ally says.

We stand and wear our gold and black with dignity.

I clap and scream for Stone and continue to do so throughout the entire first period. He's playing like he's distracted, and my stomach knots each time his stick slips against the ice.

"I have no idea what's wrong with him," I murmur.

Ally tries to come up with excuses, but I mostly shoot her down. It isn't until the Guardians are nearing the end of the second period that Stone ends up in the sin bin for knocking the opposing player on his ass.

"What is going on with you?" I shout, descending down the aisle, knowing it's about to be intermission.

Stone is breathing heavily, and when his blue eyes fling to mine, I can tell he's distracted.

"Fuck it," he mumbles.

What?

The buzzer echoes around the arena, and Stone flies out of the sin bin in a hurry.

I practically press my face up against the glass, prepared to see him get reamed by his coach, except Stone turns to me instead.

Ice flies up in his wake, and although every other player is huddling together, and the crowd is going to the concessions for refills, Stone skates to the barrier between us.

"What's wrong?" I ask.

He pulls on his glove and throws it down to the ice. "I'm distracted."

I snort. "I can tell." I glance at the eavesdroppers and lower my voice. "What's going on? Talk to me."

Stone signals for their best center, and he skates over quickly and drops something into Stone's hand.

I'm confused, and everyone is staring.

"Stone." I'm impatient and hesitant at the same time.

"Baby," he says, getting down on one knee.

What the hell is he doing?

He takes his helmet off and shakes his sweaty head. Stone Foster is just as edgily attractive as he was years ago when we came face to face as enemies. He hated me then, but I know he loves me now.

"I had this entire thing planned for after the game. The guys were in on it, and even the fucking cameraman was going to zoom in on your face so I could watch the surprise flicker across it over and over again until we're old and gray, but I can't play another second of this game without knowing you'll be my wife."

A knot the size of a hockey puck is lodged in my throat.

Stone opens his hand and shows me the ring, but it doesn't matter the size or the way the oval-shaped diamond catches the lights from above. All that matters is the desperation in his shaky voice that silently begs me to be his forever.

"Yes," I say without an ounce of hesitation.

His smooth chuckle erases his nerves. "I didn't even ask you yet."

"I don't care," I reply.

A single tear creeps down my face, but Stone has somehow made it around the glass, up the few steps, and wipes it away.

"Wren *Foster*," he whispers against my lips. "It's about time we discarded that shitty Davis last name."

I smile and nod. I barely hear the roaring crowd that surrounds us when Stone's hands cup my cheeks. Everything fades when he places his mouth on mine.

"Stone and Wren Foster," I whisper, pulling back.

It sounds like forever to me.

The End

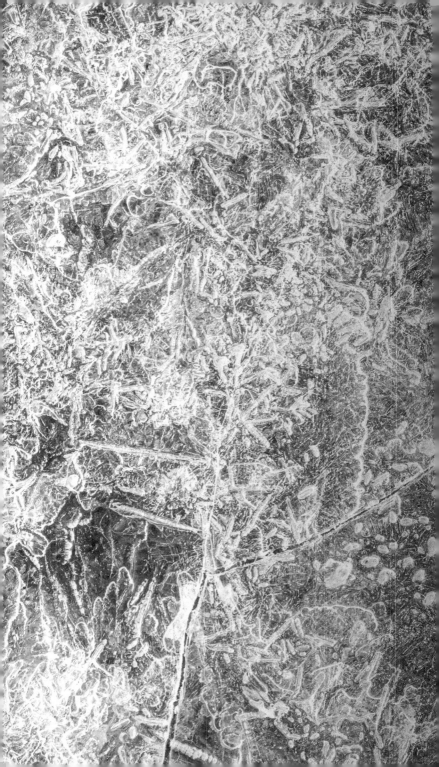

AFTERWORD

If you enjoyed Sticks and Stones and want more of Shadow Valley University, keep an eye out for our next book in the series coming in 2024!
Pre-order it here: https://mybook.to/RqBLO

LOOKING FOR YOUR NEXT READ? TRY EITHER ONE OF THESE HOCKEY ROMANCES:

Brutal Obsession **by S. Massery**

Weak Side **by S.J. Sylvis**

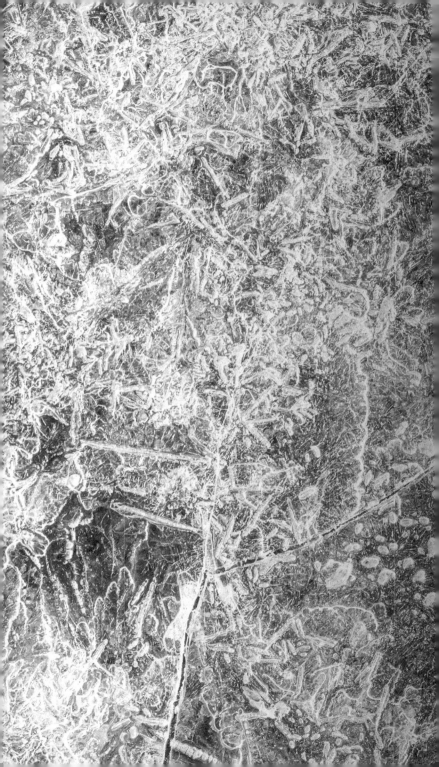

ABOUT THE AUTHORS

S. Massery is a dark romance author who loves injecting a good dose of suspense into her stories. She lives in Western Massachusetts with her dog, Alice.

Before adventuring into the world of writing, she went to college in Boston and held a wide variety of jobs—including working on a dude ranch in Wyoming (a personal highlight). She has a love affair with coffee and chocolate. When S. Massery isn't writing, she can be found devouring books, playing outside with her dog, or trying to make people smile.

Join her newsletter to stay up to date on new releases: http://smassery.com/newsletter

S.J. Sylvis is an Amazon top 50 and USA Today bestselling author who is best known for her angsty new adult romances. She currently resides in Arizona with her husband, two small kiddos, dog, and cat. She is obsessed with coffee, becomes easily attached to fictional characters, and spends most of her evenings buried in a book!

Join her newsletter to stay up to date on new releases: SJ Sylvis Newsletter

ALSO BY S. MASSERY

Standalones

The Pucking Coach's Daughter (coming 2024)

Hockey Gods

Brutal Obsession

Devious Obsession

Secret Obsession

Twisted Obsession

Fierce Obsession

Sterling Falls

#0 THRILL

#1 THIEF

#2 FIGHTER

#3 REBEL

#4 QUEEN

DeSantis Mafia

#1 Ruthless Saint

#2 Savage Prince

#3 Stolen Crown

Fallen Royals

#1 Wicked Dreams

#2 Wicked Games

#3 Wicked Promises

#4 Vicious Desire

#5 Cruel Abandon

#6 Wild Fury

Broken Mercenaries

#1 Blood Sky

#2 Angel of Death

#3 Morning Star

More at http://smassery.com/ebooks

ALSO BY S.J. SYLVIS

Bexley U Series

Weak Side

Ice Bet

Untitled

Shadow Valley Series

Sticks and Stones

English Prep Series

All the Little Lies

All the Little Secrets

All the Little Truths

St. Mary's Series

Good Girls Never Rise

Bad Boys Never Fall

Dead Girls Never Talk

Heartless Boys Never Kiss

Pretty Girls Never Lie

Standalones

Three Summers

Yours Truly, Cammie

Chasing Ivy

Falling for Fallon

Truth

Click here

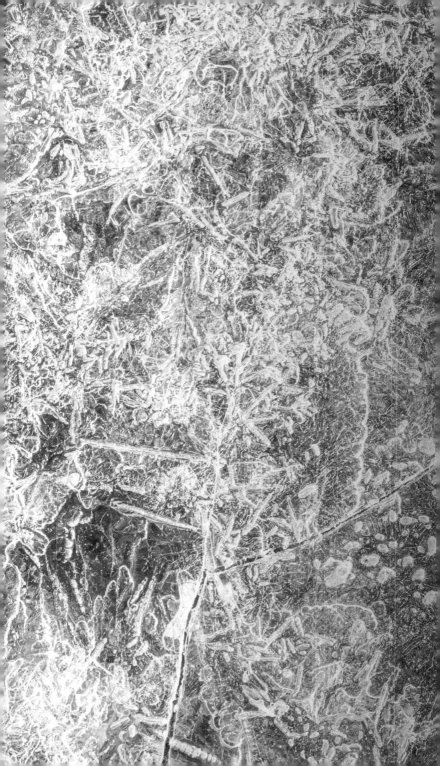

ACKNOWLEDGMENTS

Thank you *so* much to everyone who has helped and/or encouraged us to write our first book together! Writing Sticks and Stones was both challenging and incredibly fulfilling. From voice memos, text messages, screenshots, to random plot sessions — we honestly had fun every step of the way. And we hope you enjoyed reading it as much as we enjoyed writing it.

Thank you to our editors, proofers, alpha readers, beta readers, and cover designer. Stone and Wren wouldn't be as perfect as they are without your help.

Thank you to each of our PAs, and Valentine PR for helping spread the word about Sticks and Stones — and to all the amazing readers who have read, reviewed, and shared! We appreciate you so much!

We cannot wait to give you more books in Shadow Valley University world. Stay tuned!

<3

S. Massery & S.J. Sylvis